Prologue: Explosion
August, 1955

In those days the refinery never rested, but on weekends it seemed to calm down, as fewer men scurried about checking gauges or climbing steel ladders to reach separate levels on the catalytic cracking units. Tended less carefully, the pair of cat crackers looked bigger on Saturdays and Sundays, their boilers fatter, their seven stories of open-air platforms wider and more geometrically detailed against the orange sky on warm mornings.

On cold nights in December, however, each of them would glow with an enormous star, formed by colored light arrangements on the facing of its upper floors. Travelers on the four-lane boulevard that cut through the refinery would slow down to admire the decoration, looking past a quarter-mile of ground level pipelines and valves to the north. Residents of the small village which, except for the boulevard, was surrounded by the chain link fences of the plant, weren't as impressed by the lights that went up every year. To them the big plant was an unchanging landscape of steel they took for granted in any kind of weather. They were also inured to its stench and noise, for to most of them the sounds and smells of the plant were the price they paid for an otherwise convenient life of good wages and low taxes.

In the midsummer heat a newer, more formidable still, FHU-700, which the company called "hydroformer" stood even closer to the passing traffic, rising nearly 250 feet above its operations office. While the cat crackers stood bulky and wide like a pair of refrigerators, the hydroformer was a sleek bottle, relatively uncomplicated except for a cluster of gadgetry near the ground, a winding stairway on its upper half, and an adjacent tall tube which spewed flames of varying sizes, day and night. The hydroformer was quieter than other units, although periodically the pressure within it would be released with a loud, piercing rush of steam which gradually sank in pitch, as if someone were trapped inside, howling for help but losing strength.

On a hot Saturday morning in August, something went wrong. At a moment when the hydroformer would normally have released pressure, it stood soundless, its bright metal surface ominous but quiet. The flame on the adjacent tube was slight.

Dawn had only just begun to filter through the smoky air above the steel mills to the east, a first light reflecting only faintly in colors off the smooth skin of the big structure. From certain angles, it was beautiful.

Then it blew up.

Big and small chunks of hot steel flew in every direction like fragments from a grenade. A huge piece shot into the farthest corner of the village, smashing through a roof and crushing to death a 10 year old boy. Two other hot projectiles ignited small fires in the kitchens of families still half-asleep, despite the thunderous awakening. The concussion forced out windows from most of the houses closest to the boulevard, whipping shards of glass into trees and lawns, cracking foundations indiscriminately, and jarring loose a few natural gas lines. The sudden tremor knocked people out of their beds, or bloodied them with glass or strips of wood from their own houses, which now tilted crazily. Some people stepped on specks of hot metal, some poured pots of water on little fires, some simply stared numbly at the much bigger fire developing in the near distance.

Shrapnel from the hydroformer ignited storage tanks and pipelines inside the refinery, and pierced the tanks of gasoline trucks in front of a hangar-like garage on the opposite side of the boulevard. Within five minutes, fires roared throughout the eastern center of the plant, sending ripples of bright flame upward which blended into thick charcoal smoke, completely darkening the dim sky of the new day. For five men inside the refinery there would never again be a new day. Two died under a falling overhead crane, while two burned to death and another, an aging sectional foreman, died of a heart attack minutes after the initial blast.

By eight o'clock firefighters from several nearby communities had rushed in to keep the chemical blaze from spreading, or to snuff out flames wherever possible. Ambulances and trucks helped evacuate those who lived in the enclosed village. A light breeze developed, pushing the immense cloud of smoke to the southeast so that it drifted above the people as they left their badly damaged houses, making them feel like refugees fleeing a war zone. A few kids tried to turn the exodus into a game, thereby angering their parents, who told them they might not ever be able to go back home.

That possibility was a release to some, discouraging to others who had enjoyed a dirty peace in this square mile of simplicity, stuffed inside the gut of heavy industry.

OUT OF STIEGLITZ PARK

Stories from a lost community.

By Andrew Jefchak

Cover illustration by Vincent Jefchak

(Real places and names are occasionally used in what follows, but the whole of it is fiction.)

Chapbook Press

Chapbook Press
Schuler Books
2660 28th Street SE
Grand Rapids, MI 49512
(616) 942-7330
www.schulerbooks.com

Printed at Schuler Books in Grand Rapids, MI on the Espresso Book Machine®

ISBN 13: 978-1-936243-23-5
ISBN 10: 1-936243-23-7

Dedicated to Kay, Vinny, Pegeen, and Katie,

the loves of my life

1. *Two Cops, Part 1*
Summer, 1949

Stieglitz Park was an isolated subdivision of old houses stained with dried oil, a separate pocket of Whiting, in the far northwest corner of Indiana. People who spent even a short time in the grimy little community became part of its moment of life, which lasted just over a half-century. It was a flat place without ridges or slopes, and its soil gave up nothing but the dull residue of industry. Streets and alleys were both narrow, often looking like each other. The same sort of gravel covered both, and the same dark, flat specks of oil and tar covered all the grass that managed to grow. Aside from a few small businesses, the houses looked like each other, facing off like fat arrows pointing upward. In the years following World War II, no one had air conditioning, so summers allowed no indoor relief. People sat on their front porch, staring out through industrial mist, listening to factory rhythms, reading the Chicago Herald-American. Then again, it may have been the back porch, and the Tribune. Sometimes they shouted at each other, too tired and hot to walk across the street. Most of the people were fairly poor, and sometimes, even in the worst heat, they would argue about money.

Stieglitz Park never had a police station, but back then two cops regularly patrolled its streets on foot or motorcycle, stopping to smoke—always separately—next to someone's wood fence or behind the sign advertising cork-tipped Old Golds near the busy intersection of Indianapolis Boulevard and 129th Street. Asphalt on the four lane boulevard rippled and cracked from heavy truck traffic, leaving a rough road surface which made older cars rattle loudly as they came to quick stops at the traffic light.

Sometimes Chet Puntillo, the cop who drank heavily, would duck into the back room of The Clipper, a tavern at the intersection, for a shot or two, leaving his Harley outside, just behind the tavern's garbage drums. The other cop, Johnny Zmudka, was ambitious; he figured sobriety would help him get what he wanted, such as a promotion or appointment to the state police, or even better, a recommendation to a federal academy. So he saved his drinking for off duty, and he never could be seen in a public dive like the Clipper. Puntillo had a barrel chest and matching stomach in those days. He took heavy steps with his long legs, and his toes pointed outward whether he was walking or sitting on the motorcycle or a bar stool. Zmudka walked straight, perfectly postured, surveying only with his eyes, which he protected with dark glasses shaped like goggles long before that style became fashionable. He sat high in his seat while riding, never showing any interest in anything except his own sturdiness. Once in a while the two pursued together or worked on the same case, but only because they had to. They didn't like each other.

Often they chased speeders who rushed up 129th street to the lakefront steel mills, or east to the Carbide plant partially hidden by toxic steam at the Calumet channel, or west out of the big Standard Oil plant to Chicago, where streets were more clogged and rent was higher, but packaged booze was cheap. Rarely did any driver from Whiting proper—the town itself has always been much smaller than the Standard plant—ever get ticketed, although some going the other way (home to Stieglitz Park) occasionally got nailed by Zmudka, who felt no sentimental attachment to the place that was his beat.

Like the people they helped protect, the cops called the big refinery SOCO, pronounced (and often spelled) "Socko."

Not many trees had survived the years, although a couple of big maples rose about fifty feet at the east edge of the community, near the fence of Sinclair Oil, Standard's smaller rival, just outside the boundary between Whiting and East Chicago. If it had mattered to the crows and starlings that hung out on the limbs of the maples, they could look down at a complex geometry: square fields full of round tanks, groups of rectangular factory truck garages, and railroad tracks that surrounded the straight avenues of Stieglitz or curved through its southernmost edge. There were also a few parking lots, mostly vacant, including the one which served as a baseball field for local boys. They had to invent flexible ground rules to account for those days when more than a few workers would actually park their cars there, just across from Standard's south entrance. That particular entrance was used almost solely by employees from Stieglitz Park, who always walked to work, just a few minutes before their scheduled punch-in time, entering the plant as if on a neighborly visit which happened to last eight hours.

Except for lunch breaks the local boys played ball most summer days until the sun started to angle into the batters' eyes. When thirsty they'd go a few doors down Grace Street and fill up jars from the Pritchard's faucet. Other houses were closer, but they—at least the older ones—took the longer walk in hopes of seeing Mrs. Pritchard walk around, and maybe even bend over in a scoop-neck blouse and tight shorts.

The only other thing that would halt the daily game was the roar of one of the motorcycles. Freezing in their tracks, the boys would watch John Zmudka rush past, a backward-leaning avenger. In such a position he could flaunt his slim power under a fully-zipped police shirt. And, if close enough, an observer could also see the jagged scar displayed above his left eyebrow. He never denied reports that he got the wound during hand to hand combat in the Pacific, but since his induction into the army had been held up until the late spring of 1945, just before the big bombs were dropped on Japan, it more likely resulted from an altercation with a drunken driver or an irate husband.

Or the boys would stare at Chet Puntillo, whose head seemed almost to join his collar bones without the intervention of a neck. With bright teeth visible under the thick moustache, he often hunched toward the center of his handlebars as if he were suffering abdominal pains. The machine he straddled vibrated his fat-layered ribs in the tight shirt, stirring in his torso the excesses of the previous night, or any other night at The Clipper, matching drinks with Frank Connolly or Steve Kowalkowski. And while he also loved to eat, he enjoyed only one meal a day, late in the evening, unless too much liquor made him forget he should have been hungry. Occasionally he could be seen with a woman—usually one who owned a car—whom he'd take to his uncle's restaurant for lasagne; he was half Polish, but he much preferred Italian dishes. The uncle—an ancient man who still was a great cook—owned a brick storefront tavern/eatery in the southeast tip of Chicago. That area was called by its residents the "East Side," a drab triangle all bridged and girdered and covered with light ash. Parts of it looked like Stieglitz Park.

The cops' work schedules kept at least one of them on duty most of the time, but the local kids dabbled in modest lawlessness even so, especially on hot nights. They'd sneak inside the tankfield and stand atop the high mound that surrounded the tanks and ran parallel to the fence. From that vantage point they'd look inside selected neighborhood windows, hoping to catch sight of an undressed girl. Or they'd flatten the tire of the butcher, or some other surly merchant who had threatened to have them arrested for petty thievery. Once in a while they'd slip in the back door of The Clipper at a late hour, especially when Ace or his barmaid went into the toilet; they'd snatch a bottle of anything and drink it in the alley behind Richie Bowman's house, across the boulevard.

Too much alcohol sickened some of the kids, even Banana Mercer, who otherwise liked the buzz and dizzy feeling. His nickname derived from his infatuation with, as well as the size and shape of, his penis. When drunk Banana would either masturbate or cry feebly, or brag about some conversation he had had with "Johnny Z.," which no one else believed, since Zmudka never made a noise beyond an intimidating snarl to any of them, least of all to the stupidest one, which Banana certainly was. Richie Bowman was usually in on the whisky heist, and he drank more than anyone else without ever getting sick. He was a strong, dark haired kid whose happy eyes disguised his quick temper. One night Richie persuaded his older sister's friend Patsy Howard to sip the stuff with them, hoping to get her drunk again so he could get in her pants as he had a couple of months before. After a couple of gulps she moved away from Richie, since she remembered how rough he had been, and concentrated her own playfulness on some of the relatively shy boys like Wally Pierce. But Richie and Banana were obnoxious and crude, and when they began to mishandle her, she ran off.

Wally was a curious kid. One day at the Whiting Library he happened to see a pictorial article in Life magazine about a man named Alfred Stieglitz. The magazine showed him in a photo along with a painter named Georgia O'Keeffe, the caption of which described how important their relationship had been, she the great modern artist and he the guy who photographed an America without makeup. Stieglitz had died in 1946, but the article quoted him on complex ideas about line and balance. Knowing Richie liked to take pictures, Wally asked him if he had ever heard of the photographer. Richie said of course he had, and he told Wally he was stupid not to know, also, since that's how Stieglitz Park got its name.

Wally didn't believe Richie, but he didn't argue, since Richie always seemed willing to slam you with his fist if you betrayed disbelief or doubt in whatever he said. Wally thought it strange that a place like Stieglitz Park could have been named after a creative artist. But the article had shown some of Stieglitz' pictures. Among them were shots of drab house fronts and dusty streets, not too different from the place in which they lived. Maybe Richie was right.

He went to both cops to see if they knew the truth. Zmudka said it wasn't true, but he didn't know the whole story, and then he rode away, uninterested. Puntillo, who was much more accomodating to Stieglitz Park residents than Zmudka, said he wasn't sure, but that Frank Connolly, the old drunk who had lived there since year one, might know. Risking a charge of contributing to the delinquency of minors, the cop took some of them into The Clipper one afternoon, while Connolly was still alert and coherent.

boulevard turned a shade lighter after crossing over the set of tracks that cut between the plant and the cleaner neighborhood. The Andersen drug store served as a sentinel point toward all the storage tanks, diesel stills, truck garages, and barbed wire fencing which lined both sides of the pavement for about a mile until it flared out into the Stieglitz Park pocket.

The drug store intersection was almost as busy as the one in front of The Clipper. On the days Ingrid helped out in the drug store they sold more soda pop, for area boys and an occasional contingent from Stieglitz Park would come in to satisfy their thirst while they watched her walk around. Her heavy breasts shook sideways when she walked, as if rolling gyroscopically, or stabilized by her Scandinavian will. She knew the boys liked to look at her, so when they weren't ordering food or drink, she would walk slowly to the window and stare out, then walk slowly back behind the counter. She sometimes smiled as she walked, but she never looked <u>at</u> them until they ordered something.

One hot June day, while the boys sucked at bottles of fruit punch and gazed at her, she took notice when a wirey, rugged looking man came in for cigarettes. The boys didn't pay him any mind, but Ingrid knew who he was. She watched his jerky movements when he asked her where the Shore Line bus stop was. She told him it was at the market, right across from Talabay's Bakery. Only the day before, she had read in the Hammond Times about an escape from the regional prison at Michigan City. The fugitive, Dennis Hathaway, was an armed robber who had earned the nickname "Ditcher" a few years back, when he had hid in a ditch next to a highway to avoid police.

The paper carried no photo, but Zmudka had left her pictures of various fugitives, and she looked through them as soon as the man left. She was certain that the guy was Ditcher. She immediately telephoned Zmudka at his favorite diner in town, and he rode evasively on his motorcycle, through alleys and sidestreets, to the back of the drug store, where she was standing, ready to nervously expand her phoned description.

"It was him," she said. "It was Hathaway, I'm sure of it."

"Did the guy have a break in his left eyebrow—you know, a white space, from a scar? Not like mine, but short."

She wasn't sure about the scar, but she told him about the bus stop inquiry. "He just walked down that way, toward the bakery. I didn't see him cross the boulevard, but he'd have to if he wanted to catch a bus."

"What about those kids in there? Any of them react to him when he came in?"

"Not that I could tell."

"Well, go back in there and distract them. If they see me they might follow, and then they'll screw things up."

She started to move toward him for a reassuring hug or kiss, but he rode off slowly.

From the alley entry behind Talabay's, Zmudka could see the place was empty except for the old proprietor, smoking a cigar as he read a newspaper on the glass counter above the special-order cakes. He got off his motorcycle and walked carefully in his rubber-soled shiny boots along the outer wall of the bakery toward the boulevard. Directly across the wide road, filling a triangular point formed by the boulevard and White Oak Avenue, was Vasilko's Market. A small shed which served as an office rested almost in the center of the back end of the triangle. The cop could see a couple of the Vasilko men in brown jackets moving around the bananas and cantaloupe and squash, probably trying to impress a reluctant shopper with their storehouse of fruit and vegetable knowledge. About half the produce was shaded by a big tent, which billowed up and out from its vertical stakes whenever the warm wind gusted.

In the deep shade behind the office was the man Ingrid had described, wearing hornrimmed glasses and a cloth hat. The cop could see that he was probably the fugitive. The only customer in the same area was an old woman examining tomatoes. The cop waited until Hathaway turned his back, then he quickly ran across the boulevard, holding out his black-gloved palm to slow an approaching car. Once he got to the sidewalk on the other side, he drew his service revolver and held it next to his thigh as he moved toward the tomatoes, keeping the small office as a partial crease between himself and the man, who was killing time by examining produce, like any other shopper. Zmudka kept moving slowly forward, his pistol now held in both hands. The woman at the tomatoes looked up and saw him, and her eyes widened. As Zmudka motioned her to keep quiet and move away, her mouth opened, and she uttered an open-mouthed, airy sound. As she did, the fugitive looked at her, then reached into his shirt as he turned to see what had startled her.

Zmudka shouted as loud as he could. "Police! Everybody down! Don't move, Hathaway!"

The escapee himself dropped into a crouch between crates of canteloupe, then brought his hand up holding his own gun, and fired two quick shots that missed the cop, splintering one of the poles supporting the tent.

"Drop it, Ditcher!" Zmudka then dove to the pavement and, aiming through table legs, shot the man above the left knee just as he had started to straighten up. The fugitive's body twisted and convulsed, and the glasses slid off his face. He clutched the bleeding leg, the gun now just hanging from a finger.

Zmudka pushed forward under the tables, aiming again. "Drop it or the next one goes in your head!"

The man gritted his teeth and moaned, still holding the wounded leg as he let the gun slide to the concrete. A couple of the bystanders covered their heads with their arms, as if expecting more shooting.

"Drop it!" Zmudka shouted again, just as the man's gun began to fall.

Zmudka jumped up, unintentionally overturning a table full of cucumbers and peppers as he rushed to the wounded fugitive. Bending to grab the stray pistol in his gloved hand, the cop could see closeup the face he'd memorized in recent days.

Then he turned to the terrified onlookers. "You! Velasko, or whatever your name is!" He shouted to one of the men in a brown coat. "Get on the phone! Now!"

The blood ran through Hathaway's denim pants and formed a round pool directly below his twisted face. His eyes welled up and tears dripped into the blood.

Zmudka grabbed a fist-sized eggplant, smashed it against the table's edge, and threw a chunk down to his captive. "Put that over the wound. It may stop you from bleeding to death before the ambulance gets here."

Ten minutes later sirens and flashing lights rushed into the pie-shaped corner, and the intersection clogged with slow cars full of gapers. The boys who had been hanging out at Andersen's drugstore were easily able to worm their way to the market in time to see Hathaway get strapped to a stretcher and put inside the ambulance with an armed guard. They even got within ten or fifteen feet of Zmudka himself as he smoked a cigarette, biting the cork tip before each drag. Two other uniformed cops from the Whiting station asked him questions which he answered without looking at their faces as he spoke.

"Johnny Z.," said Banana Mercer.

"John Z. gets his man!" shouted Richie, in a deepened voice. "Think of all the pussy he's gonna get tonight."

Zmudka ignored them, but he did smile.

After a while, Puntillo rode up and joined the group discussing what had happened. He told the boys to get back to Stieglitz Park where they belonged. Eventually they did, but not before watching Zmudka and a few other people get interviewed by reporters from the Hammond Times and the Associated Press. Zmudka spoke in short, directly descriptive sentences. The witnesses were more emotional, and they emphasized the policeman's uncommon bravery in the dangerous situation.

Westbound traffic increased as the day shift at the East Chicago mills let out. In the midst of the surge, the Whiting police car turned on its siren and oscillating light and, with Zmudka leading the way on his motorcycle, crossed from the market on White Oak, through the obediently idling cars on the boulevard, and looped around to the northward-bound brick pavement on Schrage Avenue. To unknowing onlookers it would seem to be a passing-in-review, a short parade, or a cursory inspection of new territory by a conqueror. To the boys now starting their walk back to Stieglitz Park, it was merely an appropriately noisy end to the excitement of violent adventure. It was also the last time they ever saw Zmudka on a motorcycle.

2. The Councilman's Daughter
Spring, 1955

Before the nearly wall-size mirror Geraldine stood, turning her blonde head while holding a smaller mirror in her hand, using the multiple reflections to gaze at her own eyes while turning slowly to see the face others saw, not the inverted one. She smiled to compare the two smiles, and laughed with a slight toss of the head; the angles showed little difference between her two faces, even though they weren't quite the same. She stopped smiling as she put down the smaller mirror, then narrowed her eyelids. She preferred the image she regularly looked at, in the big one that inverted not just her face but everything. But that mirror was too fragile to pack away safely, so they were leaving it behind on the buyer's wall. Her father said she could have another just as large, as a sort of going away/welcome home combined gift now that they were finally moving out of the house.

She had always thought of it as the boulevard house, noisy in front just as the refinery—on the other side of the company fence, just a few feet away from their garage—was noisy in back. The hissing of stills, especially the huge thing SOCO had recently finished building, the knocking inside pipes, and other irregular sounds blended with the rubber tire-shrieks from quick starts by cars when the traffic light turned green a block away. One noise seemed to pitch into another to create an unpleasant dissonance. During the few years they lived in the house she had always felt threatened when standing in front of it, unprotected except for a narrow sidewalk, open to the rushing traffic..

She could hardly wait until they were somewhere else, for good, and she could finish out her last year at Whiting High School, class of 1956.

Sophie, her mother, didn't care one way or the other about the move, as she chain-smoked in the breakfast nook and read the previous day's Hammond Times. For her, one place was like another. Wherever they would go, she would most likely sit in her sleeveless house dress while working crosswords, and throw in the laundry, and juggle the meal schedule to fit the times when all three could sit at once. Wherever they went, Geraldine would still go to dance classes after school, or something like dance classes, and Henry would still do whatever he had always done, whenever he chose to do it.

He wanted to win an at-large seat on the City Council, but his chances weren't good with a Stieglitz Park address. So they bought a house on Central Avenue, in the center of what was generally regarded as the best residential neighborhood in town. In an at-large bid he could keep most of the Stieglitz Park votes he had received in his unsuccessful try two years ago, and now he would get some support from other councilmen who lived in the in-town neighborhoods, because he wasn't running against them. If they came into the State Savings Bank, where he was an officer, they would engage in conversation, but that was comparatively rare. Living on Central, however, he could meet them on the street accidentally, on casual walks or errands to the drug store. Living nearby they would be able to see the handsome demeanor of a man not yet 40, and listen to his quick ability with words, and understand his potential value on the council. And, as Sophie had told him not long ago, in a curiously scratchy voice that sounded like neither criticism nor flattery, he had become a great bullshitter. The day he had officially changed their name from Szylineczak to Stillman, she said with no discernible expression, Henry had become a bullshitter for all people, not just the polacks.

On this day he walked through the front door, clean shaven and without sweat or many wrinkles, and carefully glided through the living room, where everything was boxed up for the movers. He walked past the boxes and into the dining room, where he paused to consider the empty space where mirrors had hung on the walls. In the kitchen he paused again to glance at Sophie, who was smoking with one hand and holding a pen with the other while staring out the window, trying to think of one word or another. She knew he was there, but she didn't look up.

Then the councilman—as he already liked to consider himself—took a step down to the large back enclosure, a former porch he had transformed into a bedroom for Geraldine. The girl saw him in the big wall mirror they weren't going to pack, and they beamed at each other.

She turned and held her arms out at angles, as if to acknowledge applause.

"You look wonderful." He said the words, but they could have come from her, also. He was careful about clothes and hair and a clean shave, and his face with its well-defined cheekbones and smooth, distinct nose evidenced the sources of Geraldine's beauty.

In the adjoining room Sophie, who looked a few years older than her husband, turned away suddenly from the window to scratch her head, and unintentionally dropped cigarette ash on the table cloth. Then she straightened up in the chair and printed, slowly and deliberately, the correct seven letter word into the blank squares: "mandate."

Richie Bowman stepped into the side entrance of The Clipper. "Frank!" he shouted to the old man hunched over a tall empty glass at the bar. The man pretended not to hear. Richie walked in cocky and nonchalant, acting as if he were old enough to hang out in any tavern, even though he was barely eighteen. "Frank, your sister showed up about ten minutes ago."

The man turned with an ancient glare which would have frightened most of the neighborhood youths. "What the fuck are you doin here? Kids aren't allowed! Right, Ace?"

The bartender didn't even look up from the glasses he was drying. "He's eighteen and he's not drinking," he said. "There's no law that keeps him out if he's not drinking."

"I told your sister I'd come over here and drag you out," Richie said. "So let's go." He took the old man's arm.

"Keep your hands off me."

Richie tightened his strong grip, and the old man's angry look softened. "If you come with me without trouble, I'll let go," the young man said. "Otherwise I'll put you over my shoulder like I did a couple of weeks ago." It wasn't a bluff, for Richie ran and stretched and lifted weights daily, to keep himself strong and quick.

"You think you're so goddamned tough. If I was thirty years—"

"I know I know," Richie said, leading him toward the front door. "You could've broken me in half. But now you're an old fart who gets drunk at three in the afternoon."

When they got outside, Richie pointed to the man's sister, poking around in the front yard a few houses down the block. He continued to guide him by the arm until the man shook him off and tried to walk straight, and by himself. When the sister finally saw them Richie figured he had done the favor he promised, and he turned and jogged the other way, where he hoped to find a more pleasant encounter.

He knew the Stillmans were moving to town over the weekend, and he wanted to make some kind of contact with Geraldine beforehand. Until recently, he had never done more than make offhanded smalltalk to her on the bus, on those rare days she didn't get a ride from her protective parents. She was always politely aloof, talking softly and looking down her perfectly shaped, pointed nose, briefly flashing "bright eyes that were greener than grapevine leaves in front of the morning sun." He didn't fancy himself as a writer, but he had written that line on a matchbook when they took shape in his head. He figured he'd never impress her with words.

Then something had happened on an unusually warm afternoon, only a few weeks before. Richie worked part time for the parks department, and on that day he was helping a carpenter repair the bath house at the beach. Geraldine was out with Greg Barker, the son of the high school principal, walking on the rough sand between Whiting Park and the smaller beach they all called Sheridan. Barker was a meek sort who didn't go out for sports. People who knew him thought he wanted to become a minister.

When Richie saw her with the tall, skinny guy she was apparently dating regularly, he decided to take his mid-day break. Just for diversion, just to stare at her round ass in the yellow shorts. She and the guy moved smooth and slow, a few feet from the easy ripples of Lake Michigan. Richie was able to keep them in sight without moving off the grassy ridge just above the sand where he was working, a hundred feet above the water's edge. He watched her move gracefully, barefoot beneath her shorts and sweatshirt. Like him she was going to be a senior, but in all likelihood she was still a virgin. Maybe most of the other girls her age were the same, but she was a knockout, smoothly slender with sloping breasts, a dreamgirl every guy in Stieglitz Park was probably dying to fuck.

After a few minutes Richie stopped walking and just watched. He was about to head back to the bath house when he saw Barker tumble onto the sand. Geraldine stood still, then reached out, though it looked more like a defensive gesture than one that would help her companion, who was convulsing in a manner Richie recognized. He ran down to them, and when he got close enough he could see Barker's mouth bleeding as he shook. Richie rolled him onto his back and straddled his chest, then put a handkerchief near a crease in the guy's mouth, taking care not to get his own fingers trapped in a convulsive bite. Whenever he could, Richie pushed more of the fabric between the teeth, as the guy wheezed furiously and shook violently. He made some choking noises and Richie turned him onto his side, trying to steady his head, which jerked against the sand. His whole body tightened, then went slack, then tightened again. His trembling slowed to calm. Richie massaged his jaw and removed the bloody edge of the cloth. The guy breathed fast but lay relatively still.

"I'll run up and make a call," Richie said. He could see she wasn't listening, but had turned the special grayish shade of shock, and when he reached to help her she turned and vomited. He then held her from behind, around the shoulders as she threw up some more. She leaned against him, unsteady.

In a few minutes, Barker pushed up on an elbow, breathing deeply but in control.

"I can get you a doctor," Richie said to him.

"I don't—" Geraldine started to respond as if he had been speaking to her, but just then Barker waved his hand weakly. "I'm alright," he said. "I'm sorry to be such trouble. I didn't feel it coming on until it was too late. I should've taken my medication."

Richie's boss accompanied Geraldine and Barker to his city truck and drove them home. Richie looked at them as they rolled out of the parking lot, hoping she would turn and look at him. Just before they got to the railroad tracks, she did. It was just a brief glance, but vivid enough to bring back into his mind her helpless face and troubled eyes, gorgeous even in nausea.

Geraldine thought about Richie in the days following the beach incident. Up to then he had been just another tough-looking Stieglitz Park bum, though maybe a little cuter than others, with thick black hair. Upset as she was at Greg, who had never told her about his epilepsy, she was almost ready to flirt—momentarily, at least—with Richie, to take her mind off the sight of such a frightening seizure. When she saw him jogging at the intersection, heading her way, she went out of the house to "accidentally" run into him on the sidewalk. His sleeves were cut off at the shoulder, probably to emphasize his muscularity. He looked athletic but heavy afoot, coming down hard on heels below thick legs that didn't look as if they could cover distances fast, but could probably knock over anyone who tried to stop him. Something in his constant eye-contact scared her, but when he smiled the eyes softened and she forgot about the fear.

She smiled back and they traded small talk about his running and her moving. His face was shiny with sweat and when he again stared into her eyes so intensely she felt it necessary to look down at the pavement.

"Want to share the concrete with me for a while?" he said.

"I'm not really dressed for it," she said before realizing she was in shorts and a knit blouse, so all she would have had to do would be to replace her sandals with canvas shoes. "You'd probably leave me in the dust, anyway."

"Oh, I'd never do that to you." He grinned.

She looked past him, trying to say something without making foolish mistakes. "I feel bad that I never thanked you for your help at the beach that day."

"Well, you were upset. No need to feel anything. I'm glad I was able to help."

"You should become one of those emergency people. They always seem to know what to do when someone's hurt, or sick."

"No, I don't know anything like that. I've got a cousin who's epileptic, so it wasn't as much a shock for me. I've been around him a few times when he had a fit. There's nothing anyone can do, and really it isn't that serious."

She absentmindedly made a face.

"They look worse than they really are," he said. "In the middle of a fit, I mean."

She shrugged, then looked at him, and his eyes stared back at her, so hard they gradually seemed almost threatening. Despite her uneasiness, when he asked her if she would like to go to a movie sometime, she said yes.

Their date was postponed a couple of times, once when Sophie dropped a knife on her foot and Geraldine had to take her to the emergency room, borrowing a neighbor's car, and another time when Richie's sister Marietta refused to let him use her car, and they got into a fierce argument and he sprained his ankle running down the stairs after her.

Meanwhile, electioneering went into high gear in the summer, and Henry Stillman tried to use Geraldine and Sophie in an open display of his priorities to family matters. Sophie dressed up and went along to a couple of rallies, but she soon tired of seeing other women suck up to him as if he were a visiting movie star. Her daughter, on the other hand, enjoyed all forms of attention. So Sophie pulled back into her self-imposed privacy of cigarettes, crossword puzzles, and, increasingly after dark, scotch.

As Geraldine became energized by frantic political nonsense, she all but forgot about Richie.

The weather got warmer, and Richie grew certain that Geraldine was avoiding him. Her new house was a couple of miles from Stieglitz, but he even had trouble reaching her by phone. One or the other of her parents always said they would relay his message, but she returned none of his calls. When she herself happened to pick up the phone their conversations were short, and she was unwilling to be pinned down about the movie date. He began to think she associated him completely with a place to which she had bid good riddance. Despite his insecurity, however, she stuck in his mind so that he couldn't think about other girls, in or outside of Stieglitz.

One night as he stood at the bus stop at 119th and Schrage, he decided to jog the several blocks to her new neighborhood. Central Avenue was a street lined with maples and oaks, generally quiet in the last streaks of daylight. When Richie got to the new house, Henry Stillman answered the front door. "Geraldine around?"

"Why do you want to see her?" he said.

Although they had never met before, Richie quickly caught the disapproval in the man's voice. In that instant he remembered seeing him come out of a couple of houses in Stieglitz Park the year before, usually late at night. It hadn't especially surprised Richie, since he was sure some husbands down there, including his own father, visited other men's women. It was a small community, and there weren't many streetlights, so nights were quite dark.

"We're friends," Richie said. "I thought she might want to go for a walk."

"You're from Stieglitz Park, aren't you? What are you doing around here?"

"I work for the city. Out at the beach and in the park, trimming trees and shrubs, stuff like that. I was just on my way to catch the bus."

"Seems like you've gone out of your way." When Richie didn't say anything, Stillman moved away from the door. "She isn't around, but I'll tell her you stopped by."

Faced with a closed door, Richie wanted to kick it back open, but instead he punched one fist into his other hand, and walked back to the sidewalk. He stood in front of the house for a minute or so, looking one way then another, and suddenly Geraldine came bounding out the side door. When she saw him she stopped. "Hi," she said. "What are you doing here?"

"That's what your old man just asked me. I guess I must be out of place. He wasn't too anxious to let me see you."

"Oh, I don't think he even knew I was home. He's been wrapped up in the campaign, and he hardly knows what else is going on in the world." She was wearing a silky gray blouse that clung to her.

Across the street a woman drove slowly next to the curb and pulled out a bag of groceries. She waved, and when Geraldine raised her arm Richie looked again at her breasts. He was sure she wasn't wearing a bra.

"Where you headed?" Richie said.

"I'm going to spend the night at a friend's."

"Lucky friend," he said, brushing her arm with his as they walked.

"A *girl*friend."

He had not seen her for weeks. As they walked he looked at her for a few seconds at a time. When she looked back he could tell she was made nervous by the look, but her nervousness began to arouse him.

After they had walked a short way, Geraldine paused for a few words with an older man pulling weeds from his flowerbed. While she was talking, Richie took the opportunity to stare at her more intensely. Her cream-colored shorts were a tight knit, tight enough that he could see her labia visibly folded over the center seam.

Then Henry Stillman drove by, heading south. Either he didn't notice Geraldine behind the old man's hedge, or he saw both her and and Richie but was too caught up in his own purpose to stop.

"So who's this *girlfriend*?" Richie said when they resumed walking.

"Janey. You know her, Janey Slezak."

"Hm." He nudged her arm with his again. "You go both ways?"

"What?"

"Nothing," he said with a laugh. "I'm trying to be funny but I probably come across as a lovesick fool."

"You don't seem lovesick."

"I've learned to control it." He put his arm around her shoulders as they kept on walking.

"You're not lovesick," she said, moving out of his grip. "You don't seem like the kind of person who gets emotional about anyone else."

He took a step in front of her and then moved with her when she tried to pass. She was clearly becoming annoyed. "If you let yourself get to know me better you'll see how emotional I can be."

She didn't answer, but she didn't speed up her pace. They walked soundlessly and slowly for ten minutes, but it seemed longer. Then Geraldine crossed in front of the public library, and across a patch of grass to the block on Ohio Avenue where the Slezaks lived, a heavily shaded stretch where the Norway maples blocked much of the light from the street lamps.

In the darkened space Richie walked ahead of her again, and then faced her as he walked backwards. He stuck out his hand and held her forearm. "This isn't going anywhere, is it? Look, Gerry, I mean—."

"I don't like to be called Gerry." She tried to pull away, but he held onto her arm, and they moved even slower than before.

"Why? It's unusual. It's—I don't know—friendly."

"It's a boy's nickname."

"Hey, that's not necessarily true. When I was in the 7th grade at South Side School, there was a girl named Gerry Grenchik. She didn't look like a boy, and you sure as hell don't." In the dim light he could see how the bright shorts spread smoothly across her flat abdomen.

"I'm reassured," she said, trying again to pull away.

He pushed her with gentle force, backward against a tree trunk, then pulled her forward against him. "You know what you do to me, don't you Gerry?" he said as she tried to squirm out of his arms.

Then she pretended to weaken even as her fear intensified, and she let him kiss her. When his grip loosened, she pulled away suddenly. "I'm going to my friend's house."

"Hey, come on back." He caught up with her just before she got to the Slezak house. "Look, I'm sorry. I just think we can get something going between us."

She didn't look at him. "I'll think about it," She said cautiously. She went up the stairs, pulling the screen door open so quickly the pointed lower edge of it scratched her leg, and she winced.

"Are you okay?" He started toward her.

"I'm fine. I have to go."

He moved up the steps just as she got inside the screened outer porch. "Look," he said, "what I'd really like to do is a series of pictures. You know, you in natural settings. "

"What do you mean?"

"Photography, it's my, well it's more than a hobby. I really think I could put together something interesting with you as my subject. I'm not talking about nude stuff."

"I don't know," she said. She flicked the latch on the screen door.

"We—we never had that date we set up."

"Richie, let's talk about it some other time."

"Why? Why not now?"

"Let's just—skip it."

"Goddamn it!" Richie slapped one hand against the door frame.

The porch light went on and the inner door opened. Geraldine went inside, away from his angry eyes, and she closed the door behind her.

Richie backed away, but he could hear an adult voice ask if something was wrong. He couldn't hear Geraldine's response. He turned sharply toward the street and furiously kicked the first thing he saw on the ground, which happened to be a brass lawn sprinkler in front of a coil of hose. But the sprinkler was unattached to the hose, so his kick sent it across the sidewalk, bouncing up from the fringe lawn, then crashing down on the windshield of a parked car. The noise of cracked glass prompted a couple of people to turn on their porchlights, which sent Richie running off instinctively. Swearing to himself as he ran, he headed toward the corridors of the highschool complex, remembering how, when he was eleven or twelve, having picked up a wallet from under the bleachers during Whiting's game with East Chicago Washington, he and his buddies ducked into the same darkness between buildings as if it were a smalltown Casbah, tight enough to thwart any police car's spotlight. Then and now, once beyond the dark spaces, he carefully made his way to 119th street and darted across, rushing quickly into another set of dark alleys.

Near the Community Center, a multi-purpose recreational building, he sat deep in the shadows, wishing he had a cigarette. He hadn't smoked since August of the previous summer because he didn't want to give the football coach further reasons to get pissed off at him. Richie wanted to quarterback the team, but the coach had no intention of moving him from his center/linebacker dual role. Richie knew he was good both defensively and offensively, but he longed to play the control position, where he could influence the whole offense.

For a half hour or more he sat against an empty barrel in the semi-dark and thought about football and Geraldine in the tight shorts. The next southbound bus wasn't scheduled for another 45 minutes, so he decided to run home through town, straight down the boulevard, not sprinting but just bouncing on each foot to shake off some of the fat he had collected eating lunches at the beach stand.

Few motorists were around that night, and surely none of them thought to look suspiciously at a solitary young man running along the SOCO fencing adjacent to all the big tanks. On the other side of the boulevard the refinery hissed with steam and exhaust.

Richie's heavy steps eventually slowed to a walk as he got to the first gravel street in Stieglitz Park, directly opposite the hydroformer, looming in the dark. The relentless noise of the refinery could generate a sense of danger in someone passing through. But Richie, having lived nowhere else in his life, felt secure surrounded by it, hiding his mistakes. It helped cloud the thought that Geraldine wasn't ready to trust him with intimacy. He admitted to himself she probably never would be ready. Yet he retained a dream in which she was his co-star.

At the corner of the boulevard and Ann St., he almost ran into Puntillo, who was walking back to his motorcycle after doing something, probably taking a leak, in the empty property behind the billboard advertising Old Gold cigarettes. Puntillo said nothing, which was fine with Richie, since he knew the cop hated him.

When the early sun began to glow in the polluted blur above the garbage dump east of the E J & E tracks, near the edge of Stieglitz Park, Doug Steymaier carried a couple of trays of doughnuts and pastries into the back door of his grocery store on 129th street. He set down the trays momentarily on the top of a trash can in order to work his key into the lock, and when he reached again for the trays he saw the inverted face of a man lying on the ground, about ten feet from the back door. The eyes of the face were fixed in a stare. Doug moved to look directly into the dead face, and he could see big bloodstains below, on the shirt and trousers. His routine stability shattered, Doug shook his head and looked around, without knowing what to look for. Then he looked again at the face, and he recognized it as the handsome man who had gathered his family and moved away. Doug also remembered seeing it once in a while in recent days, even so, long after the family had paid their grocery tab and moved into their new place in town. It didn't seem possible that the dead, bloody body could belong to Henry Stillman. But there it was, frozen in eternal surprise.

3. Murder
Summer, 1955

In the years after the shootout at Vasilko's market John Zmudka had become a special agent for the FBI, legally changing his name to John Saunders. He had originally wanted to change it to Zale, but his section leader at the Bureau office advised him against it, for it would seem to suggest a family connection to former middleweight champion Tony Zale, who had grown up in nearby Gary. Zmudka had no problem with that, but he took the suggestion anyway, fearing the section leader might think badly of him if he ignored it. As always, he wanted approval from the right people.

As Saunders he occasionally stopped for gas or cigarettes in the Whiting business district, but he avoided Stieglitz Park. He had no reason to go there.

During the same years, no one replaced Zmudka in Stieglitz Park. As the sole law enforcement officer in the sector, Chet Puntillo was issued a new motorcycle which ran quieter and faster. At a regular physical exam, the doctor told him sternly to stop drinking and lose weight. He took the advice on both counts, and over the course of a year or so he dropped 40 pounds. Sobriety led him to take the people aspects of his job, as well as the community, more seriously and personally. He even moved into a house in Stieglitz Park.

On that warm morning in 1955 after Doug Steymaier's shocking discovery, the death of Henry Stillman was officially ruled a homicide. The Whiting police chief ordered Puntillo to lead the investigation for several reasons: because the corpse was found in Stieglitz Park, because none of the detectives on the force knew much about the area, and because he knew Puntillo to be a working stiff who wouldn't seek headlines. But the victim had been a politician, so the headlines came anyway. The Hammond Times assigned two of its reporters to interview people in Stieglitz Park and keep a close watch on Puntillo. From the start he acted as if they weren't there. He stored his motorcycle, figuring a police cruiser would be quicker and more useful in avoiding people, or tracking them down, to say nothing of space needed for his young assistant on the case, Billy Tomczak.

He spent a surprisingly short time on what potentially would have been his most difficult task, informing the widow. When he made the grim announcement to Sophie Stillman, her expression seemed to hover between a sneer and a snicker, and then changed to tired exasperation. She shrugged when the cop asked about enemies. He guessed she was exhibiting symptoms of shock. He would pursue the questioning later. The atmosphere in the house changed sharply when Geraldine arrived, having been driven home by her friend's mother. For several minutes she screamed as if she herself were being attacked. Sophie's passivity changed when she embraced her daughter. She even began to cry, though Puntillo guessed the tears were more for the daughter's shock and grief than for the dead husband. Mrs. Slezak stayed with Geraldine, along with two plainclothes cops, while Puntillo drove Sophie to the Baran Mortuary to identify the corpse.

Then he returned to Stieglitz Park. After questioning Steymaier, he went to the Bowman house, just beyond the intersection of Indianapolis Boulevard and 129th Street. Richie's mother told the cop her son was still at his job somewhere in the lakefront park, or at the beach. She didn't seem particularly concerned over the policeman's inquiry, even though word about the murder had spread since the first moments when chaotic colored lights from several vehicles spun through the morning mist.

"What time does he usually get home at night? From the job, I mean." Puntillo spoke in a loud, distinctive tone.

"I don't know. It varies." She scratched her neck and stared emptily. "I think he punches out at eight, but he doesn't always come straight home. He catches the bus."

"Do you know what time—"

She continued her sentence under his question. "The Shore Line 4-B, the one that goes through Goose Island."

"—he got home last night?"

She shook her head. "I fell asleep watching television. I can't even remember what was on. What did he do?"

"I don't know. Maybe nothing." Puntillo walked away slowly, half expecting her to give the standard motherly plea about what a good boy he was, and so on, but she said nothing else.

Puntillo drove into town with his quiet partner Billy, deciding at the last moment to see Richie before going back to the Stillman house. He found him shirtless on the south slope of the park, in the waning sunlight, digging up shrubs to be transplanted.

"Looks like you're working hard to get your mind off things," Puntillo said.

"No, just to make money."

"What were you up to when I ran into you last night?"

"Nothing. I was just coming home from town."

"Your mother told me you punch out at eight. It was just before eleven when I saw you. You were sweaty and out of breath."

"Well, I missed the bus and I jogged home. I had kind of a date. But it didn't work out."

"Did everything *work out* by the time you got home?"

"What do you mean?"

"Henry Stillman was murdered some time last night."

"Yeah, I heard about that. Jesus."

"The coroner's early guess is that Stillman was killed right around the time I saw you, all sweaty."

Richie shrugged. "And right around the time I saw you." He smiled, but Puntillo didn't think it was funny.

"Does that clever shit impress girls? Or is that why your date didn't work out?"

Richie wiped his face with his shirt, then he put it on. "Look, I saw him last night, but it was at his house on Central Avenue. After that I took a walk with his daughter and I saw him again, driving off after we had gone a few blocks."

"The daughter was this date that didn't work out?" Puntillo took off his glasses so Richie could see his suspicious face more clearly. "What exactly didn't 'work out'?"

"We had an argument."

"About her father?"

"No. Look, you've got to be kidding if you think—"

"Shut your trap!" Puntillo spoke the words close to Richie's face. "Always keep in mind, smart ass, that I know what kind of a punk you are." He walked back toward the cruiser, which was parked on a gravel service road at the foot of the slope. "I'll get back to you."

Puntillo may have thought seriously that Richie had personal reasons for killing the man, and he had always considered the kid to be a sneak and a bully, with a love of blood that drove him to take pictures of bad traffic accidents right in front of his house. But he probably wasn't dumb enough to lie about what went on during a two and a half hour stretch of time, and shortly after. The shortly after might be a mystery, but the rest would be easy to check.

By the end of the day Puntillo wasn't sure of anything. The crime may have been committed elsewhere and the body carted over to the alley behind Steymaier's. There was some smeared blood on the back wall near the trash cans, suggesting the body had brushed against it, but there were no other signs of struggle there, not even foot scrapes on the dirt alley. The murder weapon probably was a knife, but the forensic report indicated it might have been a big screwdriver which had been sharpened, since the cuts were narrow but uneven. The report confirmed the victim had been dead several hours before the grocer found his body in the alley. That meant Stillman had indeed been killed right around the time Richie Bowman could have reached his house near the intersection of the boulevard and 129th street, just a block from Steymaier's grocery store.

Puntillo interviewed Geraldine as it was getting dark. Inside the house it was also fairly dark, at her insistence, but the cop could see her face was red and puffy. She nervously described the walk through the neighborhood with Richie. Puntillo could see she was rattled by questions about Richie, and he wrote himself reminders to follow through, to find out what she was leaving out by talking to her again a couple of days later. He was about to leave her alone when her expression changed.

"What did he look like?" she said quietly.

"Who, Richie?"

"No, my father."

Puntillo looked at her sympathetically for the first time. Even in the dim light he could see she was emotionally lost. He started to tell her that her mother could answer the question, since she had seen the cold face at Baran's. But then he realized she didn't really know what she was asking.

"Look, kid." He held her gently at the wrist.

"I saw him walking through the kitchen," she said. "He was scratching his head. And he stopped and looked like he was thinking about something not so serious, not about the election or anything. He smiled about something, and I realized he probably didn't even see me leaning against the counter. Then he went to the phone in my bedroom. He knew I was going to sleep over at Janey's, so I just walked out the side door and let him be his candidate self in private."

Puntillo wanted to question her further, but he held off as tears ran down her cheeks and she looked down.

"That smile—a sort of nonchalant smile, maybe he was thinking of me. Maybe he knew I was there," she said almost in a whisper. "I'll always keep that look in my mind, my memory."

"Did you—" Puntillo started to focus on the phone call.

"Has he been cremated yet? He always said he wanted to be cremated, you can ask my mother."

She started to tremble, and he put an arm around her shoulders. "We can't—"

"He needs to be what he will always be. For me, it's that nice smile. You know?"

"We can't allow the cremation just yet, Geraldine. He was a victim of a crime, and we need to complete the investigation."

Suddenly she stiffened and moved away from him. "You need to examine him for clues. For marks of a struggle."

Puntillo nodded.

Her tears welled up again. "He was a good man. I don't care what some people—" She clearly was about to say something defensive, but she caught herself.

"I need to ask you about the last minutes when you were in the same room. You said you were going to sleep over at your friend's. So your father didn't know you were going out with Richie Bowman?"

"No, because I *wasn't* going out with him. He was on the front sidewalk when I got outside, and we just took a walk. It wasn't anything planned."

"What did your father think of Richie?"

"I don't think he even knew him. Just as a neighborhood boy in Stieglitz Park."

"So they didn't have an argument or anything? And the phone call your dad was making—"

"I didn't hear any of it." Her expression changed again, and this time she looked right into the cop's eyes. The light wasn't bright enough for him to see the color of hers, but it occurred to him they were the same shape as her mother's. He touched her wrist again.

"You alright? Why don't you sit down."

She did, but the cop remained standing. "I think he's a violent person."

"You mean Richie. You think he could have killed your father?"

"No." Tears welled up again. "I don't know. I see something dangerous in him. I think he's capable of brutal things."

"Did he try to force himself on you?"

Geraldine hesitated, then shook her head. "It's just that— I didn't feel safe with him last night. I don't know."

"Don't worry, kid. I'll see what I can do about keeping him away from you."

Sophie came into the room, pulled her daughter down to a sofa and hugged her, then gestured to Puntillo to hold off further questions.

"We'll continue another time," he said, giving the girl's hand a gentle squeeze. "But let me talk to your mother." He walked back toward Geraldine's bedroom, where the dead man must have made his last phone call. He saw himself in a big mirror and, recognizing his own fatigued shabbiness, turned away, only to look into a couple of smaller mirrors. The colors on the bed and walls were subdued—mostly gray or tan. When he left the room he could see Geraldine on the top concrete step outside the front door.

Because Sophie's reaction to the murder had not been what Puntillo would have expected in a wife of many years, he couldn't avoid thinking she had something to do with it. He realized it was a dumb thought, dumber even than suspecting Richie. She seemed a pleasant, good-natured sort of woman, but early in their conversation she brought up Henry's philandering. She did so in whispers, to prevent Geraldine from hearing.

"You're certain he was seeing women?" Puntillo asked, in a loud whisper.

She poured herself a glass of scotch and took him into the back yard, farther from the distressed daughter. As she talked to him her eyes wandered, as if she were following the fireflies in the increasing darkness.

"It used to be painful to me, his womanizing," she said. "It hasn't hurt for a long time." She leaned against a catalpa tree. "It's been years since we argued about his sexual games. Sexual needs." She looked back at the house. "He considered himself very special, and it was clear I didn't share the view, or that I didn't understand. God, what a cliché. The wife who doesn't understand."

Then they sat on a backless bench. She lit a cigarette, the first puffs of which must have scratched her throat, for she coughed and her voice changed slightly, giving a sting to her words. Puntillo tried to sound casual in his questioning.

"Do you know any of the women? Any of them live in Stieglitz Park?"

She took a long drink and the lines on her face softened. He didn't think she would answer. She wore a flimsy dark blouse and vertically striped shorts. Her legs looked almost athletic, youthful.

"Be careful about drinking at a time like this," he said.

"It doesn't matter. I drink pretty much the same way all the time. Now that he's dead I guess I have one less excuse."

"About the women."

She took a deep breath. "There were at least two in Stieglitz Park. When we lived there."

"How do you know that?"

"I saw him in the car a couple of times with different girls. I asked him about one of them, but he said she was a precinct worker, or something. One time a loving neighbor of mine told me about someone named Sylvia Sanchez he was seeing. I don't know if she expected me to go after them with an axe, or what." She laughed weakly, then stared at Puntillo as she took another swallow of scotch. "That's the only name I know, but I never saw them together."

"Sanchez. She still lives in Stieglitz Park?"

"I think so. I don't know where. She and her husband split up some time ago. They might even be divorced."

Puntillo wrote some more notes, then shifted to things which had nothing to do with the murder. He had a feeling, despite the woman's resigned attitude toward her husband's behavior, his murder, and the possibility of a connection between the two, that she was holding back an emotional response—regret, laughter, an angry tirade.

"You and your daughter do a lot of things together?"

"Not much outside this house, except here in the garden." She looked back toward a modest array of color. "The previous owners didn't plant much. Geraldine and I just got the perennials started when Henry began campaigning. And then she was off with him, whenever he needed a female presence, especially a young one he could claim as his own. He used to talk about higher office—congress, governor. If he had ever made it she would have been a much better first lady than I. She took to that stuff a lot more enthusiastically than I did."

"Did any of his political enemies hate him?"

She laughed quietly. "Do politicians actually hate each other? I think he was popular. I disconnected the phone a couple of hours ago because when people got the news it wouldn't stop ringing. Not just relatives and friends, either. Such a great loss, they would say. Lots of people have dropped in, but Geraldine has been in such shock that I finally asked them to leave, and we'll see them at the wake."

"I'm sure they didn't mean to overwhelm you," Puntillo said.

"I don't know about that. Maybe that's the way it is with political people around here—everything in large quantities. But you can only take so much pity all at once."

He didn't answer, but he frowned.

"I guess I sound cynical," she said. "I promise not to say such things at the wake."

"That's a good promise, if only for Geraldine's sake."

She finished what was left in her glass, then got up and walked, a bit unsteadily, to a skinny sumac, and touched its outermost branch with one hand. They talked for a while about Geraldine, the things she liked and her serious interest in politics and culture. She was a good student, a good writer and speaker, but Sophie worried that the death would make her last year at Whiting High emotionally difficult. Not that money would be a problem, for the dead man had provided both of them with adequate support, plus enough savings to see Geraldine through four years at one of the universities, probably Indiana, with its relatively cheap tuition.

Before leaving, Puntillo offered help. "Don't be afraid to call me," he said. "Even if it has nothing to do with the killing. Tell your daughter the same thing. If she needs any kind of help at all, even someone to sound off to, keep me in mind." He handed her a card. "I do need to get one other promise from you, Sophie." He was going to reach for her hand, but he decided a smile was enough.

She said nothing. She didn't even look at him.

"I stopped drinking a few years ago, and I think it was the smartest thing I've ever done. I lost some weight, I feel good every day, and I don't worry about anyone getting an advantage on me. Promise me you'll give some thought to that."

"What's your first name?"

"Chet."

"Well, Chet. Thank you for your concern. I'm sure I'll see you around."

For someone who didn't take great care in dressing or making herself up, she was oddly attractive. While she climbed the back stairs, Puntillo glanced up at her. Her legs were just as attractive when she walked, and the smoking and drinking apparently hadn't done much harm to her figure. He took the sidewalk around the house to the front. Geraldine was still sitting on the top concrete step. Puntillo approached her slowly.

"Share things with your mother, " he said, trying not to make it sound like advice.

"Will you get the person who did it?" She asked quietly but without a crack in her voice. It was the first time he sensed a touch of real anger in her voice.

"Yeah," he said.

It was just after eight, so he decided to go to The Clipper, to see if he could get anything from the gossip of drinkers. He had gone into the place only a few times since swearing off alcohol, so when he entered in uniform the ambient noise lowered to a hush, as if it were a remote saloon in the old west, and he was looking for a shootout. He pretended not to notice, and even slapped one beer drinker on the back.

"Keep your count down, Dinky," he said. "You've only got three blocks to make yourself seem sober for your cute little wife."

"Jesus, Chet, I thought maybe they sent a new cop down here. You lost some weight."

"A little." He knew the guy was buttering up, for they had already seen each other a few times since the weight loss.

Nothing had been replaced or even rearranged over the years. The linoleum tops of some tables looked worse than ever, with taped-over cracks and discoloration, and carved obscenities on some of them. The air was stale with smoke and alcohol breath, and some of the more wobbly chairs made sticky noise as a leg or two lifted up from the stained floor.

A couple of older guys were mumbling things to each other, occasionally in rising inflection punctuated by a fist on the table which made beer splash and cigarette ashes float. The cop put a hand on the shoulder of Frank Connolly.

"How's it going, Frank?"

The long-faced man looked back and squinted. "Jesus Christ. Go fuck yourself, Puntillo."

"Why would I want to do that, Frank?" Puntillo's tone seemed to mock the old man.

"You're fucking up a good man's drink, snooping about Stillman."

"I'm not that powerful, Frank. I can't ruin your booze."

Because Connolly talked in such a loud voice, Puntillo didn't ask him anything. Instead, he walked to the far end of the bar and sat in the space where it curved around to meet the wall. No one was within ten feet of him as he sat and signaled to Ace.

"I'd ask why you're here, but I already know," said the bartender. "Still on the wagon?"

"Ginger ale. No ice. And I need your help."

Ace brought him a glass and poured it in front of him, then looked at him with wide eyes but an otherwise blank expression. "That's a buck."

"A *buck*? If ginger ale costs a buck, I'm glad—. I need to know something, Ace, so I won't argue that you're overcharging me."

"I'm not the one to tell you. I don't know anything."

"Just answer my questions. I'll determine whether or not you know something." Ace said nothing. "I can make it worth your while."

Ace's laugh seemed silent in the midst of growing background noise. He pointed to the dollar bill Puntillo had put next to his glass. "Nineteen more of those might help stir my memories."

"I don't have a budget. Come on, Ace, I can help you out. Say how, and just talk to me."

"My wife got a ticket last week."

"For what? Speeding? That's easy."

"No, not speeding. Reckless something or other."

Puntillo raised his eyebrows and puffed out his cheeks. "I don't know. Okay, okay. Give me the details before I leave, and I'll see what I can do. Just let me hear what you know."

"What if I really don't know anything?"

"I've already given you a promise. Did Stillman ever come in here?"

"No. I wouldn't even know what he looked like except for pictures in the paper."

"What about Steymaier?"

"The grocer? He lives in Cal City. He never comes in. If he needs a drink he probably sneaks one from a bottle he keeps in the meat locker, or wherever. What did *he* do?"

"Nothing, but he found the body. Listen, you must hear lots of conversations going on in here."

"Just near the bar. Otherwise it's too noisy."

"What about late at night? You know, when there's just the hard core drinkers left, and some of them have had too much. Maybe even some guy trying to impress his girlfriend with what he knows about important people. You overhear anything about Stillman? Anything at all."

Ace tended to a female customer who wanted to pay her tab. It probably wasn't her money, since she left with an older man. "I could tell you that story," Ace said, gesturing toward the exit, when he returned to the end of the bar.

"Does it connect to Stillman?"

"No, except for that fact they're not from around here, just like he wasn't."

"But he was, up until a few months ago."

"Yeah, but he never came in here, so from my standpoint he wasn't from Stieglitz Park."

Puntillo was getting impatient. "Come on, Ace, did you ever hear anyone that sounded like they really disliked Stillman, or like they knew some dirt about the guy?"

"Well, there used to be talk about him when he lived up on the boulevard."

"Such as?"

"Fooling around. There was a woman who worked at the bank, where he was an officer or something."

"What was her name?"

"I don't know. Really, I don't know, but I heard she was good looking. She wasn't from Stieglitz. You can get the name at the bank."

"Okay. Do you remember hearing about anyone with a name?"

"Let me think." He took care of a couple of other customers, then called over a guy who was in the middle of a card game in the far corner. When he returned he had some names. "Mildred Milosevich was one, a big woman. She used to live down on 131st Street. I don't know where she moved to, though." He spelled the name as Puntillo wrote it down. "And then of course there was Sylvia Sanchez."

"Why 'of course?' "

"I figured you knew about her."

"I know who she is, but why would you say 'of course'?"

"I just figured you knew about her and Zmudka back in '48 or '49. She was still married to Pedro back then."

"We didn't talk much."

"Is that right? I figured Pedro's temper was one of the reasons John Z. got out of here. Pedro's always been a guy who gets pissed off easily."

"They're divorced now, right? Where did Pedro move to? Is he still in Whiting?"

"I don't think so. I should have asked him when he was in here last week. He's probably gone by now. To wherever he lives."

"Sanchez was here?" Puntillo jotted himself a note, but he put the pad away quickly when he saw one of the Hammond Times reporters enter the front door. "What about Sylvia and Stillman? Was that a recent thing?"

"I think so. It seems to me the gossip was about sex and politics."

Puntillo turned toward the wall, so the reporter couldn't make out what he was talking about. "I need one more favor from you, Ace. The guy that just walked in, with the baggy sport jacket and red shirt?"

"Right."

"He's from the Times, and when I leave he's going to ask you where I just ran off to. Tell him I went up to the White Castle. To question a possible witness."

"Right."

Puntillo gave him a sheet from his small notebook. "Write down the details about your wife's ticket, but tell the reporter you were giving me information about the suspect at the White Castle. If he asks."

Once outside, Puntillo drove to the alley behind the Bowman house and picked up his young partner Billy Tomczak. They sat in the dark at the end of the alley, where they had a clear view of The Clipper. Billy started to talk about Richie, but Puntillo told him to forget Richie and look up an address for Sylvia Sanchez. When they saw the reporter exit the tavern and drive north, they drove south.

Sylvia Sanchez lived in a well-painted house on Ivy Street. The shades were drawn, but there was at least one light on inside. Puntillo got out alone and approached slowly, while Billy drove into the alley in the rear. As he crept up the front steps, Puntillo could make out two voices, one a baritone.

He rang the doorbell and he could hear quick movement inside. He rang it again.

"Who is it?" the female voice asked, close to the door.

"Police." She opened the door as far as the chain lock would allow. Puntillo smiled and showed his badge. "If you're Sylvia Sanchez, I need to ask you some questions." She said nothing. "A man was murdered last night, and I'm trying to find out how and why."

"Wh-what does that have to do with me?"

"Perhaps nothing. Can I come in, please?"

As soon as he walked through the doorway he smelled cigarette smoke. She wasn't smoking, however, and there weren't any ashtrays in sight. She was a mildly pretty woman with sparkle in her eyes and teeth, but her face showed concern, probably fear, and there was an evasive flatness in her expression. Most likely she had spent too much time in her life defending against men eager to get her, as if she were a prize in an ongoing contest. She nervously clutched the cord of her robe while he moved around the room.

"Do you know Henry Stillman?" He asked.

"No."

"Well, we're not off to a very good start," the cop said. "You knew him very well, and even if you've been holed up here all day, you probably know he's dead."

She said nothing, but continued to look nervous. A faintly audible child's voice came from below.

"You have a son," Puntillo said.

"Yes," she smiled, but briefly. "Xaviar. He—he loves to play by himself."

"He's probably an imaginative kid. How old is he?"

"Twelve." She spoke with a gasp, and the fear in her face was stressed.

"Why don't we go down and watch the game he's playing."

"No!" She spoke in a loud whisper. Her eyes widened and she put out both hands spread-fingered, as if to prevent him from going anywhere, even though he hadn't moved an inch. "No, please." Tears welled up. "I don't want him to be hurt. Please."

Puntillo stared at her. She couldn't disguise the terror in her voice. He whispered back at her. "Is your ex-husband down there? Does he have a weapon?"

"I don't know. I don't think so, but he'll hurt Xaviar somehow. He's crazy."

"He'll hurt his own son?"

"He's crazy."

Puntillo doubted what she said, but he still felt the worst thing he could do would be to charge down into the basement. He also figured the child had probably been safer before he came to the door, and that Billy Tomczak would play it cool for the time being. The last was a hopeful guess, since he had only been working with the young officer for a matter of hours.

"Look, Mrs. Sanchez," he said, still in a loud whisper while pulling her farther away from the basement door. "Sylvia. Where's your car?"

"In the garage," she said in a trembling voice.

"The garage is a separate structure in the back, right?"

"Yes, but he'll—"

"Just stay calm, Sylvia. I'm going to go outside, and I'll slam the door, but then I'll stay in front, behind that hedge out there. Okay?"

"Yes."

"After I slam the door you wait about sixty seconds, then call downstairs to Pedro. Tell him I've gone to get a search warrant, and I'll be back soon. Give him the impression I don't know he's here."

"Okay. But what if he—" She began to sob, but she stifled the sound, even so.

"He'll probably want to take your car, but I've got a man in back." He watched her bite her lips, then cover her mouth. "A good man," he added, again hopefully.

"What if he doesn't believe me? What if he comes up the stairs and gets a knife?"

"Keep your voice down. I can see inside through that little patch of screen in front. Just leave the door ajar, so I can rush in to get him, if necessary. Okay? I'm going out now. The best chance for your son's safety is you. Behave calmly. Deep breaths, and keep your voice steady."

Puntillo slammed the door, then set himself in the darkness between a tall hedge and a screened window which was open a few inches. He could see her standing near a corridor, looking at her watch. He hoped that the absence of a police car out front—presuming Sanchez would look out there—would tell him he had time to save his skin.

After what was at least twice the time he had told her to wait, Sylvia moved out of Puntillo's sight line and opened a door. But before she could enact his plan, her son rushed up the basement stairs to her embrace, which continued as they moved to the front door. Puntillo opened it and, seeing the boy was unhurt, guided them into the front yard. Then he drew his revolver and went back into the house and down to the basement, where he found Pedro Sanchez sitting on the floor next to a stationary tub. Both of his white tennis shoes showed brownish spots and blotches, as well as pale smears indicating an unsuccessful cleaning. The glazed look in his eyes suggested fatigue rather than emotional disorder.

"Okay, Sanchez. Let's go." The tired man gave Puntillo no trouble as they went upstairs.

Late that night Sanchez confessed to the murder, so the case was solved not long after newspapers even announced a crime had been committed. While the chief of police explained details to reporters the next morning, Puntillo was taking a nap in the station's lunch room. A fit of relaxation had come over him after another visit to Sophie and Geraldine, to whom he promised to get a restraining order preventing Richie Bowman from any social contact.

4. Two Cops, Part 2
Late Summer, 1955

The place Puntillo had bought a year earlier was a one-level, boxy frame on Louisiana Street. It looked like most of the other houses in Stieglitz Park, and it needed repair, or at least more care than it was getting. He bought it from the estate of an old Turk named Ajas Rushet. The family who buried the reclusive man wanted no part of the place, and were eager to dump it at any price, along with the empty lot next to it, which was partially dug up so that it sported a long trench and a hill about fifteen feet high. There the neighborhood kids sledded in winter and, when tall weeds bloomed furiously, played war in the summer. Puntillo bid $5300 for the house and the adjoining lot, and Ajas' descendants gladly took it.

Knowing only basic facts about joists and studs, the cop marvelled at the seemingly advanced carpentry skills of his next door neighbor, Louie Fronczek, who worked irregular shifts on the big stills at SOCO. Puntillo was further amazed at how much energy and time the guy could devote to his own house and property after putting in a night's work at the plant. Only after several weeks did he learn Louie got more sleep on the job than he did in his own bed. He also earned a 30 cent differential for each hour on the midnight shift, for which he was a regular volunteer. For Louie the midnight to eight a.m. slot provided him all the benefits of employment and some of the special leisure of unemployment.

When they first met, Louie shook his hand, then shoved his own hands into his pockets while putting on a wide grin. He pointed out how his wife's name was Lois, that their two kids were named Louis, Jr., and Louisa, and that they lived in a house on Louisiana Street.

"Ain't that somethin? All the 'Lou' sounds. He laughed, and Puntillo laughed with him simply to be cordial. He understood the neighbor's sense of humor even less after Louie added they had had another daughter, named Lizzie, who had been dead for a long time.

Louie's wife seemed friendly, but she talked loudly, sometimes shouting things, such as her admiration for his nationality ("eyetalian") and her secret recipe for spaghetti sauce, which contained no tomatoes at all, and how safe! she would feel living next to a "person of the law," apparently trying to sound respectful. Then Louie himself shouted reprimands at their nine year old son, who was digging up turf in the yard with his feet as their dog playfully pulled the laces of his shoes. Actually, the boy was pretending to be White Sox star Chico Carrasquel, sliding into second for a stolen base, being tagged too late by Yankee infielder Billy Martin, played by the dog. Then the wife shouted at Louie to keep his voice down, even as she berated him for worrying about the grass.

"It's just grass!" She yelled. "Where's he supposed to play? He could be out getting into trouble, and you're moaning about the lawn!" But they were an openly affectionate couple, notwithstanding their occasional bickering. More than once Puntillo saw Louie kiss his angry wife, thereby softening her frown, and even getting her to laugh while he stroked her buttocks. She may have seemed a bit wacky to the cop, but for Louie she was a queen.

About then the daughter, eighteen year old Louisa, came out in the dress her mother had just completed for her, and the mother shrieked. "Oh, my God! How beautiful that is!" Turning so quickly to Puntillo he thought she was about to assault him, she shouted, "Officer, doesn't she look pretty in that dress? I made that for her! A high school graduate, no college though. She's gonna get a good job soon." The girl rolled her eyes and went back into the house.

Puntillo agreed the new dress and the young girl were pretty. He couldn't understand why the woman screamed everything, since he never heard loud voices from inside their house; they apparently shouted to each other only when they were outside in the yard. After a couple of meetings, the cop noticed how Mrs. Fronczek also seemed eager to discuss all things indefinitely, so that she relied not only on loudness, but also free association. Sometimes, to interrupt her loud rambling, he would pretend that his phone was ringing, giving him sufficient reason to rush into his own house.

Actually, the Fronczeks may have had good reason to raise their voices out in the stinging air. The refinery stills closest to the boulevard, particularly the enormous hydroformer, did seem louder that summer, as if the company were trying to enhance the volatility of their ultimate fuel products through higher decibels. Occasionally, the constant flame from the hydroformer's exhaust tower would flare up, as if some giant fire wizard were demonstrating high-octane gasoline by spitting it over a Bunsen burner to the amazement of carnival customers.

"You work on those stills, Louie. I've often wondered—what causes that flame to get so big once in a while?" Puntillo asked one day when Louie was watering his snapdragons. Flowers didn't usually do well in the prickly air, but Louie watered his snapdragons each day and they survived. Maybe the excess water kept the toxicity away from the pink and red petals.

"Ah, it ain't nothin'," said Louie, about the flame. "You get used to it after a while, just like the smell."

"You mean it's supposed to do that?"

"Oh, yeah. The gas, you know, the stuff that builds up inside the pipe," Louie started to explain, then realized he was saying it wrong.

"What pipe?" Puntillo asked, looking up at the big silhouette against clouds in the north.

"The pipe!" Louie said it louder, as if added volume would clarify matters. "The gas builds up in it, just like in the sheds up there, so we got to keep canaries in them."

"Canaries? Where? In the pipe?"

"No!" Louie's shout seemed to shift to a different key, and he gave a quick smile over the short fence they shared between properties, and then a strangely serious face. "In the sheds over there. Over there. And when the canary dies over there we know there's too much gas in the air!" He seemed perplexed he had made an impromptu rhyme, and he stuck out his jaw and brought his lower teeth up over his upper lip. Puntillo could see no patterns in the man's gestures, so he tried to understand again through words.

"So that's why you can't smoke inside the plant?"

"Yeah," said Louie. "But I don't go to no smokehouse for a cigarette. I just chew snuff. And then I light up outside the gate at twelve midnight, or eight in the morning."

Puntillo smiled and nodded. He had had similar conversations with his neighbor about the nature of life inside and outside of the plant, but the cop never learned anything that clarified the processes or made the neighbor's explanations understandable.

One hot evening he sat in his full uniform on a webbed chair next to the front door of his house, watching as a highschool football star from uptown drove down for a date with Louise, who was all lacy and slim in the outfit her mother had raved about. Before leaving, the bright-grinning young man lofted a pass to Louie Jr., who caught the spongy football in full stride and headed for an imaginary endzone, his barking dog tugging at his cuffs. As his father watched, Louie Jr. then lost the ball to the dog, whom they called Mousie because he was small, gray, and quick. The dog darted this way and that when the boy tried to get the ball back.

"You gotta move around just like Mousie," the father said, "then you'll be a big shot just like the boyfriend, there." He motioned toward the departing car.

The boy then zigged and zagged after the dog who had the spongy football in his mouth. The energetic, short-haired beast always managed to evade Lou's clutches at the last moment. His father smiled and then waived at Puntillo, who walked across his yard holding a coke, his uniform unbuttoned at the chest.

Then the man paused before speaking to the cop again. "Loafing on duty, huh? And *drinking!*" Louie then laughed to emphasize his joking tone.

"It's coke, and I'm not on duty. The department runs a patrol down here on Friday night. So this is my easy night. I'm just too tired to take the suit off."

"You oughta put in a outside shower like I did," Louie said, pointing to his shanty in the back. "Man o man that is really *it* on a hot day."

"I don't have your plumbing skills, Louie. Or the necessary material and equipment."

"Ah, I just pick it up here and there. You know, if I do a government job or something. And my brother Mikey sometimes brings stuff over."

"Government job?"

"Well, you know what I mean. When we get together and help each other out, you know. Privately—it's when we do the government jobs. At home."

"Oh."

Puntillo wasn't sure if he were missing some nuance of factory jargon, or if once again the neighbor was getting tangled up in his own partially formed sentences. It may even have had something to do with the sleep Louie would get at the factory when he worked the night shifts: five, six hours a night, just enough to make him well rested for his "government job" at home. Something like that.

The cop forgot about the conversation until later, on another hot evening after a dirty, windy day of arguing with merchants and motorists. For relief he had taken Sophie and Geraldine to his uncle's restaurant for an early supper, and then to the lakefront for ice cream sundaes. Sophie seemed quite sober and pleasant; the girl still was withdrawn and quiet, as if she were waging a battle inside. She ate very little, but spoke when she was spoken to. He avoided talking about Sanchez and the case, since it was clear the girl was still clinging so thoroughly to an idealized image of her father.

When he got home just before dark, a neighborhood kid and Lou, the youngest Fronczek, were building something like a temporary screen against the garage, near the alley to provide a safe backstop for pitching. It was rough-grain screening that Lou was about to cut with pliars.

"That's brand new. Won't your dad get angry if you ruin it?" the other kid said.

"Not if we just use a little bit. It didn't cost anything, anyway. It's for a government job he's working on."

The other kid squinted, for his own father worked in a steel mill. "I thought your dad worked at Socko."

"He does, but he does government jobs, too. And he needs lots of this stuff in the shanty for that."

Hearing this, Puntillo walked to the fence next to the open shanty, where the glow of the setting sun shadowed some things and highlighted others. He could see the shower Fronczek had mentioned, a clean white stall with what looked like new stainless fixtures and a raised tile floor. Next to the stall was a wall full of hanging tools, and spools of wire. On the floor were neatly stacked bags of unopened cement mix and several lengths of conduit.

Later that same day, after thinking about the shanty and the stuff inside, he decided to question Fronczek.

"Hello, Officer Puntillo," Lou said, smiling.

"Hello, Junior. Where's your daddy?"

"He had to work a double shift tonight. He went in at four. Some guy got sick."

"Too bad."

"Do you want me to give him a message?"

"No, I'll probably see him in the morning."

Puntillo took another look in the shanty, and then in the garage, before going back into the alley. The boys played on. Puntillo took a deep breath and kicked some dirt. He couldn't escape the obvious: his neighbor had stolen a significant number of things from the refinery. For years he had heard scattershot rumors at The Clipper about the ways Socko employees would embellish their paychecks by smuggling out miscellaneous stuff. He may have even heard the term "government job" tossed around before but had never been interested enough to attach importance to it.

Now he had seen the goods Fronczek had brought home. It would be an easy matter, certainly warrantable, to jot down specifications and lot numbers of any equipment or tools in the guy's shed, and then contact plant security to match numbers against a master list of stolen or materials unaccounted for. Still, he had never heard scuttlebutt about equipment losses or storage theft at the Whiting plant.

What good would it do to report stolen materials from a factory, Puntillo asked himself. The neighbor would get fired, or worse, and credit for busting the case, if there was a case, would most likely go to the security people inside the plant. He himself would become a Judas figure in Stieglitz Park. He had enough to worry about without searching people's houses for stolen materials.

He considered going next door to warn Fronczek by way of his wife, but he gave up on that idea, too, when he imagined how she would rant and rave, or weep and go for her rosary, which he occasionally saw her carrying. Like others of her generation in Stieglitz Park, she was a relentless Catholic, often transforming the devious pranks of her son and daughter into major moral offenses, as clearly condemned in the Baltimore Catechism. "The devil will be happy if he could see you now," she would tell them, her tone a chant that rose on the musical scale to the irony of "happy," then descended to the "now."

The cop didn't want to ruin anyone's life, even though as part of the daily routine he had done just that many times, like most other cops on any street. Risk-taking punks eventually did themselves in and justice got stamped on them, the natural order of things. But not these lives, not the Louisiana Street Louies. He didn't want to ruin these. Ordinary working class folks. Some of them needed protection against themselves, against their own stupidity.

Maybe, Puntillo thought, he could set things straight by going next door one of these days and threatening the fool coldly, staring down into those baggy eyes of his, scaring the shit out of him.

And then what? Puntillo knew little about the middle-aged man with the thin brown hair. He was a guy who walked heavy on his heels so that his head bobbed up and down. He talked loudly with his wife. He called his son Junior, or Sunny. He got a lot of sleep on his job. He took stuff from the plant. He built his garage by himself, and fixed up his house by himself. Maybe those weren't government jobs. Puntillo actually hoped the guy had paid for everything, and that it was all a big mistake, coincidence.

Still later, on another Friday, Puntillo couldn't shake the jitters. The case against Pedro Sanchez looked like a sure thing, and he was developing a friendship with Sophie Stillman, a widow who in many ways was relieved to be a widow, even under such violent circumstances. But Geraldine was hard to read. She kept so much inside he felt he didn't know her at all. He had temporarily taken care of Richie Bowman's possible threat to her, but she was still stuck somewhere between grief and fear. She had a whole year of high school left. He hoped she was strong enough. He reminded himself she wasn't his daughter. He had no children, and probably wouldn't ever have any.

"No kids," he said out loud, at about one thirty in the morning. There was some noise in front of the Fronczek place. He looked out his window to see Louisa walking to the front door. A car—probably her boyfriend's—did a U-turn, kicking up gravel as he drove away. He thought of going over there to see if anything was wrong, but immediately changed his mind, since an intrusion might waken the mother.

"Kids." He shook his head in relief, even as he recognized the gap in his life. "No kids." The gap put knots in his stomach, and he decided to open the bottle of Old Grandad he had bought a year ago to test his refusal to drink. He poured some of the bottle into a coffee cup and raised it as if it were making a toast. "Louie's got two kids and a job, and he's probably sleeping on that job this very minute," he said. "Dreaming away on some oil-stained cot. Here's looking at Louie."

He drank what he had poured, then stopped himself from pouring some more. He had thoughts about Sylvia Sanchez. He might have been attracted to her but for the murder, and anyway she had been the mistress of Zmudka, who now called himself Saunders. It was enough to quiet whatever passion he felt at the moment. He drank another shot, put away the bottle, then leaned back on the flowered, fat chair in the middle of his screened back porch, listening to the many noises of Stieglitz Park. After months and years he had gotten used to all of them. Within minutes he was asleep.

No one saw the fiery burst against the early morning dark: strong, strange noise crashed into the collective unconscious, sudden and painful to sleepers throughout Stieglitz Park. The blast pressured out windows and cracked structural foundations within a half mile. Little Lou Fronczek was knocked out of bed in the loft room his father had completed—a government job—the previous November. Banana Mercer whispered obscenities as he shook his head, for he had been having an erotic dream when the blast rocked his bed. Pete Strecsko was knocked down just as he flushed the toilet, and now one of his bathtub pipes shot a spray across the small room. The fall gave him a quick headache which he tried to shake off, but then fear seized him when he saw flames, for his gas station bordered the plant at the 129th and Indianapolis intersection. He imagined devastation.

The blast broke hard into Puntillo's blurred dream. He opened his eyes to the streaked blackness of early morning, and to unsteady brightness flickering on the walls, frightening shadows that seemed to fold the big noise and pull in its echoes—ripples of sound that swirled, fire flashing against the star-strewn sky. Even in his disorientation the cop knew it was an explosion—a heavy crack which seemed to linger still, as if it were a big rock rolling around an immense steel bowl. The force of it had knocked him off the chair, and from the floor he could look out and see that the early morning stars were real, not visual specks of sleep. There was no longer a roof on the porch just beyond his chair. He could look up and see a huge glow, and flashes that rose up to the dim sky. He moved across the hard floor to look past the Fronczek back yard, and then his eyes squinted at the bright source of the noise: a mass of flame spread out, orange and terrifying in the near distance.

Then there was another threatening flash, and then ripples of black and orange that jerked malevolently, followed by hissing and honking, and lesser blasts. The explosions seemed to have sucked up the ground-level chill and made it swirl with the heat from the fire, so that the dark air was alternately cool and hot.

In the quickly rising ripples of the burning refinery he could see no silhouette of the hydroformer, no spike in the skyline. The big still must have disintegrated, and flames were shooting up from nearby tanks that had apparently burst from pressure, heat, hot sparks, or some combination of all of them. Across the yards of this part of Stieglitz Park and up through the branches of scrawny sumacs and mulberry trees, the cop saw another unit flare up and spread flames almost geometrically across pipelines to those nearby structures that probably had lost pressure. The atmosphere got brighter and hotter.

It was early Saturday, an otherwise lazy time. Factory sirens initially installed to awaken the community to an attack during the war now deafened everyone with shrill, aggravated warning: get up and get out.

Lois Fronczek screamed in horror when she saw the fire's glare, then screamed again at the glass and debris spread all over the main floor of their house. She moved without a physical idea, forward and then in a circle. She had read in Reader's Digest how people sometimes panic by running toward danger. Her screaming made her daughter Louisa tremble, especially since the girl had been out late that night, with the boy named Chuck, who was handsome but too cocky. But Lois gave no thought to the night before, for the inferno overwhelmed her senses. Little Lou cut his foot on glass, and left bloody footprints on the back porch as he looked for the dog Mousie. When Puntillo came over to help, the front door fell against his shoulder and insulation spilled from a big crack in the doorway. Lois wept loudly, suddenly realizing Louie was still at work, somewhere behind the wall of flames.

As if to demonstrate the Reader's Digest article she had read, Lois ran outside and took several strides toward the back fence—thus, toward the factory—before Puntillo caught up to her and convinced her that the flames were real, and she should go in the other direction. He then assured her he would go to the plant and find Louie. She looked at him as if she had no idea what he was talking about, but then took another step toward the plant again before Louisa caught her and hugged her, and they both cried before being led away by the cop.

Telephones weren't working, so after helping the Fronczeks--including the dog, who was shaking with fear--into a neighbor's truck for evacuation, Puntillo put on his uniform and rode off on his motorcycle. He knew the evacuees would get temporary sanctuary about a mile and a half north, in the basement of St. Adalbert's church, the "Polish church" as it was called by anyone who wasn't Polish. But they had to first go west, and cut through Goose Island.

Puntillo rode south of the fire. The plant entrance at that end was near the destroyed unit, and therefore couldn't be approached because of intense heat. He needed to find a safer entry. At the corner of 129th and Indianapolis, Pete Strecsko's filling station sat broken, dark, unoccupied. The doors to the lavatories had been pressured out. Just behind the station, inside the plant fence, several night laborers were on their knees, scooping coarse dirt, frantically trying to dig their way out, creating a separate exit. When they first saw the cop they looked ready to panic, but he told them he wanted to help, taking some basic tools out of his pannier pack. They looked relieved as he used wirecutters to make a slit in the galvanized chainlink. He asked about Louie Fronczek but after giving him some general directions they rushed through the cut opening and headed toward The Clipper, which was relatively undamaged and had just opened to serve the night shift from the steel mills. Puntillo shook his head. Seeing that the laborers yearned more for booze than safety, Puntillo pushed his motorcycle through the cut fence and headed down cinder paths farther east and north, to the other side of the flames and black smoke. Ordinarily he would need a warrant or an invitation or at least a visitor pass to get inside the plant, but now he gave no thought to procedure. Most of the men he came across looked terrified, primarily because they couldn't leave; they had to stay on the job to help contain the fire.

Shriller new howls got louder as fire trucks from outlying areas joined the ones already inside the refinery. Gradually the noises merged in the near distance into a steady sound of confusion, and as daylight advanced the flames seemed to hide inside the dark smoke, only to shoot out at irregular intervals, hot orange streaks like tongues out of the black fur of a monster.

By late morning, when the danger of further explosions lessened, Puntillo finally found someone who knew the whereabouts of Louie Fronczek. He was with some others in a black cindered field where pipelines and valves stood above ground in multicolored, perfectly geometric formations that looked from above as if they might have been inspired by Mondrian.

"What you doing here?" Louie said, with a worried grin under the brim of his hard hat. His hands were trembling. "Chet, anything wrong? Lois? What about my house?"

He told Louie everyone was safe, but when he said the house was badly damaged, some color noticably left Louie's face, and he looked sick. He walked away from everyone else, in the long strides that made his head bob up and down. Puntillo walked after him until the worried man stopped and said something that sounded like "what did I do?"

"What do you mean?" Puntillo started to pursue something else he didn't understand, but just then a fire truck moved away from a nearby smoking ruin, sounding its siren.

"I wasn't sleeping by that still, you know," said Fronczek. "The one that blew, I was way over there, over by the buffalo side." He took a couple of deep breaths, as if suddenly reassured he hadn't started the fire.

"The buffalo side," Puntillo said. He understood this to mean he had been in the area of the plant that was closest to the lake. He had never learned why SOCO workers sometimes called it the "buffalo side." Buffalo itself was hundreds of miles to the east, and bison had permanently moved west 150 years ago. And he couldn't figure why Louie felt some kind of guilt.

"That wasn't no checkpoint for me tonight," said Fronczek.

"What do you mean?"

"The hydroformer—I, uh, that wasn't on my log this time."

The cop could see he was confused. He told Fronczek he would go to St. Adalbert's and tell Lois and the kids he was okay. As he rolled his machine away he could still hear Louie moaning, as if the catastrophe fell heavier on him than anyone else.

Even after the flames diminished, thick smoke rolled upward, then drifted east in the wind, which had begun to swirl more unpredictably. Firefighters kept at it with retardant and water, to anticipate further heat pockets. By the time Puntillo returned from St. Adalbert's the sun was sinking in the opposite direction of the thick charcoal smoke. Even a mile beyond the source of the explosion the charred stench of steam and acid in the air made tense throats itch.

Puntillo stopped in The Clipper to check for inside damage, but all he could see was a badly cracked mirror. Ace the bartender, perhaps thinking to establish credibility in an insurance claim, told Puntillo that 25 bottles of liquor had been shaken off the shelves by the big blast. The cop looked around. A dozen men sat on barstools or at tables, and a few nodded in agreement.

Ace had his radio tuned to a music station. "What's the latest word on deaths and injuries?" Puntillo asked him.

"Three inside the plant."

"Four!" A customer corrected him. "One guy had a heart attack."

"Yeah, and the kid over on Berry Avenue," said Ace. "A big piece of the still went right through the roof of his house and killed him."

"Where on Berry?"

"The far end. Near the fence."

"Near the fence. Jesus," Puntillo said angrily. "Some innocent kid."

"Well, Socko didn't exactly get off lightly," Ace said, gesturing toward the front window. "See for yourself."

"Shit," said Puntillo. "Think about it. That kid was killed by a piece from a 250 foot bomb. Right next to the boulevard. Jesus Christ." He kicked a chair and walked away.

Outside, Puntillo saw Richie Bowman just inside the fence the cop had cut earlier.
He was using a telephoto lens to take pictures of the firefighters and the rubble at the site where the big still had stood.

"Hey, Richie!"

Richie walked the other way, pretending not to hear.

"Get out of there!"

Richie took a few more shots, then slipped back through the fence. The cocky youth walked toward the road where the cop was standing.

"I figured I'd get some shots the bureau might buy if they find it was sabotage. You got another restraining order?"

"Just obey the one."

"I haven't gone near her."

"I better not hear that you have. What do you mean, 'bureau?'" Puntillo asked.

"The Feds, the FBI. Big Johnny Zmudka himself is back, I hear. J.Z. the fibbie. Only he calls himself Saunders now. You see him?"

"No." Puntillo squinted. "What's he doing here?"

"The gate watchman said he heard the fibbies had a warrant to look through every house in Stieglitz."

"Look for what?"

"I don't know. They must think someone sabotaged the plant."

"Christ," said the cop. "*Socko* did the sabotaging." He shook his head, then focused on Richie's camera. "What the hell do you think you're doing?"

" I was thinking of getting a head start. With my camera, I mean, just—"

"Just nothing," Puntillo said. "You stay away from those houses. If I catch you looting I'll lock you in someone's cellar, and then forget about you. And then I'll go check the serial number on that big lens you're using, and match it against lists of stolen goods from camera shops in this area. You get the picture, cameraman?"

Richie said nothing.

"Saunders," Puntillo said out loud to himself. "By any name, an asshole."

Puntillo rode across the empty intersection of Indianapolis and 129th. Traffic from the south and east had been rerouted since before daybreak, away from the thick black cloud. Since the early morning evacuation of most residents, Stieglitz Park looked like a village battered by war. Shortcuts were easy to find, and he took one of them to his house, checking for looters along the way. He saw Pete Strecsko pushing up on a garage door, but it was his own garage, so the cop left him alone after seeing that he needed no help lifting it.

Three of the windows at Puntillo's house were cracked but still in place, not pushed in by the force of the blast like so many others, including Fronczek's. The cop thought of what Richie had said about the FBI search. Maybe the punk was making up the story, but Puntillo didn't want to take the chance that an overzealous agent like Zmudka/Saunders would develop a federal case out of Louie's illegal stockpiling.

He stood still at the low fence near Fronczek's shanty, which itself had sustained some damage. He could see the same materials inside he first noticed the night before.

He brought up a couple of trunks and boxes from his basement--they had only been empty for a short time since his move--and carried them over to the Fronczek shed. He filled them with anything that bore any connection (manufacturer's registry plate, chalk markings, etc.) to the plant. He carried them to the trench at the bottom of the hill in the lot he had bought along with his house. Then he dragged bigger articles like conduit and plumbing tools to the same spot, and covered them all with sand from the hill. Luckily no one saw him. He had no interest in the stuff, and—now that everyone would have to move out—neither would Louie Fronczek, a stupid, nice guy with two nice kids and a nice lunatic for a wife, all under the same roof, but the roof was no good anymore.

As seen from the southern edge of Stieglitz Park, the refinery took on the sharply contrasting tones of a bold canvas. The sunset beyond the tankfield, cooled by hoses, was a deep orange which faded in cloudy, purplish ridges above the near-empty streets. Closer eastward the sky turned a hazy gray above the structures that were still burning. The closer a viewer got to the fence the more offensive was the air—dirty mist combined with wet smoke and the residue from burned oil, pinching soft skin and irritating eyes.

The ex-cop who now called himself Saunders walked down a sidewalk near the corner of Indianapolis Boulevard and Louisiana St., just across from the acres of burning rubble and twisted steel. He and two other agents, all of whom wore picture-badges clipped to their smartly tailored jackets, surveyed all the houses that fronted the boulevard and the factory fence, all blackened and wrinkled. Saunders sent his colleagues a block north to 128th Street for a house-to-house check. They had been ordered to seek out any information or evidence which might suggest a plot to blow up the hydroformer, or to destroy anything else in the area.

Just as the FBI entourage paused to look at a man-hole cover that had apparently been dislodged at the corner, the two former partners saw each other. Neither showed any acknowledgement at first. Saunders squatted, holding a piece of jagged asphalt, while Puntillo pulled his motorcycle over to the dirt shoulder of Louisiana and stared at the asphalt.

"What the hell are you doing here?" Puntillo said.

Saunders said nothing as he put the piece of asphalt into a large cloth bag. Then he gave the bag, along with muffled instructions to the other agents, who continued the survey westward down the boulevard.

Saunders walked with a quickened pace down Louisiana Street.

As Puntillo caught up with him, he stopped walking and turned quickly.

"What am I doing here, you ask. I think a more important question would be what were *you* doing inside the Standard Oil facility earlier?" He gestured forward, to the middle of the block. "And what's that truck doing in front of your house. That is your house, isn't it? I was told you bought a place here."

"I'm flattered you take such an interest in me." Puntillo recognized the truck as one belonging to Fronczek's brother. "Look, I--" he started to say.

"You cut your way inside the plant, didn't you?"

"It was an emergency."

"You don't determine emergency, officer Puntillo," Saunders said loudly, as if he were addressing a room full of recruits. "This refinery fire--"

"Where do you get off lecturing me?"

Saunders now pointed a finger at the cop. "Let me finish, Puntillo. This refinery fire really has nothing to do with Stieglitz Park. It's too important to leave to firemen or to the simpletons who make up the local authority. National security, Puntillo. National security depends on installations like the Standard Oil refineries. The fact that this one is in Stieglitz Park and Whiting, Indiana is really immaterial. It's not the *where,* but the *what* that's important here. I don't suppose you ever gave thought to that. We're talking about possible sabotage, possible activity by organizations that would gain a lot from such a fire! Foreign organizations, perhaps."

"Spies," Puntillo said, squinting as if he were lost.

"Sure, spies. Communist sympathizers. You've been locked up in this industrial slum for so long you may have forgotten about the world outside it."

"Communists," Puntillo said with a disbelieving giggle.

"That's right," Saunders said, moving down Louisiana Street, in the general direction of Puntillo's house—and the truck. "So just sweep up the glass, or whatever you're supposed to do here, and stay out of the way. One of the guys who was working near the unit that exploded actually lived right down this street. Right down there somewhere, near your own place."

Puntillo ignored the words, and took Saunders gently by the arm, steering him toward a vacant lot from which the Fronczek truck couldn't be seen. "Let me get this straight. You're saying the bureau thinks this is a communist plot? Some bomb-tossing red came out of the bushes to start World War Three?"

"Puntillo, don't try to understand something you're not trained to understand."

When Puntillo pulled Saunders' sleeve, the agent reached back for a weapon. Instinctively, Puntillo brought his knee upward and swept out with his left arm, knocking the pistol into Louisiana Street. Puntillo rushed to cover it with his foot.

"Who the hell do you think you are?"

Shaken, Saunders slowly straightened up. "Don't get yourself into worse trouble, Chet. Stick to solving what you're trained for, like small town murders."

"I'll tell you what I'm trained for. I'm trained to recognize a horse's ass." He stood on the pistol and looked to see if the other agents were in view. He didn't see any, but he did see Richie Bowman behind a shrub in a nearby yard, shooting away with his telephoto lens.

"Just move away and let me do what needs to be done," Saunders said to his former colleague.

"You're telling me straight faced this is a plot? For an FBI man, you're really dumb. Open your eyes! Everybody who lives in Stieglitz Park, their whole life is changed because of this, caused by a goddamn company that put an experimental monster right across from their houses—a stone's throw from houses with people in them. You know there's a kid who lived over on Berry Avenue that got crushed to death by flying steel? You know that?"

"If anything was done deliberately it wasn't the company that--"

"It was deliberate they erected the thing in that spot. Why don't you investigate why they picked that spot?"

"You're not making any sense. I haven't been around here for years, but even I know most of these people depend on Socko for paychecks. So don't act like some kind of village champion!" Saunders bent down. "Give me back my weapon and we'll call it even."

Puntillo kicked the pistol hard, and it bounced next to the fence where Richie was taking pictures.

Saunders stared at him. "What's this all about, really?"

Puntillo shook his head and looked down in disgust. In that pause, Saunders dove and tackled him around the waist. They rolled over each other on the pavement before Saunders brought up an elbow to Puntillo's chin. Puntillo fell back, but managed to kick Saunders in the face. Saunders sprang up bleeding from his mouth, and caught Puntillo with a hard right at the corner of his left eye. Puntillo needed a few steps to right himself, but just when it seemed he was going to stop, he lunged forward and tackled Saunders. Each struggled to get an armhold on the other, but for a few minutes both sets of arms and legs just slid off. Then Puntillo brought his right fist hard into the flesh next to Saunders' ear. Saunders moved away on all fours, bleeding from the nose and mouth.

"Great fight," Richie said, straightening up from a crouch and approaching them, carrying Saunders' pistol. "Right there on the field where we used to play football. Remember, Chet? That time Wally Pierce tried to tackle me and I gave him the stiff arm and he fell on a broken bottle. Jesus, cut his knee like raw meat. Remember? You rode in and carried the kid back home, bleeding all over your leather jacket."

Saunders got up and moved toward Richie. "Give me that gun. And the camera."

"Hey, what? I'm just recording the scene," said Richie. "It's a free country—ask Chet."

"Leave him alone," Puntillo said, snatching Saunders' pistol from Richie's outstretched hand.

"Leave him alone? What is this, some kind of blackmail plot?" Saunders looked wide-eyed at them.

"Leave him alone," Puntillo said again, moving between Richie and the agent. "You worried you won't get a medal for courage this time? The bureau doesn't like its people to look like fools, does it? You'll never get invited to Hoover's house for dinner this way."

Saunders looked intently at Richie. "What do you want?"

"He doesn't want anything," Puntillo said. "But I do. I'll walk you back to your buddies and give you your weapon before we get to them. Later I'll give you the film in that camera, undeveloped. Leave these people alone."

"They—"

"They did nothing except live here, and it's a miracle they're all not dead right now. Some of them have come back for special trinkets and chairs. Jesus, some of them have a lifetime of memories to gather here. Even a self-serving bastard like you must understand that." He took a deep breath. "Hell, maybe you don't. But you leave them alone."

"I—"

"Keep in mind you don't have any friends on the Whiting force." He looked up at the black smoke blowing toward the north. "*My* report could slow your climb to stardom."

Saunders wiped his mouth with a handkerchief.

"Let's go back and find your buddies and tell them there's nothing much to write up except the obvious," Puntillo said. "You don't even need to take notes. The insurance people will be out here soon enough. And oh, yeah, you slipped and fell against a fence post. Meaningless, irrelevant. What's important? The big still blew up, and the concussion ruined most of these houses. And the plant fire is still burning. No sign of sabotage. End of report."

The two former associates then walked across the field to an alley, and then back toward the boulevard. Puntillo saw Richie trailing them. They stopped and he went back to the young man.

"You go to my house and wait in front," Puntillo said. "Give me the camera."

"What for?" Richie said, pulling it back.

Puntillo kept his arm outstretched for a few seconds, then moved it to his belt. "Go to my house. Just go there. If you're not there ten minutes from now, you'll regret it." He ignored the camera, and went back to Saunders.

After emptying the shells, Puntillo gave Saunders back his pistol before they reached the others, just as he said he would. The agent put it away slowly. Puntillo turned and walked briskly down an alley to the back end of his place, looking fully confident but actually not sure if Richie would be there, nor if Saunders would follow him.

Louie Froczek walked home against a background of thick black smoke streaked with flame. His brother Joe had driven in past the junkyard west of Stieglitz Park, to help him load canned food and other non-perishables. Nine year old Lou was with him.

Richie was next door in Puntillo's yard, taking pictures of the broken house and Lou, whose bandaged feet didn't stop him from hitting flyballs high and deep over the back fence, imaginary home runs that moved him to limp around imaginary bases under the dark sky. He waved at Richie, and grinned as if it were an ordinary day. Richie didn't wave back because the cop was approaching him.

"Empty your pockets," Puntillo said to Richie.

"Why?"

"Just give me the damn film." He held out his hand.

"I've got two other rolls here that are old."

"Give it all to me, I don't trust you. Take the roll out of the camera, too."

Richie turned over all the film he had.

"Get lost." Puntillo said. "And if you bother Geraldine you land in jail. Don't forget."

After Richie walked away angrily, Louie Fronczek came out of his shed with tears in his eyes. His brother was walking with his arm around him.

"What the hell they gotta do a thing like that for?" Louie sobbed.

"Forget it, Louie." His brother said. "Everybody's okay, and that's what counts."

Puntillo approached. "What else is wrong?"

"Ah, some looters came through here. Took all my tools, even that little table and stool I just put in there last month."

"Yeah, well, like your brother said—" Puntillo tried to put in.

"Ah, shit. Nobody cares. I thought when a cop moved in next door nobody would bother us, but—ah, shit." He kept going, past the damaged house and on to the truck, which was loaded with chairs and a table and several boxes of laundry soap and canned goods.

For the moment, Chet was sure he'd never tell the disconsolate man that he himself had stolen the "looted" stuff.

The youngest Fronczek took one last swing and hit another deep drive, but the baseball hit the top of the wooden fence and bounded over toward Puntillo, who caught it and then tried unsuccessfully to do an arm-trick with it. It rolled into a gouged section in the front yard, where Lou picked it up.

"It's a crazy bouncing ball, fans," the boy said, as if he were announcing on radio, "but Minnie Minoso scoops it up and air-mails it home to catcher Gus Niarhos. And they got him!"

When the boy saw Puntillo looking at him with a smile, he stopped pretending.

"You should rest those feet," Puntillo said. "You don't want them to get infected."

"They don't hurt much. My mom put iodine on the cuts." He walked to the fence, then jumped over and walked toward the street with the cop. "Did you grow up in Stieglitz Park?"

"No," said the cop.

"How come you moved here?"

"Well—" he didn't know what to say to the kid, so he just shrugged.

"To make sure," the boy added, as if it had been part of his original question, "that everything went okay?"

"I think so," said Puntillo. "But it didn't work out, I guess."

"You did your best," the boy said as he continued on toward his uncle's truck.

Puntillo wanted to say how much he appreciated that, but the boy threw his bat and ball into the truckbed and climbed into the front seat. The cop waved at him as the truck rolled away.

5. *Louisa's Needs*
Spring, 1959

Once in a while Louisa Fronczek thought about the boxy house in Stieglitz Park, but only in connection with her brother Lou. When the place got wrecked by the refinery explosion four years earlier, they had to be evacuated, and she was glad to leave it. But whenever she looked down from an upper window, any upper window anywhere, down at long shadows, she could see her brother Lou, his little body in the big yard, hauling imaginary freight.

In those midsummers before the explosion he was a train. He was the black iron steam engine, and the wheels on the rails, and the man with the striped denim cap that operated it. At dusk he was most dramatic, locomoting slowly in the reddish sunlight, imaginary steam rushing laterally out the sides of his bare feet, heavy wheels rolling slow and straight toward the wide pine planks of the back fence. Beyond that was the alley, and farther away to the west the tank fields, flat black against the sunset. And to the northwest and west there were the silhouettes of the huge refinery stills that roared and spouted steam. Her brother seemed to function somehow in that whole scheme, and she would sometimes watch from above, in his room, the room their father had built for him in a section of the attic. When the family moved she took away with her that picture of him, framed from above by the window.

Looking away now from her book she saw through a newer window a smaller yard than the one in Stieglitz Park. The air here wasn't mixed with smoke and chemical process. It was thick and humid at the edge of Wolf Lake. She waited in the fade of day for Talbot Spencer, who would drive with her in his shiny new 1959 Pontiac across the state line to Cal City and John's Pizzeria. In Illinois she could legally drink Black Russians even though she wasn't yet 21. Women were granted adulthood in taverns there at 18.

After that they would go someplace and hold each other, perhaps intimately.

Louisa paused at the end of a chapter she was reading, an end muddled with the confused thoughts of the main character, Don Carlo Zaragossa. Handsome Don Carlo was a man of passion whose boldness and strength quickened a woman's pulse, and Louisa could imagine his sweat, trickling down the sides of his face, his dashing behavior punctuated by gleaming eyes. She could hear orchestral sounds as she watched dust float through the last streaks of sun above the bed.

Down on the grass of this small yard, her brother came into view, standing still, looking around as if in deeper thought now that he was thirteen. But she could still picture him shorter and bonier, chugging away toward the back fence, moving straight and determined. Their father called him Sunny, sometimes just Sun, but for her he was Lou, a train in the yard, his mouth both whistle and engine, his arms pumping parallel to the ground, moved smoothly by steam, rolling the wheels steadily toward Joliet and points east as warm night covered the industrial hum.

Watching him play train when he was little had always been a pleasant distraction for her. All that peculiar rigidity, dedicated to imaginary commerce. Sometimes he would reach quickly, randomly in the midst of his scheduled journey, into the elastic front of his shorts and scratch or shift his private parts. Very briefly, not like he was playing with himself. In those days he couldn't have known what they were really for, or what his arms or hands were for, either, the arms and hands that churned and chugged. Older now, maybe he was beginning to know. He wasn't any longer a train, and never again would be. But she still liked to think of him in that preoccupation, a boy in his own world.

E J & E was the actual railroad that had originally inspired him, the one their father always pronounced as two distinct but confused units: eejay nee, making it sound like an ailing joint. Back then the Elgin, Joliet and Eastern company's track had been close enough to be seen from the upper floor of the Stieglitz Park house, where Lou could look out and transfer into his imagination the sight of actual slow trains.

She knew her brother had liked that place, probably as much as she had hated it. But she loved him, and she never called him Sunny, just Lou, or sometimes kid. He looked like the kind of boy people called kid, funny but innocent; always appearing ready to laugh or shout, never looking bored. His eyes seemed bigger because his lashes were long; they almost looked fake. He was a good-looking boy, but he was unsure of himself. She didn't mind that their parents favored him, and had favored him even before their sister Lizzie, three years younger than Louisa, died of polio when Lou was just an infant. She knew that Lou didn't like being favored. Their mother's loud, overdramatic style of affection always seemed to embarrass him.

She turned away and took up the book, looked at the faces on the cover, then threw it back down on the bed. Against the pale pink bedspread the dark shades of the book cover seemed to turn into a single blemish, and she moved to another window, and another picture took shape against speckled asphalt. In her memory no one else was around except Chuck, who was getting into his dark blue car, lighting a cigarette. She could feel herself on the gray driveway, face down in despair, wet cheek in the dark on the hard concrete, four years in the past but so recent she could still taste the dry dust on the pavement, and feel the rough surface scratch at her skin. That driveway was unyielding, cruelly scratching and bearing upward against her as she lay still except for trembles of sorrow and fierce regret.

Lights from a tan car moved directly at the house but cut toward the curb in a quick easy swerve, indicating the driver was indeed Talbot, not some lost person looking for a different house number. Talbot's father, a superintendent at the refinery, had expedited the Fronczek claim several months after the explosion, or about the time Talbot himself was trying to make a good early impression on Louisa, without much success at first. But then she let him into her life at about the same time her father moved them into the new place, a 20 year old house in a thickly crowded neighborhood, crowded at least when compared to Stieglitz Park.

She walked with Talbot down the concrete, past some chalk marks. Her father and brother talked in the yard, her father quite loud. Talbot said a final something to her father with a smile at the car door, but she didn't hear what it was.

He talked as he drove, but she didn't hear any of that, either. Her head was against the seat, a soft, fake velvet fabric which in her hard thoughts became hard as concrete. She stretched her arm to the triangular vent but she decided not to open it. Her arm held out to another time, the time she had been thinking about just before he drove up.

On the remembered concrete she stretched her arm to the rocks at the edge of the driveway as Chuck got into the car, shaking his head and taking a deep breath. Her tortured misery turned angry after he drove away, the tires kicking up gravel, little white rocks that bounced up and around the driveway. One hit her on the wrist she had extended, and the sting of it made her want to retaliate. She gripped a border rock and sat up to throw it at his car, but he was already down the block, toward the stills that hummed and steamed against the dark sky. She slammed the smooth rock back into the soft earth next to the driveway, and her anger evolved into convulsive weeping, and she began pulling at her clothes, unable to free the persistent desire trapped inside her misery like sickly sweet nectar caught in a cluster of thorns.

She hit the glove compartment of Talbot's car, which made him laugh, since he had no idea what she had been thinking about. Talbot was a quiet, sweet man with blond slopes that descended in layers from the part in the middle of his head. More pleasant and handsome than Chuck, whose features were jagged and distinct, he liked to turn to her whenever they stopped at a red light, and touch her cheek with clean hands and manicured nails. Sometimes he told her how eager he was to give her joy and a good life. She often lamented what she called her own dirty brown hair, significantly less than black or blonde, and never fluffy. But Talbot called it deep silk, fresh walnut. He promised to give her jewels every birthday.

When they first had sex she controlled him without saying anything. She knew he was urgent, but she didn't let his passion get too far ahead of her own. A couple of times she mentally framed their lovemaking with memories of Chuck and his roughness in the back seat of the dark blue car, and it gave her strange pleasure—as if she were getting even with the bastard who had left her on the driveway.

She didn't want to go to college. At least she hadn't yet thought of anything so serious as higher learning or a career. Her high school grades were good and she loved to read, but the only thing that really interested her was the thought of living in a sorority and meeting girls who drove their own cars and lived in big homes. She would soon turn 21, and figured to save some money from working at the refinery's main office where she had met Talbot after he graduated from Earlham in the southern part of the state.

Then she got pregnant. She didn't immediately tell her parents, but Talbot confided in his father because he knew the man liked Louisa very much. The trust proved especially helpful to the young couple, for George Spencer promised them various forms of help as a collective wedding gift, most notably the down payment on a home in the Chicago suburbs.

"Find a good neighborhood not too close to bars and restaurants, or any place with crowds of noisy people. Get something with a nice yard so I can play with my grandchildren." He gave Louisa a hug around her shoulders. "You've got to have at least two or three, since Margie keeps saying she doesn't want any part of marriage or parenthood," he said, referring to Talbot's 18 year old sister. Talbot's father also helped out by getting him an intermediate level accounting position with a SOCO subsidiary headquartered on Michigan Avenue in Chicago.

Spencer's generosity often ran contrary to the senselessly tight budget his wife Wilma chose to keep. Hence neither he nor Talbot told her immediately about the promised gift, or Louisa's pregnancy, for that matter. Wilma was pleased that Talbot was marrying an attractive, well-mannered girl, whom she saw as a good example for

Margie. Still, Louisa couldn't understand Wilma's unpredictable frugality. When Louisa visited for dinner, Wilma served everyone as if they were all on strict diets. One baked potato was split between two people, as was one small cornish hen and the stuffing inside it. When Louisa casually described to Talbot how her own father required a full size chicken for himself, preferably cut up and breaded, Talbot explained that everyone in his family had gotten used to his mother's serving habits and, rather than argue uselessly with her, they all secretly snacked before and after meals.

The weekend after he started on the new job, he and Louisa drove into the suburbs looking for the right kind of house. She remembered thinking how the Green Avenue house was a great jump up from Stieglitz Park, but that feeling had died soon enough, and now she needed to get out of the whole industrial corner and into someplace clean. All the suburbs had crisp, natural names, but finding their way through to the correct Forest, Park, Ridge, or Grove wasn't easy. Talbot was ready to deal for any of the places they looked at, but each time Louisa looked at a house she liked they'd enter another which she liked twice as much. It took them a month of weekends before she finally decided.

By then the wedding plans were settling, and she knew she'd have to tell her parents about the baby. She anticipated problems, especially after Talbot had informed his mother and she behaved uncharacteristically cold toward them for a few days afterwards.

Louisa guessed her own mother would respond more emotionally. She did, exhaling slowly as she moved her head in a clockwise arc, deeply and in a thin wail that rose and fell like the shriek of a suddenly disturbed cat. Her disappointment echoed off the walls of her kitchen.

"What will they think? What will they say about me?" she said, in generalized pain.

"Who?" Louisa knew it was no one definite, but she asked because she couldn't think of any other defense.

"Anyone! My gosh, what kind of mother will they say I am when they find out?"

"It's not you that—"

"I can just see, O God, I can see Mary Hospody counting the months on her fingers! And oh, she was pregnant! And oh, her mother must have told her to do anything to get a man. And oh, like animals they couldn't wait!"

When Louisa tried to leave quietly she was shouted back.

"Such shame! And how I think of myself, innocent and dumb I was on my wedding night! And you, just going and—" she leaned against a chair and wept with clenched fist, and when Louisa tried to calm her with an embrace she turned away. "You're just lucky we like him, even though he's got that ritzy phony name."

She was indeed lucky both her parents liked Talbot, but that didn't stop her father from objecting, based on what she considered predictable grounds.

"If that's the way you're gonna do things," Louie said later, "then I'm not gonna cough up all that money for the hall and the food and all the rest of that. If he don't care no more about giving you a child that's lejamit, then—"

Lately she had stopped correcting his mispronunciations of multisyllabic words, but this time he made it sound as if the child would have fudgy limbs. "God, dad, the baby *won't* be *illegitimate*. We're getting married!"

"Yeah, well I'll walk you down the aisle, but I can't afford to pay for no big wedding."

Money was the heart of the matter, Louisa could see. He probably wouldn't have wanted to pay even if she had been perfectly chaste, for her father knew the Spencers were well off and could spend a lot more. "What the hell, he's the big boss in the big building," Louie said.

She was unhappy for about a week, and even gave some thought to getting an abortion. She knew a couple of girls who had had their problems taken care of while still in high school. She could lie to everyone and say she miscarried. But it was too frightening a thought, a dangerous desperation. And Talbot was eager to be a helpful father. Things would work out, she thought, and she began to anticipate having a little boy who might well grow up to be as pleasant and lovable as Lou.

As the weekend in late September drew near, most of her friends were away at school but she was able to get Ellie Novak to come home and be her maid of honor. Talbot's attendants were in their mid- to late-twenties, so Louisa was able to get bridesmaids by advertising the coolness and maturity of their temporary partners. Mr. Spencer paid for everything except the band. Louisa's father picked up that bill eagerly because a fellow worker of his who owed him a favor had a son who was an accordionist with a band that played parties cheaply. They also specialized in polka music, not the stuff Louie feared Spencer would like.

Like many other weddings this one featured the dividing of friends and relatives in social clusters belonging to bride or groom, without much intermingling. But the two sets of parents did sit together for a while, and the four of them discussed other daughters—Margie, the Spencer who was potentially wild and, as Wilma said, probably sipping booze secretly somewhere in a dark corner of the hall; and Lizzie, the Fronczek who had been dead for so long they rarely spoke of her except in terms of Lois's sometimes inventive expressions of guilt. The wedding reception conversation ended after neither of the Spencers responded to Louie's lament over the size of Lizzie's hospital bills, and how the insurance didn't pick up everything, and how he had to keep on paying even years after the girl was dead. His wife stared at him angrily.

Almost ready to leave, the bride and groom ambled over, Talbot kissing Louisa on the neck as they got near.

"You take good care of her now," Mr. Spencer told his son with a smile.

Louisa turned to her father, whose own smile seemed more polite than she was used to. Louisa hugged her mother, who reminded her in a straightfaced whisper that *her* wedding night wouldn't be anything special. "And you know why," she added, but put one hand to her mouth as soon as she said the words.

She told Talbot he was more handsome without the bowtie, and with his shirt collar open. Wilma agreed.

Louisa didn't argue with Talbot when he said they should pretend the wedding night would be their first intimacy. But when he came to her naked and erect she couldn't simply ignore that she already knew what he looked like and how it felt when he went into her, and how his kisses quickened in porportion to his breathing, and how his pleasure grew more dramatic at the first movements of her pelvis. He had never been rough, perhaps because she always took him without strain or effort.

As her handsome husband slept against the soft junction at her armpit, her thoughts got up from the marriage bed and anxious memory took over once again. She thought of Chuck and their first time, when his car was in the shop and he had walked her home in the late sunset, past the refinery lights and noise, the derricks topped with exhaust flame. Halfway home, even as passing headlights streaked across them, he had leaned into her against the tankyard fence and kissed her, sliding his tongue through her lips and pushing her buttocks toward him. When she twisted away he grinned and held his arms out to his sides and sang something about the night and the music, rhyming it somehow with the lights and periodic clangings of the big stills.

She laughed, but it was a nervous laugh, and he kissed her again a few times before they got to her father's tool shed in the back yard. By then it was too dark for any onlooker to see inside as they clutched and fondled each other, and he lifted her up to a workbench. She heard the sound of latex and she touched the slipperiness, then held him with both her arms and legs, and the brief pain turned warm, with his quick strength pushing inside her. When they rested they saw through an open window the big still, a noisy observer.

Several months into their marriage, as Talbot sat in shirt and tie finishing his coffee, looking at the middle pages of the Tribune, she felt sickly distress. Not the kind that in the early months of her pregnancy would make her rush off to vomit, but rather an unnerving pressure to steal into his apparent comfort as he perused the gossip columns.

She moved her head quickly, as if to shake off pieces of a dream. When she looked around at the bright room and its white cabinetry and white countertops, Talbot took notice.

"What's wrong?" he asked.

"I'd really like to make a big room," she said breathlessly. "Something like a leisure room, with soft drapes and bookcases and a fireplace."

He smiled. "Sure, anything you want."

She didn't look at him, however. "Something in peaceful shades, and we'd enter it right here, next to the refrigerator. We don't have to enter from the yard. There's nothing out there in the yard, anyway. Could we do that?"

"Anything you want," he said again, then looked in the direction she was looking. "The foundation would have to be extended, so that means cement trucks for a while, and heavy—"

"Oh, but that would be too expensive, wouldn't it?" she said. "Your father would think we were irresponsible."

"Why would he think that?"

"Well, he gave us the down payment, and here's more debt, and so soon."

"He'll be happy. And we wouldn't be borrowing from him again, if that's what you mean. I'll just sell some stock."

"Stock?"

"Sure. Standard Oil of Indiana."

"Wow. Stock." She smiled, curiously. "How did you get stock?"

"My grandfather left me some shares, and dad gave me some more when I turned 21."

Louisa had known from early in their relationship that Talbot wasn't poor, judging by his parents' house and the cars they drove, and the places he took her for dinner. But until now she hadn't thought of herself as a direct recipient of anything so gaudy as accumulated funds.

And even though he was her husband, she still marvelled at what seemed like impromptu generosity, the very idea of giving for no better reason than her need for something. After a short lifetime of frustrating arguments with her own tightfisted father, any sign of gracious giving took on the glint of high mystery. In the secrecy of her conscience she had decided, even before she learned where babies came from, that any children of hers would get the clothes and dolls and toys and other playthings they desired, without waiting for annual price-slashing sales. But that thought was mere fanciful invention, like getting dramatically kidnapped by a masked horseman who was secretly a duke. This suddenly available money certainly changed the options. For her, it clearly changed life.

Workers started the remodeling of their Glen Ellyn house in early March, but Louisa still had her family over for dinner on Easter Sunday. As soon as she answered the front door Lou put the palm of his hand flat against her stomach and grinned, for when he had last seen the stomach it had not protruded so. He apparently wanted the baby inside to move, but it didn't. He laughed, perhaps to hide his embarrassment. Then Louisa laughed and kissed him on the cheek, and everybody laughed. Her mother and father stepped up and she hugged them both, reminding them how long it had been since their last visit.

Talbot had known from the start of their relationship how to make small talk with her father. In this case the subject matter was the route taken between Whiting and Glen Ellyn, and all the detours at the state line and into the western suburbs, plus the heaviness of the traffic. Lou sat down and read a magazine article on baseball, which by now had supplanted his train fantasies. Her mother joined Louisa in the kitchen and gave her advice about heartburn and back pains, both of which had intensified recently. Louisa listened to her words before responding that brisk walks worked best for her. As for the heartburn, she would try anything. "Drink ice water and baking soda," her mother said. "And pray for strength. You should pray anyway, a lot, and you know why. It's Easter, and Our Lord died for your sins, too." Louisa never felt like discussing sin with her mother, so she quickly changed the topic to meat batter and deep fat frying.

For her, especially in her advanced pregnancy, heartburn was accelerated and intensified by fried foods. But because of her father's craving for it, she had to fry or listen to him nag about the good flavor he was missing. So, whereas the centerpiece of her Easter dinner was a classic stuffed bird, she added a platterful of crisply fried, breaded turkey drumsticks and breast slices. The intransigent old man never wanted to see on his plate turkey or chicken that had been stewed, roasted, grilled, or broiled. Anything that once wore feathers had to be dipped in egg batter and cracker meal, and fried in lard or Crisco.

During dinner everyone except Louie chatted idly. He said nothing even when passing a dish. Through the years he had often proclaimed, "if you're gonna eat, eat! Never mind monkeying around or yakking away." With big meals such as this he hunched over his the plate and chewed, looking up only with eye movement, as if he were protecting a kill from approaching wolves. Steadily he stripped the bones and tendons of the turkey legs, waiting until he had eaten everything before wiping the grease and flaked crust from his face. When he straightened up and looked around curiously, Louisa was sure he wanted more fried dark meat, but there wasn't any left. She could offer only the roasted variety.

"Nah, that's all right," he said. "I'll stop on the way home and pick up something."

"Well, here's some fried breast, dad," Louisa said.

"Nah, I don't like that dry white stuff. I'll just have some more of that bread."

"Try the dressing," Talbot said, reaching. "Louisa makes great dressing."

"Nah, I never liked that," he said. "Stuffing is like bread, and I'd rather eat good bread." He sliced some off the end of the loaf.

"Look how much he's cutting," his wife said in a deep, rejecting voice and frown usually reserved for television actresses she didn't like.

"I like the kronka," he said, referring to the end of the hard crust.

"Kronka, like heck," Lois said. "That's more like half a loaf."

"Mom, there's plenty more," Louisa said, trying to encourage pleasantries.

"You keep eating bread like that," Lois said, "and you'll have to buy all new clothes."

"Ah, bunk," he said. "It's Easter, so I'm celebrating the end of Lent."

"We should all celebrate," Talbot said. "Let me get some wine out here."

"Nah, no wine for me," her father said through a cheekful of bread. "I don't drink much."

"Oh, him. He's too cheap to drink," her mother said. "I'll have a teeny bit, though."

When everyone finished Louisa cleared the table, put away the food, and started to do the dishes with her mother. But Talbot pulled her away from the sink and told her to sit. She wanted to walk, instead, and she got her brother to go along.

"Look how cute he looks!" her mother said loudly when Louisa told her they were going out. "He's the cutest boy in Whiting. Thirteen years old, already!" She took his face in her wet hands and kissed him as he twisted away.

"He *is* a doll," Louisa said, messing his black hair. "If he weren't my brother, I'd—" her joking tone abruptly halted, as she realized her mother wouldn't appreciate any kind of double-entendre or dirty talk, even in jest.

"So, do you have a girlfriend?" Louisa asked when they got outside.

"Huh?" He squinted and didn't look at her.

"Well, you *are* the cutest boy in town. You just heard the proclamation."

He slowed down. "I'm going to walk on the other side of the street."

She grabbed him by one shoulder, then hugged him. "I won't tease any more, I promise."

He had grown a lot in the nearly four years since the explosion. Now she had to look up to see into his dark, round eyes, with the long lashes. Sometimes when he glanced downward his eyes showed sadness and devilishness at the same time. Now as always he was quick to give a closed-mouth smile, the only facial characteristic he seemed to have inherited from their father.

They reached a set of railroad tracks that had not been used for years.

"Do you still play train?"

"No." He smiled, and when she turned to him he looked away as if to hide. "Do you?"

"No, I don't." He was still smiling.

"You're not a very good liar."

He broke into a laugh. "Honest, I don't. I'm not lying. It's just that it's so stupid, I can't help laughing. My friends would really let me have it if they knew I did that. Even if I was just a little kid then."

"So what are you now? A *big* kid? You're only thirteen."

"I don't like fantasies and games."

"Okay, okay. Well, your secret's safe with me. Anyway, it's not stupid. I used to like watching you, as if you wished you had been born an engine, or something."

He touched her stomach again. "What does that feel like?" he said.

"You mean the baby inside?"

"Yeah, when it kicks or turns. Does it hurt? Is it like when you have to fart?"

"Lou! It doesn't feel like that at all. It feels like—what it is, a baby moving around and poking its elbows, and so on." She took a deep breath and exhaled. "And it seems to get heavier every day."

He made a puzzled face again, but he also showed the beginning of another grin. "I heard that babies are scrunched up inside a bag of water, or something. Can you hear splashing?"

"No. I mean there isn't enough for the baby to do the backstroke."

He made a face. "Come on, I'm serious."

"You don't like my explanation?"

"I like the idea of being an uncle. I'll be the only kid I know who is an uncle."

She put her arm around his waist and left it there as they walked another block, where the sidewalk ended in front of a big field that was being dug up. Then they walked back toward the house, past smoothly finished concrete driveways and newly-seeded lawns and houses with labels still stuck on the window glass.

"God, look at the size of that one," Louisa said, moving toward it. "I'll bet it's got five bedrooms in it."

Her brother looked at the big place but said nothing.

"Do you miss the place in Stieglitz Park?" she said.

He shrugged, then nodded. "My room upstairs was big."

"You liked that."

"Yeah. My room and the attic. I had a whole floor."

"So you could hide."

"Yeah, and see everything. Like the big fire through the crack in the roof."

"What a thing to wake up to. You got thrown to the floor by the explosion, didn't you?"

He nodded. They walked without saying anything else until they were just a few doors down from her house.

"Well, that's my exercise for the day, " she said.

He stopped, and stretched his arms forward and then outward, as if he were readying himself to fly. Then he stood perfectly still, his eyes big, and stared at her.

"What?" she asked. "I know. You play <u>airplane</u> now."

"I do not." He looked away.

"What's the matter?"

"I saw you that night on the driveway," he said softly.

"Hm?"

"The night before the explosion, you came home real late. And you were angry, and noisy, and I woke up. I never heard you get angry with that guy Chuck before, so I thought it might be someone else, instead. But I got up and looked down from my window and I could see it was him, and you pushed him away and called him a bastard. He kind of snickered like he was surprised you were angry, and you tried to push him again, but he moved out of the way and you tripped on something and fell down on the driveway."

She trembled, for the scene was immediately unsettling because it was her brother recalling it. The fact that he actually saw and remembered compounded new pain because here he was, the softly funny, delightfully reserved pubescent little fool. He was telling her he had been secretly aware of something she couldn't rid herself of, showing and telling it from a new angle, a new view. He was describing what she had never told anyone.

"You were up there, looking down?"

"Yeah. You were on the concrete, and he bent and said something I couldn't hear—"

"He said 'you're too childish to understand this is just ordinary.'" She trembled some more. "And he said how he had to go out into the world and find out all he needed to know, from tough people and exciting women, about things that mattered. Or something like that. What he meant was that <u>I</u> <u>didn't</u> matter, but he didn't say it. He said I'd get over it."

"I couldn't hear anything," Lou said.

"Maybe he didn't say quite that, but that's what he meant. I should have spit at him. Or thrown something as he went to his car. I tried to, actually."

Her brother looked puzzled, but he went on anyway with his recollection. "I came downstairs and unlocked the door, and I was going to go out and help you if you were hurt. When you got up I went back upstairs. He was driving away. And then I heard you come inside."

That wasn't all of it, she thought. Could he have seen the screams she was muffling down there, her mouth at the abrasive surface, biting her lips to suppress a cry of outrage, clutching the rocks next to the concrete.

"You saw," she said, in a delayed whisper.

"You were crying. I heard it. It sounded like a squeal. I thought he hurt you."

"He did."

"He did?"

She could see his confused concern, and she reached a hand to touch his chin, then rested it for a second on his cheek. "Not physically."

They walked toward her front entrance, which was open behind the screen door. From inside came her father's voice, loudly telling Talbot about the different route he planned to take on their way back home. The wheeze and changing pitch of his voice made the explanation convoluted even though it should have been simple. Louisa smiled, then stopped and held her brother's arm as she looked up. "Talbot's going to make the house bigger."

"Just for the baby?" He laughed nervously.

"For me. He's going to give me everything. That's the way he is."

They walked across her driveway and up the lawn to the front steps.

Talbot grinned in the doorway, rolling his eyes at Louisa, then forcing a frown at Lou. "Where've you been with my wife?"

6. *Moral Turpentine*
1958-59   School Year

"The novel is loaded with the kind of irony which is easy to perceive as irony," said Professor Stephen Coble. "Right from the title to all the rotting fruit imagery, and on to the ending, when Rosasharn, even though she's got nothing to give, gives." He cautiously got up from his chair to walk around the long seminar table. Actually it was two tables pushed together, for the registrar had mistakenly enrolled twenty students, twice the optimal number. A few, like Geraldine Stillman, were not even seniors. He stood right behind her chair and threw out his ultimate, end-of-the-class question. "But what about the irony Steinbeck didn't intend? You know, the stuff he couldn't have known about, the historical irony. The stuff <u>we</u> know but he couldn't have known unless he was one strange visionary."

No one looked ready to respond. To Geraldine the question sounded as if it were designed to stir cleverness; she never tried to be clever in this class. A few of the seniors in the room liked to intimidate other students through scornful laughter if they thought a stated opinion was stupid, or founded purely on emotion. She usually kept quiet.

"No one? Come on, we've been together all these weeks, and you're still afraid to make a fool of yourself?" About half of them laughed nervously. "You realize, of course, that you're forcing <u>me</u> once again to make a fool of <u>my</u>self, and how will that reflect upon the collective wisdom of Indiana University, which granted me tenure years ago? I'll have to write another book, for god's sake, to make up for the exhibition of foolishness. Come on, there's no right answer, so make up something erudite."

A young man seated in the middle of the room began speaking as he half-raised his hand. "Are you looking for something like 'Lincoln was a racist'?"

"No. Lincoln knew his own feelings about blacks. Whatever gets dug up by scholars is based on what Lincoln said or wrote. What we've got here is just the opposite."

Students stirred and put their notes and books in order, clearly wishing to get up and leave. Another young man spoke. "Do you mean something like this— Steinbeck couldn't have known how his own writing was going to change after *The Grapes of Wrath*?"

"No, I don't mean that, but you're headed in an interesting direction. I'm referring to the historically implied future of his characters. What does that sound like? The historically implied future—write it down, somebody, in case I forget it. It's a good phrase, I think. The historically implied future of the transient people, Okies especially. They're courageous, self-sacrificing, helpful to each other, purveyors of Manself! and so on, a true picture of what Steinbeck himself observed in his travels with them, as far as we know."

He then paused and bit his lip, even as the rest of his face looked like it wanted to smile. Looking at the clock, he then spoke louder, more dramatically. "But we *also* know—now, that is—that those *same* people eventually worked in war plants and put together a nice nest egg and bought property in the late 1940s and forgot about Manself. And they worried about the influx of migrant workers from Mexico. And they became republicans. And they voted for Eisenhower. Twice. And therein lies another kind of tragedy."

There was some low-toned laughter. Geraldine immediately thought of her father, who had distrusted Stevenson but voted for him anyway. Others in the class, after many weeks fully aware of Coble's politics, rolled their eyes or didn't react at all, and got up to leave.

"One more thing before you run off," Coble said. "I'm generally pleased with your papers, but unfortunately I haven't finished reading all of them. I'll definitely return them to you after the Thanksgiving break, so you'll have plenty of time to revise them before Christmas," he paused noticably, surveying the room quickly with eye movement, "if, of course, you need to do so. Have a nice long weekend." As the others walked out he gestured toward Geraldine, who was putting her jacket on, a bulky black thing that seemed to serve as a hiding place, but made her hair look golden above it.

"Miss Stillman, could I talk to you?" He didn't wait for her reply, but turned abruptly and walked to his front desk and reached into his briefcase.

Geraldine suddenly felt cold and fearful. Perhaps he was rejecting her paper, aiming his "time to revise" comment especially at people like her. She knew very little about his grading policy, although since he was a popular teacher the odds were that he wasn't too tough. Other girls in the class thought he was a self-styled curmudgeon who had secret affairs with female colleagues. Geraldine thought he looked like a steelworker she once knew, a physical man whose hands were never completely clean, not even when he shook hands at political dinners. But Coble's hands were clean, and he spoke beautifully. She liked his thick black hair.

She could see pencil marks and words in the margins of her paper as he took it out of his briefcase. Her hands trembled and she clutched them together.

"Dr. Coble, I know I could have said some things differently."

"How do you mean?" He didn't look at her, but held her pages and shuffled them, as if searching for a specific passage.

"Well, this is the first long paper I've ever written in a literature class. And— uh—I don't even know if I want to major in English."

He said nothing, but kept on leafing through the twenty sheets, clasped differently from the way she had submitted them the week before. He seemed to have pages mixed up. Then he pointed to something, nodded, and finally looked up at her. For an instant his eyes moved as if he were studying her. Up to now she had sat at the far end of the big table; this close, his stare frightened her a little.

"What's that you said?" he asked.

"I'll make any changes you suggest."

"No, no. Why would you do that?" he moved a chair for her to sit on. "This is a wonderful essay. I've read it three times and it gets better each time."

She sat, and the fear immediately left her, as if it were a deep breath she had been holding. She made a nervous face, then briefly covered her eyes with both hands, a childish twitch that made him laugh. When she brought down one of her hands to the desk as if for support, he instinctively put one hand on top of hers, just for a second.

"It's very good," he said.

"Oh," she said with a wide grin. "You really mean that."

"Of course I do. Hasn't anyone ever told you you're an excellent writer?"

"Not really. I haven't written very much."

"You haven't?" He looked genuinely surprised.

"I had to keep a journal in a phys ed course, but that's about it."

"This is far and away the best paper in the class. But keep that to yourself. The prima donnas want lots of feedback, so I couldn't return all of them today."

"The prima—"

"Never mind. I have a couple of questions. Not really objections, but just some things I'm uncertain about. Most importantly here, in the middle of page 17. Why do you suddenly bring yourself into the body of the essay? I quote, 'Someone once told me it was dangerous to be beautiful. I wish I could go into these books and whisper that warning to the doomed people inside. I would be a helpful ghost, spooking warnings to them while they slept, not knowing the next day will bring death. Despite his ill-purchased flash and desperate wealth, Gatsby is a gorgeous dreamer who certainly doesn't deserve to be killed.' Let's see, dum de dum de dum, I'm skipping here."

"Okay," Geraldine said, dumbfounded by the sight and sound of him reading the words she had written.

"And here, 'I can't resist the juvenile urge to pull Joe Gillis out of the pool and breathe life back into him, because he isn't really a cynic. He has been wounded in so many other ways—' Jesus! You bring in *Sunset Boulevard*!" He laughed.

She squirmed a little. "I'm sorry. But you didn't say we *couldn't* use a movie."

"It's okay. It's wonderfully outrageous, and Joe Gillis fits your context perfectly. Besides, that's one of my favorite films."

"Oh, mine too. When I think about the things he says to Betty at the end, I just hurt."

"You mean Norma."

"No, Betty, the girl he writes with. Nancy Olson."

"Oh yeah. I haven't seen it since it first came out." He stared at her again and nodded his head slightly. "Look, I have a suggestion. I want you to think about tightening up the whole paper—shorten it—and re-direct some of it so you can submit it to the annual Humanities and Culture Conference. They devote three or four sessions to student presentations."

She felt confused. "A conference?"

"Right. It's held each year in late January, in a different city. This time it's in Key West. You'd have to get the paper to them before the Christmas break, but I'm sure you can do it."

Geraldine tugged at the zipper of her jacket. "I guess I'm not following you. I don't major in English. Why—"

"That's probably for the best. I've been to presentations by grad students in English and their stuff is mostly shit, anyway. What you need to do is tighten it up, make it shorter so it will fit into a slot that's 20 minutes long. More importantly—the point I was going to make earlier—the way you bring yourself in, as if it were suddenly a sort of narrative. Why not do that throughout the paper?" He smiled and paused, but she didn't grow nervous. In fact, she smiled back.

"It isn't silly to do that?" she asked.

"Not at all. Your personal comments certainly fit what you're trying to say about violent death. Violent death," he repeated. "A surprising topic coming from someone who's—as far as I can tell—mild-mannered, gentle, whatever. I'll bet you love animals."

She squinted.

"Forget that. Why did you write about violence?"

"Well, when I finished each book it seemed to stand out in them. For me, at least. To the point that I couldn't analyze them without first saying something about death. And they're all terrible deaths, I mean the people who die are the ones who really should live."

"You are passionate about that in the paper. Why?"

He seemed to be encouraging her to feel something, which was unlike the English teachers she had written for in high school, and certainly unlike the few others she had been exposed to at Indiana. "I love to read. I guess I get into the books too personally. If a character I like is wronged, I feel hurt, in a way."

He leaned back in his chair, his black hair mostly flat against his head, like tamed fur. He kept his eyes on hers. "Why?"

In the easy quiet of the empty room she could hear his slow breathing. She wanted to tell him things. "My father was the person who told me it was dangerous to be beautiful," she said. "He said that in any part of the world, any situation got more risky when beauty entered into it."

"That sounds like another movie. *King Kong*, I think." He waved both his hands, as if trying to erase his irrelevant comment. "Don't mind me."

She stared ahead at nothing, and for a moment she didn't seem to be breathing. She felt her face drooping.

"He was killed, " she said. "My father was murdered."

Coble's eyes widened and his mouth froze, partially open, and he slowly moved forward. He couldn't pick the right words to say. It didn't matter to her, for she went on.

"It was four years ago. He was running for the city council in my home town. The man who stabbed him was convicted and sent to prison. He killed himself last February, so it's all over. Except that I think about it often."

Coble reached out and took hold of the same hand he had touched earlier. He looked at her and she felt a kind of freedom for having told him. Without being asked, she told him other things about her father: the way he looked when he knew she was lying, or how he could appear interested in something when in fact he wasn't really listening to her words. She described his deep voice, and how persuasively he spoke.

The classroom was unscheduled during the next hour, so they stayed and talked. She told him how she loved her father and how she still missed him, and when tears came to her, Coble didn't intrude on her grief. He sat and listened and let her stop when she finally got it all out. At the same time, he felt she was explaining her place in such a course. She was bringing her life into American Literature, and he was accepting it as a legitimate entry.

Before she left he assured her he was serious about reworking the paper for the conference. She wondered aloud about the cost of going to Key West. He told her not to worry, for the department had funds for such contingencies.

Her mother and Chet Puntillo drove down to Bloomington for Thanksgiving. They took Geraldine to a small restaurant on the road to Brown County, and they openly talked about the possibility of commitment, just to see Geraldine's reaction. She didn't really care if they got married, but she didn't want them to *see* she didn't care, so she just smiled. With Puntillo and Sophie sitting side by side in the leather booth that curled around a table full of wine and turkey and bowls of other things, Geraldine said she would be happy if they were happy. However, a noticably nervous Sophie told her later, when they were alone, that she wasn't sure she would go through with it. She liked him as a good friend, and that was that.

They stayed until Saturday in a University guest house. Because they were in separate rooms, Geraldine joined her mother in one of them. All the dormitories were practically empty, and campus life was a void for the four day break. Geraldine told them a paper of hers was being considered for a conference in Key West, but she said nothing about Coble or his encouragement.

Nor did she mention to either of them that, the day after Thanksgiving, she had seen Richie Bowman just outside a coffee shop. He was writing something on a clipboard. For no particular reason she took a few steps in his direction and he saw her. He was thinner and tan, and his eyes were less intense than she remembered. For a few seconds they looked at each other, and then Geraldine, using the years since they had last seen each other as a sort of safety barrier, shook her head with a slight, curious smile.

"What are you doing here?" she asked.

He laughed. "Do you ask that of everyone, or just me?"

He told her he was a freshman, taking advantage of the Korean G.I. Bill before the politicians did away with it. He had pushed up his number for the draft back in '56, spent some time on Okinawa and the Japanese mainland, then drove a truck around the midwest after his discharge. For the time being he was taking the usual freshman courses, plus an intro to journalism, but his main interest was still photography. He told her he sold a picture of a car accident in front of the main library to the *Daily Student*.

"You're still taking pictures. Did you do that in the army?"

He shook his head, then finished writing something on the clipboard. "I've got a job with the journalism department. Have to make a living while I'm going to school."

"But you get the G.I. Bill?"

"That isn't much. Not enough to have fun on, anyway." He looked at her more casually than he once did, but he still made her nervous. "You probably don't have any trouble having fun. Guys still beating your door down. Especially now, you're legal."

She turned away, rolling her eyes, then cautiously looked back at him. "I'm kind of interested in one, but it isn't serious. I've got to go." She regretted the lie, then compounding it, as if she were inviting a phone call.

"Yeah," he said. "Good seeing you, too."

Geraldine found it surprisingly difficult to cut things out of the essay. Every time she went to the library to look again at one of her sources, she got a new idea which tempted her, if anything, to expand it. To resolve her confusion without having to wait for the next class, she went one cold, windy afternoon to Coble's office. English professors were spread randomly around the campus while the new Arts and Letters building was being completed. Coble was temporarily holed up in the basement of Hollingsworth Hall, an old classroom structure, just across the snowy lawn from Ernie Pyle Hall, the journalism building.

She speeded up her walking, pretending she was lost in thought, when she saw Richie coming out the front of Pyle. But she had to slow down a little as she approached Hollingsworth, for there was Coble, talking through the opened entrance to a slender woman wearing sunglasses. Her coat and shoes looked as if they had been designed for no one else, and she pushed back her dark hair with a hand inside a tightly fitting leather glove. When they finished talking Coble ducked inside quickly, and the woman went down the concrete steps in a smooth, deliberate pace. She carried herself perfectly, confidently; Geraldine couldn't guess her age.

Geraldine tried to walk smoothly and deliberately into Coble's office. He barely looked up, and didn't even seem surprised when he saw her, carrying her scribble-revised essay. He gestured for her to sit.

"Why do you want to bring in Edmund Wilson here?" Coble spoke with a touch of exasperation after looking through her revisions. "Enough people are already quoting him at any given minute of any day. He doesn't belong in this."

"But he says the same things about tragedy as—"

"Who cares? Keep it fresh—keep it your own. You've done some nice chiseling in this. Don't invite Wilson or any of those guys into it."

Her shoulders drooped. "Doctor Coble, I was always told that—"

"You were told wrongly. Erroneously." He laughed. "The people who told you whatever they told you weren't looking at this particular paper, this personal essay, when they told you you should do this and you shouldn't do that." He appeared to be staring at her forehead. "What is your first name? I know, Geraldine. It scans nicely. Geraldine, I don't like to be called 'doctor.' I don't wear a stethoscope and I don't diagnose. Professor Coble will be fine. Or mister. Or Stephen, for that matter."

She didn't know how to take his suggestion, and she was relieved when he continued to offer other ideas about letting the personal tone dominate throughout, and how this would always make the cutting easier. She confessed to second thoughts about sending off the paper to Key West, and worried about the expense to the department of English. He said her worry was unfounded, since the department would receive a lower budget next year if they didn't spend all of this year's funds. Anyway, another IU student, a graduating history major, had already had a paper accepted, and she could share a room with her. And he assured her the conference organizers would spill over with enthusiasm when they read her essay, and would want to know who advised her. Ultimately, he would then be looked upon as an extraordinary judge of talent.

Before leaving, she asked him if the woman she had seen him with in the doorway was his wife. He acknowledged it was.

"She looked very. . .dignified. Sophisticated."

"Expensive," Coble said. "All of the above. I'm not being sarcastic. It's her money, and she earns it. Nicole is an interior decorator. She spends half her time in Chicago and Indianapolis, driving her creative minions to productive exhaustion. She's quite successful."

When she got back out in the cold air, she angled back across the snow toward the Women's Quad, ignoring Richie, who was loitering across the street. He didn't follow her.

During the Christmas break Geraldine made some spending money working at a jewelry store on 119th Street in Whiting. She impressed the owner with her ideas about advertising techniques. He encouraged her to work for him the following summer.

A few days before she got on the plane to Key West—only the second flight in her life—she had met Valerie Turner, the history student who was going to be her roommate. Valerie was plain-looking but she had an easily animated face, and she shared some of her own sexual history much earlier in their conversation than Geraldine would have expected. Geraldine, however, didn't respond in kind. She didn't like sharing intimacies with anyone.

She had to admit to herself, at least, an unsettling attraction to Coble. Before takeoff he introduced her to a stout gentleman named Wahlberg from Northwestern, who had written a few books on Robert Browning. Geraldine was polite to him, even though he looked at her with a kind of hunger, glancing down at her breasts while praising Coble's talents and saying how he valued their collegial friendship.

After Wahlberg moved off to the rear of the plane, Coble sat in Geraldine's window seat, since she seemed nervous about the view. "You get used to it," he said. "I like to look at the rivers from up here. Like a big map." He smiled at her, and she smiled back but said nothing. "He's a horse's ass," Coble said of Wahlberg, "but he can give you connections if you decide to major in English."

"He doesn't know anything about me," she said.

"That doesn't matter," he answered quickly, and patted her hand, which was resting on her thigh. She knew she should be offended by the implication of what he said, but instead she simply enjoyed his warm touch.

Early in the flight they talked again about her father. Coble seemed sensitive and genuinely concerned when he asked her about the crime, and cautious enough that she knew his interest was personal curiosity, rather than something he would eventually exploit. When he asked about her father he seemed, in fact, fatherly.

"What kind of hopes did he have for you?"

"You mean, as a career? He never spelled anything out. I think he wanted me to be a little like him. He was a leader, and he thought I could be a leader."

"Leading what? You want to go into politics?"

She shrugged the shoulder nearer to him. "I don't know." She shrugged again, nervously. "I guess I don't show much leadership in our class."

"Well, you should. And you probably will, now that you know you've got something to say. A lot more than some of those jerks in there. They think they're funny, but they're just scared of failing."

She looked at him and he looked back. "You don't—" she hesitated. "If we had just met, I wouldn't guess you were a professor. Not of English, anyway."

"Why? Because I talk dumb?"

"No. No you don't. But when you refer to those guys in the classroom—the ones who sit at the far end of the table and, I don't know, act—"

"Supercilious," he interrupted. "Self-consciously arrogant."

"Yeah." She grinned, searching for a way to seem perceptive. "But it doesn't impress you. I think they talk that way because other English professors like to hear it, but you don't." She shook her head and waved her hand, cutting off his interruption. "I'm not saying you betray your feelings to them, because you don't. But you—I don't think you like English majors."

"Well, I don't know if I'd go that far. I don't like many of them, I suppose."

"That's terrible."

He laughed heartily.

"It *is*," she said, turning directly to him. "You must not like what you do, even though—"

"I *love* what I do. I absolutely love teaching. But I don't have to approve of everyone in my classes. Some of them I simply don't like. But I like you."

She moved a bit toward the aisle. "I'm not an English major."

"Yes, but maybe I'm secretly recruiting you, using reverse psychology because I see great analytical potential in you."

She laughed, and he laughed back at her. She found herself truly enjoying each bit of conversation with him. It may have been a reckless enjoyment, but it sustained her for the rest of the flight, at least.

She asked him why he decided to teach, and he told her again it was the G.I.Bill, a money thing. She recalled what Richie had mentioned about government money, but Coble was older, probably in his mid-thirties. He acknowledged he had been in actual combat in Sicily, and then later had an easier time of it in Belgium near the end of the war, in the spring of 1945. She wanted to ask him if he had killed anyone, and if the killing had made a difference in his life. But she could tell he was more interested in making her laugh, so she laughed, and looked at his hair and the parts of his face she hadn't looked at before.

He told her that by the time he went back to school, after the war, the only thing he really wanted to do was write, so he got a degree in English as the easiest fit, and then a doctorate from the University of Chicago, with help from Nicole, whom he married while still an undergrad at Illinois. Nicole impressed the hell out of everyone she ever met, he said, including people at the university who wanted to hire her, and one who actually did, and for a good salary. Meanwhile, he transformed his Ph.D. dissertation on James T. Farrell into a slim volume for Greenhouse publishing. After taking the job at Indiana he wrote a series of essays on T.S. Eliot, Ezra Pound, and other poets. They were always in two parts, followed by a somewhat comic epilogue. First he would argue a point, and then he would point to flaws in his earlier argument. Finally, as if he were settling a game which was tied at the end of regulation, he would end up favoring one side or the other, but only in totally new terms—new "evidence" uncovered at the last moment. For whatever reason, Greenhouse liked them enough to gather the essays under a single cover entitled *Yes and No,* which sold 3,000 copies and was a key factor in getting him tenure.

"I look back at it as a bunch of crap," he said. "But the reviewer for the *Delta Philology Quarterly* must have been consumed by it. He wrote something like 'classic detachment which challenges notions of reader reality and structural purity.'"

"I don't think I understand," she said.

"Neither did I. I doubt if the reviewer did, either. He was just fulfilling his own expectations."

She laughed nervously. He went on with his condensed autobiography. Shortly after the book came out, he promised himself he would never again write anything which could be construed as literary criticism. He then wrote two novels, one about fighting and dying in sub-zero temperatures, the other about labor-management conflict in a Chicago warehouse. Both received positive reviews in a few sources but didn't sell many copies.

"Did you demonstrate 'classic detachment' in them?" she asked.

"Hey, you're catching on," he said with a laugh.

"I couldn't resist," she said. "Seriously, I'd love to read them."

He started to say something, perhaps to ask why, but then turned away and looked out the window as the plane swept through the feathery white heavens above South Florida.

Geraldine barely got to know Valerie, her appointed roommate, who fully intended to spend most of her time with her boyfriend, who just so happened to be a graduate student at the University of Florida, and was also attending the conference. So Geraldine was left alone with her apprehensions over presenting a paper to a group of presumably bright, critical people. What if, she wondered, they were like the "supercilious" guys in the Modern Lit seminar? They might ask questions hoping to see her buckle under pressure, or watch her make up a confused answer to cover for her stupidity. Perhaps Coble—Stephen—would rush in to the rescue, with suitably great sarcasm.

It was a thought she kept privately, in a daydream featuring his face, closeup, the lower half of it encased in short black stubble, giving his skin the look of passionate fatigue. She recalled how his unexpected praise for her writing had made her own skin grow warm, and she felt a special satisfaction and pride, feelings previously brought on by comments about her looks.

According to the printed program she had received on arrival at the Bayfront Hotel, Coble was scheduled to take part in a 60-minute panel discussion on Literature and Motion Pictures just before lunch the next day. Her presentation was set for an afternoon slot, running from 4:10 to 5:30, hers being the third and final paper, to be followed by general questions and discussion. They had misspelled her name, giving her one "l" instead of two. She was thrilled, even so, to see herself officially cited.

She decided to commit her paper—all ten and a half pages of it—to memory.

Coble called to ask if she and Valerie would dine with him. Geraldine said she needed to be alone with her paper and she would get something from room service. He offered to be an audience to her practice reading, but she declined in as appreciative a tone as she could muster. She didn't tell him Valerie was never around, and she didn't tell him she was memorizing her paper. He said he felt responsible for her, and he insisted she call him if she had any problems.

On the following morning the Bayfront hummed with activity. Beyond the lobby was a big room devoted to publishers' exhibits and presses from various universities. But the check-in area was itself so crowded with desks and representatives who were selling several college-oriented ideas or text approaches, it reminded Geraldine of the time she and her parents had gone to Las Vegas. To pull your luggage to the front desk you had to negotiate a maze of slot machines set up at different angles. The security people there weren't especially friendly, while these men at the Bayfront desks grinned and spoke to everyone pleasantly, but their intentions were the same. They both hoped you would get so tired of figuring out how to get through that you'd simply stop and plug in some quarters, or pick up a monograph and listen to the seller's prepared sales pitch.

A woman from a Texas college spoke with gestures to a representative about something she had written about a New Yorker story called "Territory of Ice," but her accent made the key word sound like "ass." Still nervous, Geraldine mustered up a smile, then walked up a short flight of stairs to the mezzanine, just to see the meeting room in which she was to present her paper. She wore a gray knit dress with a necklace of strung pewter, trying in vain not to look too young, for most of the women who walked past her looked older than her mother.

In her mind she had blocked out areas of her paper to the extent she could associate one thing with another, thereby allowing her to recall a passage which she might momentarily have forgotten. She was talking to herself when Coble caught up with her from behind.

"You know," he said, "for someone who's never done this before, you're pretty independent."

"What? Oh—"

"You're pretty, in fact. I didn't mean to sneak up on you. But you look wonderful."

"Thank you. I—" She felt strangely uncomfortable with his sudden stress on her appearance. All her life people had complimented her, but Coble's words made her nervous.

"You want a cup of coffee?" he asked.

"No thanks, I just had some with toast. Too much of it makes me. . . jittery." She actually meant it made her go to the bathroom often, but she chose not to share that detail.

"Is the paper ready? Maybe that's not the right question to ask."

"I've pretty much memorized it."

"What? Why would you do that?"

"To give myself more confidence."

"Well, I'm not sure about that. But if you've done it, you've done it." He looked at his watch. "Are you coming to the Lit-MoPic panel?"

"Of course. How could I be so ungrateful to miss it?"

"Hmm."

"Oh, I didn't mean it that way," she said, quietly embarrassed.

"I promise you won't be excessively bored. Wait for me afterwards and I'll buy you lunch. And we'll talk about this memorizing." He said the word in a low tone. Clearly he disapproved.

The Literature/Motion Pictures panel was so heavily attended they had to bring in fifteen or twenty more chairs, and the session started several minutes late. Geraldine sat in the midst of a faculty group from various places in the south. The woman she had run across in the lobby sat nearby reprising her enthusiasm for "Territory of Ice." The man sitting behind her leaned forward with a puzzled expression and asked "territory of what?" Geraldine felt like laughing but forced herself not to, seeing that no one else in the immediate vicinity seemed to think it was funny. The same woman rambled on about other presentations she wanted to attend, such as the combined Marxist/Freudian approach to *My Antonia,* and another person's analysis of Gogol's "The Overcoat" which used a medical approach to moral/ethical dilemmas in literature.

"That's the idea where literature is a cure," a slender man with a narrow nose chimed in. "I've read his work. It's very unusual. He works from a theory that literature which provides a cure, or the suggestion of revitalized health, is therefore great literature because it transcends leisure and vaults itself into the realm of life-significance."

"A sort of *roman a remede,*" added another voice, with a snicker.

A sensitive looking young man, looking uncomfortable in a three-piece suit, asked Geraldine if she had attended the multi-media presentation by Ahib Hussein the previous evening. He grinned lazy-eyed, making his question sound like a proposition, and she just shook her head with a smile. By then the session was ready to start. Coble leaned forward to say something about procedure to a gentleman at the other end of the long table.

Each presenter—four men and one woman—spoke theoretically about the transformation of literature into motion pictures, using one or two examples such as *A Tale of Two Cities* or *The Sun Also Rises*. One at a time, they talked about the inherent qualities of printed story and filmed story, and then they addressed questions and comments, sometimes argumentatively, and went silent at the behest of the first speaker, who thereafter served as moderator. Then the next person would do the same, followed by questions and comments. Coble spoke last. He thanked the moderator for saving some time for him and, as a reward for the attentiveness and good will of the audience, his presentation would be short.

He began by uncovering four lines of poetry on the chalkboard behind the table:

Humpty Dumpty sat on a wall
Humpty Dumpty had a great fall
All the King's horses and all the King's men
Couldn't put Humpty (Dumpty) together again

"This is one of the first pieces of literature I was ever exposed to, and in the oral tradition, no less, for I was about five or six, and I couldn't read yet. In the elective course I teach called 'Film and Fiction,' I start with Humpty Dumpty because students can read it in ten seconds, and then I ask them what they see, in their mind's eye. Not surprisingly they see an egg, because that's the visual equivalent which the toy-making, cereal-selling, children's reader-shaping corporate machine has permanently forged into their—OUR—brains, right? Does anyone here *not* see an egg?"

He paused long enough that some in the audience realized it wasn't a rhetorical question. One young man, clipboard in hand, obviously was taken in by Coble's introduction. "You're saying the first movie versions of literature exist in our heads before we know anything about either literature or movies?"

Coble hesitated and looked down at the floor. Then he turned sharply to the young respondent and said, with a look of honest surprise, "You know, I wasn't saying quite that until *you* put it into those words."

The interchange drew puzzled laughter, from which Coble effectively launched a presentation unlike any of the others. He seemed to be talking off the cuff, even rambling, but what he said had structure and it connected to the session's topic. He rushed through angles of interpretation within the nursery rhyme, such as the crude possibilities of "hump" and "dump," along with the tragic undertones of "had a great fall" and "couldn't put . . .together." In deference to grammarians and devotees of perfect rhythm, he showed how "Dumpty" could be eliminated in the last line.

He hung on the chalkboard some poster-sketches he had prepared of Humpty Dumpty with a Hitler moustache, Humpty Dumpty as Oscar Wilde with giant sunflower, and Humpty Dumpty as Hamlet, atop a wall of indecision. And another sketch, this one of Humpty being mourned by effeminate King's men, raising the question of why the King would delegate his best guards to help a weakling. Surely, he said, Humpty must have been the King's favorite.

"But even if your mind's eye insists on seeing an egg, can it not also understand something life-affirming, in a symbolic sense, when the delicate thing drops down? Consider what happens within a woman's body when the egg falls and is fertilized, and eventually becomes a new person."

In all of the words of this time-honored piece of children's literature, he summarized, students can be informed about the possibilities of film through their own understanding of literature in its simplest forms.

When he finished there was a flurry of responses and questions, most of them about the practical pedagogy of using books and equipment in a way that celebrated both. Geraldine didn't pay much heed to the conversation, for she was struck so totally by Coble's simple dramatics. He had brought into this professional circumstance the same casual, mildly disrespectful attitude he gave in the classroom, but here it clearly was unexpected. He was like the guy who brought liquor to the company picnic, making other people wonder why *they* hadn't thought of it.

"You were so great!" she told him as he, tray in hand, approached her at a lunch table.

"Thanks. Actually, I've done that routine dozens of times. It works better if I can get some animated film passages."

"Oh, I thought it was great just the way you gave it."

"I appreciate your appreciation. Now what's this about memorizing your paper?"

"You don't like the idea."

"That's beside the point. Why would you want to do that? Do you have a good memory?"

"I do."

"What if you slip up here and there?"

"I'll just ad lib. Isn't that what you were doing? You didn't even use any notes."

"Not true." He reached into the inside pocket of his jacket and pulled out a folded piece of paper, on which were scribbled words like "Freud," "fall," and "Clemson." "I always give myself reminders, in the order in which I need to bring them in. You could probably do the same thing, especially if your memory is good."

"What's 'Clemson'?"

"A few years ago I went to a conference session where a psychologist from Clemson University did a great paper on the egg as an overriding symbol of just about everything. I stole pieces of it and adapted them for my own purposes."

Geraldine sneered. "You'd probably fail a student for not citing a resource."

"I usually cite her, but I forgot to today. I admitted it to you because I trust you. You won't tell all your friends."

"They wouldn't be interested. 'Her.' The Clemson person is a woman? Is she a friend?"

"Actually, I can't remember her name. Maybe that's why I didn't cite her."

With his head bent slightly downward, he looked at her with a sort of controlled devilishness. She looked back at him while chewing on a salad of lettuce and cucumber.

Still nervous about presenting, she delivered parts of the paper a bit later to Coble as they sat on a straw sofa in one of the Bayfront's outdoor porches. She tried to ignore his facial gestures, by which he probably meant to calm her, just as she tried to ignore the inclination to be fascinated by brown pelicans, flying low above the rippling Caribbean. In the end he told her how good it was, and what good judgment she showed in making cuts. But she truly relaxed only when he stood behind her and gently rubbed her shoulders and neck. The element of touch momentarily took her away from words and vocal stresses. She knew it was probably wrong for him to touch her this way, or at least unprofessional. But it felt good.

After a minute she stood up, took a deep breath as a sort of self-signal to readiness, and turned quickly. Before she turned he had moved closer to her, leaning forward far enough to kiss her, but then he merely smiled.

"You're beautiful," he said. "Go get 'em."

In another frame of mind she might have recognized it as condescension, but now she felt only a romantic thrill and gratitude for his encouragement.

Her presentation went well. Having adopted Coble's suggestion that she scribble some key words to keep on track, she finished in 24 minutes, though no one in the audience looked upset that she had run over. Each of the comments and questions which followed (all except one from male attendees) was accompanied by a smile, to which she smiled back and provided a response which in a more austere environment might have sounded shallow, if not embarrassing. But this was a student, after all, and an undergraduate at that, and they apparently felt she merited approval. They applauded warmly at the end, and some added their own private praise as the session broke up. Two of them gave her their addresses and suggested they discuss further with her the idea of death in literature.

When she felt ready to collapse mentally, Coble intervened and guided her away, urging her to relax and forget everything and everybody else. Nonetheless, he accompanied her to her room, and once inside he took her in his arms, gentle and smooth enough to have been rehearsed. Experienced only with crude clutches and embraces that were all bones and teeth and jabbing fingers, she had never felt such comfortable holding, and she tried to return the professor's knowing touch. Had she not been so eager at that instant to give herself to him, she might have suspected he had arranged the trip for the sole purpose of going to bed with her.

As he took off his shirt, she sat down at the foot of the bed and seemed to merely watch him, passively.

"Anything wrong?" he said.

"No."

"Do you want me to help you?"

"I don't know." She stood up, and he embraced her. The skin on his upper back was damp, and it made her smile as she leaned against his shoulder. She tried not to seem too excited.

He put his mouth against hers and she readied for a kiss, but then he pulled back to look at her eyes, which had been closed but now opened. "Have you ever done this before?" She didn't immediately answer, and he pursued: "Are you a virgin?"

"Yes," she said. It was a lie.

Without a pause or a flinch of surprise, he proceeded to pull up her dress and, unsnapping her brassiere with one hand, lowered her to the firm bed and kissed her breasts. With his other hand he slowly pulled down her panties without any help from her. There was an ease to every one of his moves and, while she was breathing nervously, he was nearly soundless, even as he unwrapped a condom and put it on.

To herself she justified the lie. No one had ever touched her with such knowledge, such respectful desire as this. She remembered the few instances when noises and pokes culminated in regretful annoyance rather than pleasure. Curiosity had led her off a couple of times with one attractive boy and another, neither of whom knew anything besides their own urgency. With Coble it was a first time, a true initiation, and when he moved around within her he watched her face as if to gauge the joy she might be feeling. Before long she pulled his face down to the nape of her neck as she bit her lower lip and strained upward against him as hard as she could. With an airless, inner scream she released some pleasant seizure which had long been lodged in a cautious pocket. Even as he peaked with a low, throaty kind of growl, he continued to move with slow, abrupt jolts. She held on, but now it was as if she were rolling, floating. She kissed his ear and hair, and licked his eyes, and tasted the moisture on his cheek.

They lay quietly, breathing the close heat between them, and the cool breezes through the screenless open balcony door above the steady Gulf waves.

"Could we get in trouble for this?" she asked after a quiet rest, when he pulled her on top of him so that they pressed together the whole length of their bodies, and their faces stared into each other, inches apart. He laughed silently, and the muscles needed for laughter made the fleshy layers of them move both horizontally and vertically. "I'm serious. Could we?"

"Not 'we,' Miss Stillman. You're an innocent victim. It isn't likely you'll have a problem. But I will. Moral turpentine."

"What's that?"

"Moral turpitude, actually. An official decree, nationwide. Scandalous conduct which is detrimental to the university and to the profession. By fucking you I have abused my position of power and destroyed the natural trust which must exist between teacher and student."

"But I wanted to, too." She kissed him on each corner of his mouth.

"You wanted to what?"

"I wanted to make love."

"That's not what I said."

"I don't like that word." She kissed his lips and his chin. "What did you say at first? Turpentine?" She laughed, and the layers of them quaked again.

"When I was in Chicago I taught a few night classes, and there was this guy named Waldo who worked in the library. He was a dirty old man, but funny as hell. He had big feet, and walked with his toes at right angle from each other, as if he were sweeping the floor as he went. Anyway, he'd flirt with just about any woman who came in with a question."

"So that made him a dirty old man?"

"Maybe not just that. Actually, he *told* me once he was a dirty old man, like he was proud of it. He said as soon as he started work each night he would dream up a sexual fantasy, and then keep modifying it, and that would stand him well throughout his shift."

"Why would he tell *you* that?

"Well, actually that's part of the answer to your question about the term. We were talking about one thing or other and a particularly voluptuous older woman, a student in one of my classes, said hello to me as she walked by. Waldo said he perceived a hungry look in my eye, and he warned me of 'moral turpentine,' which he said was the stuff administrators brush on situations in order to get rid of nasty stains."

"*Did* you look hungrily at the woman?" She pushed against him from the waist down.

"I can't remember. What difference does it make?"

"I don't know. Maybe you're *often* 'hungry.'"

"Actually, now that you mention it, my appetite for you is starting to return."

They could have returned to Bloomington the next day, but they decided to stay on and enjoy each other more fully. Besides, the weather was spectacularly beautiful, with temperatures in the low 70s, under a bright blue sky spotted with fluffy clouds blown by an almost fragrant Caribbean breeze. In the afternoon they rented bicycles and rode out to the airport and the other beaches on the island, stopping occasionally to kiss or talk about pelicans. And they rode into the older section of town and ate dinner in a Cuban restaurant which Coble remembered fondly.

"On New Year's Eve," he said, "nothing can touch Key West for parties."

Back at the Bayfront, they stayed in his room, and she surprised herself with her eagerness to have sex again and again. It aroused her that Coble was almost as eager each time.

After a nightcap of brandy, they pushed one of the twin beds closer to the opened doors of the balcony and lay naked, open to moist air blowing across their skin as they touched each other. The orange sun set slowly behind clouds streaked with gray and maroon, invasive residue that made it more beautiful. For Geraldine it was the happiest time ever.

When the weather began to moderate and white trillium poked through the southern Indiana leaf mulch, Geraldine's opportunities for pleasure diminished significantly. Coble was teaching only one class, a required senior seminar for which she was ineligible; he was also putting together a new course in popular culture. Despite his relatively light schedule, however, she had difficulty seeing him in his office. By the Easter break their affair had stalled; he didn't phone her at all. She was very reluctant to call him at home, which was her only other option, since all his office calls were handled by the departmental secretary. During the whole month of March they had sex only once, and that in the leather front seat of his Olds 88. It was exciting fun, deep in the woods south of the campus; but to her it was also a reminder of unromantic times with stupid boys who, she could now understand, didn't really know what they were doing. That same night, perhaps out of fear, she asked him how his marriage was going. He said things were okay, but he then elaborated as to how tension in his relationship with Nicole was a key reason he didn't want to see more of her. That, and the demands of developing the new course. She grew anxious after his explanation, for she had anticipated him talking softly, with a soft, insecure stammer. But his response was quick and almost polite.

Never in her life, not from fourth grade on, had she ever experienced anything like rejection from a boy or man of any age. If No was to be said, it had always been she who said it—either directly or in a note, or through some friend. Now this professor, who had clearly—she told herself now with certainty—had clearly orchestrated their sexual occasions, was pushing her out of his life for reasons of his own, without consideration for her feelings, without consulting her about other possibilities, without her being ready. He had even spoken the breakup words in soft tones, that romantic cliché of mature understanding which especially sickened her now that she was the wounded party. At random moments, even a couple of times in the neutrality of a classroom, she yielded to tears of anger and frustration.

She had always taken satisfaction from looking at herself in a mirror, if only to verify or confirm the desire and admiration she saw in other people's eyes. But Coble's eyes no longer gleamed on those rare occasions when they ran into each other on campus, and consequently she saw in her mirror only lines of fatigue and unhappiness. She tried to lose herself in coursework, but in her favorite class the key work was *Madame Bovary,* and she found herself quickly identifying with the doomed, self-deluding heroine.

Another matter was less weighty but still disturbing. Richie Bowman must have somehow been keeping track of her connection to Coble, for he phoned her a couple of times and made pointed references to her as the man's protégé, and even to her conference junket to Key West. She did her best to make it seem that he was on the wrong track, but he wouldn't be put off. After the fourth call, she unplugged her phone for a few days, but then he began popping into view as she walked from one building to another. She considered telephoning Chet, but that would have required explaining her time with Coble, and she certainly wasn't ready for that.

"It's none of your business!" she shouted at Richie when he approached her directly, this time with what seemed like sincerity.

"Look," he said, "I just want to help, and I think you need help." When she said nothing, he handed her a picture. It showed her with a saddened face, standing at a campus bus stop. "I used a telephoto lens for that. I hope you—"

She threw the picture back at him. "Stop spying on me!"

Her angry response seemed to shake him, and for days afterward she didn't see him.

With spring term drawing to a close, Geraldine finished what she had to do in each of her courses and felt reasonably sure her grades would be good, barring any disaster on final exams. In the middle of exam week she worked up the nerve to go and see Coble in order to retrieve her first semester paper; under his advice she had further revised it after the Key West presentation. He had yet to give back to her.

"Look, Geraldine," he said, after digging it out of a file in his desk. "Let me have a copy made of this, just so I can send it to—"

"Please, just give it to me," she said, as angrily as she could, even though he couldn't have missed the slight crack in her voice. "You could have had a copy made long ago if it'd really mattered to you."

"It *does* matter. I can get it to the editor of Modern Fiction Studies. You might be a star before you even get to graduate school."

"I don't *want* to go to graduate school. I may even change my major to business, or advertising. At least those phonies and liars don't hide behind a cloud of intellectual honor."

Tears began to well up in her eyes, and she backed up toward the entrance to his office. He started toward her with the manuscript in his hand, but then turned his head slightly, and his expression went from concern to annoyance.

"Look, whatever you want, this isn't a good time," he said, his eyes looking past her.

Geraldine turned to see Richie Bowman in the doorway.

"Oh, I think it's as good a time as any." Richie said in a voice with a rough edge that reminded her of Stieglitz Park. "Give her back the paper."

"Richie," she said in a calm yet emotional tone. "Just leave it be. Please go away. If you're really concerned about me, go away. There's no reason for you to be here."

"Well, maybe not, but I'd like to find out what stud professor here has to say. I don't see why we should be reasonable if he's holding on to something that's yours."

"Who are you?" Coble asked, standing firm beside his desk.

"I'm an interested friend of hers."

"You don't look very friendly to me."

"To *you* I'm not friendly. You're taking advantage of her."

"Oh, for Christ's sake!" Coble started to move toward the door to shut it in front of the visitor, but Richie quickly moved inside the office.

"Richie, please, this isn't any of your business," she said in a shaky voice.

"Who knows? Maybe it *is* my business. Right, stud prof?"

Coble went back to his desk and dropped Geraldine's essay in the middle of it. Then he came forward to escort the intruder out of his office. But as soon as he touched Richie's arm the younger man hit him with a quick right to the chin. Coble's hips glanced off the edge of his desk as he straightened up, looking shocked, then angry.

Geraldine moved back toward the door, thinking she should get help from somewhere. But just as she was about to go out into the hall, Richie moved forward to deliver another punch. The dazed Coble dodged most of it, though it caught him on the shoulder blade. He shoved the other shoulder into Richie's chest, knocking him back toward the bookcases which ran alongside the desk, against the wall.

"Stephen!" Geraldine shouted. Coble went into a semi-crouch, and he stalked the younger man as if driven by a rush of instinct. Richie looked like the same young thug from the old neighborhood, but Coble was new and strange. His eyes, wide with readiness, waited for Richie's slightest movement.

Richie faked with his right hand and launched a long left which Coble ducked under as he pushed his shoulder into Richie's midsection, causing him to flip over and onto the floor.

Slowly he got up.

"Enough of this bullshit, buddy, " Coble said, still hunched forward, cautious but ready. "Get the hell out of here."

Richie went toward the door, but after two steps he lunged again at Coble. Ready for any move, the professor twisted like a matador and stuck a leg in Richie's path, kneeing him behind a thigh, thereby pushing him back toward the bookshelves. Richie hit the face of the shelves hard, bringing some of the books down as he himself fell to the floor. The free-standing shelf rocked a bit with the force and vibrations, and a crystal cupid Nicole had brought back from Galway the previous summer fell down from an upper shelf and, just as the younger man came to a rest on the floor, struck him with its point in the right temple. Blood rushed from the wound.

Coble started toward the motionless body, then stopped and froze, trembling. All color faded from Geraldine's face as she leaned against the front of Coble's desk and looked down at the blood coming out of the skull of the Stieglitz Park tough. A couple of women came in from down the hall. "Is anything wrong?" One of them asked.

"Yes," said Coble.

7. *Letters for Lou*
Spring, 1966

Like all Friday afternoons this one was for wasting time and, in the case of Lou's musically inclined housemates, for fooling around with talent. Lee, the sax player from Amish country, tickled his own fancy with random notes in between puffs on a joint that was getting hot and short. Jake, the cynical bassist, rubbed his hand flat against the strings and tilted his head, as if listening to something no one else could hear.

"On Fridays Vietnam is farther away," said Lou, "even if my grades don't get better."

"Yeah, but the induction center hasn't moved, and they'd prefer that you flunk everything," said Jake. "Forget about that world and go get those letters on the table downstairs. You're the only one around here who's gotten any fucking mail in weeks, and you won't even go and read it. Go, and find out what criminal chaos is raging in Da Region." He hit the bass and sang, "it's ragin' in da region, outside that toddlin' town, tra la."

"Oh," said Lou. "You're talking about Chicago. I don't think Whiting toddles. Maybe that's why I get letters from people there who are so disappointed in my lack of direction. How can they say that when I'm a theatre major? I have to take <u>courses</u> in directing."

Lee looked surprised. "You're a theatre major. When did you decide? I didn't know."

"None of them know, either," Lou said. "I'd tell them, but they'd only bitch about me pursuing something useless."

"Theatre major," Jake said, stressing the syllables, then slapped the strings for stress. "Thee-" Slap. "Thee-ah" Slap. "Thee-ah-tah" Slap! "Thee-ah-tah-may-juh, then shift to minor key—" He strummed a quiet adventure on the bass, then looked at Lee, who could only grab a couple of bars before he laughed, accompanied by a saxophone snort.

Lou also laughed, and took in the last of the stub, shaking it off scorched fingers. "I wish I could play an instrument," he said. "That would be the best way for me to say what I feel."

"You don't need to play anything to explain," Jake said. "It has nothing to do with thee-ah-tuh-may-juh. You're simply worried your girlfriend is getting hosed by some defrocked priest up at Marquette."

"With bourbon on his breath," Lee added, then played six notes, one for each syllable in the line he had just spoken. "The bourbon on his breath/Scares her half to death. Uh."

"Oh, Christ," said Lou. He then walked out of the room and went downstairs to get his letters. He could still hear Jake: "If you spell theatre '-re' instead of '-er,' you have to change something." He hit a discordant note.

One piece of mail was from a car dealer, which made no sense, for he had never owned a car. The other three were letters. He started to open the one from Maggie Conroy, the girl who was finishing up at Marquette in Milwaukee, but then decided to save what would probably be the best for last. He figured the other two would be further complaints about his seemingly aimless life. He opened the one from his sister Louise.

Dear Lou:

I don't know why you don't get a telephone. You've got that night job cleaning whatever it is you clean. I hope it isn't toilets. Well, I'm probably going to have to go to work myself soon. My world is basically falling apart. Your niece and nephew look up at me and want to know what's wrong, and I don't have the right words for them. Talbot was arrested for fraud, or embezzlement, I don't know which is worse. The police said he set up transactions between the company and a non-existent outfit in Chicago. It had better be nonexistent, or the FBI will step in and we'll be in *real* trouble, the kind his father can't bargain him out of. The amount is just over $100,000, but the company won't press charges if Mr. Spencer comes up with the whole sum. He's already bailed him out, but Talbot's fired, needless to say. Mr. Spencer has been wonderful and kind, but my dear mother in law doesn't even look at me. She says it's <u>my</u> fault for pressuring him to get a raise or play the market so I can have more things. Our own dear mother agrees with her, so I feel like I'm being gang-blamed. Doesn't <u>everyone</u> want a better life? Believe me, I never told him to break the law.

What hurts the worst is I don't know where the money has gone. Our style of life hasn't changed much. Maybe he's been spending it on someone else. A girl I used to work with at the mill saw him lunching not long ago in a

Chicago restaurant with a flashy blonde. When I finally got enough nerve to bring up the subject he said she was a head-hunter for some corporation, interviewing him for a better paying job. That's probably crap—the corporation is most likely the one Talbot invented. It turns out she's from Stieglitz Park, of all places, and about seven years ago she was one of the witnesses at the hearing, or grand jury thing, when they set that professor free after Richie Bowman got killed. I could never figure that story out.

Maybe you were too young to remember, but she was also the one whose father got stabbed behind the grocery store a long time ago. Stilwell, or something. I never could stand her, she thought she was hot shit. Talbot denies he did anything with her, but I think he's lying. She's the kind that goes through life ruining men.

I don't know what to do, except get a job, since we can't depend on Talbot. I wish I had gone to college. If you still pray, Lou, say one for me. —
Love, Louisa

Lou sat down on the steps and read the letter again, shocked by the idea that a doting mouse like Talbot Spencer was a big-time cheat, an embezzler. He felt sorry for Louisa, but when he thought of going down to the drugstore and using the pay phone, he immediately remembered he had little money until his meagre check came next Friday, and he certainly didn't want to reverse the charges. Worst of all, he had no idea what to say to her. He imagined she was lonely, even with the kids.

Since it wasn't a full-fledged emergency, he didn't want to ask to use the phone of old Ed Adams, who owned the house and lived on the main floor. As he sat thinking blankly his other housemate rushed in and accidentally slammed the door, then made a fearful face and glanced through the french door to see if the slam had upset Adams. There was no response, so apparently the old guy wasn't around.

"Jesus, I always forget how fucking loud that door is when it slams shut."

He was a keyboardist, another member of the upstairs group who also sang, mostly standards. He also acted as manager of the band, which sometimes included anywhere from three to five others who lived elsewhere. He proudly called himself The Great Bob Milnah! in an accent out of somewhere between Boston and Brooklyn.

"Why do I always forget about that door?" When he saw the concerned look on Lou's face, he added, "What's wrong, Loopy Louie?"

"Nothing."

"Somebody die?"

"No, it's nothing. Family complications."

"Well, cheer up, 'cause I got us a great gig for tonight. Ten O'Clock at Alpha Tau fucking Omega. Come along, you can hook up with one of their chicks. Most of the fratboys will be stumbling, puking drunk by then, and the chicks will hunger for a cool man from Da Region."

"They won't let me stay if I don't play an instrument."

"Not to worry." Milnar stepped around him and went upstairs. "We'll dig up a bongo and you can thump it whenever they look suspicious at you. And look stoned, so they'll think you've got rhythm."

Lou opened the letter from his mother. She liked to underline any words which bore, to her thinking, some spiritual or inspirational significance. She also dotted some of her i's with circles, as if to show a streak of youthful self-expression.

> My Dearest Lou:
>
> The news I have for you isn't pleasant, and maybe your sister has already written you or phoned you about it. But you don't have a phone. <u>Why</u> don't you and those other boys—they're <u>so dirty looking</u>—pool your money and get a <u>phone</u>!!!???
>
> The news is terrible, and I don't know how I can look other mothers in the face after this. I've been making novenas and praying especially to <u>the Blessed Virgin</u> for help in my pain and worry for my precious grandchildren, who are so innocent.
>
> I knew there was going to be trouble when Louisa <u>had</u> to get married, because she and that <u>weakling</u> couldn't control themselves! And now he's <u>sinning</u> with another woman and stealing money from the company and going to jail. Oh God, (forgive me, Jesus) how horrible and <u>shameful</u> this is for a mother to think about. And that <u>other woman</u> –to think she actually baby sat for you one time when Daddy and I had to go to a funeral for Eugene Matlowsky, what a nice man.
> I can't tell you how much pain

There was another page, but Lou couldn't take any more exclamation points and stressed phrases. He crumpled the sheets and threw the paper aimlessly over his shoulder. He briefly re-visited the chief reasons he didn't go home very often. He thought again of his sister, and wondered if there were some kind of pleasantry he could deliver to her, in the distance. If only they could sit and talk about funny things the way they once did on the porch in Stieglitz Park. If only she would tease him about his hair, and she could quiz him on geography, his favorite subject. He vaguely remembered Geraldine the babysitter. She was blonde and, to his recollection, kind of scary-looking.

With geography on his mind, he opened the letter from Maggie Conroy and remembered how shabby was her knowledge of even the simplest, map-connected problems. She was a proud, strong-willed Irish girl, sure that she was superior to him in intelligence and dedication. But the fact she admitted to him her feeble confusions about maps and topography was enough to encourage him and sustain his romantic dreams about her. He recognized the admission as a statement of trust one would only give to a special friend. He also felt it was a weakness that made him somehow necessary in her life.

He tore open the envelope slowly, fearing it would contain something worse than what he had already read. He rushed quickly through the first page, a short sheet only as big as a paperback rectangle, just to check for new disaster. As always, her penmanship was inconsistent, with some B's looking like M's at an angle, and some words looking like shorthand symbols.

But they announced only affection, and he was glad she didn't join in the complaint about him not owning a telephone.

> Dear Lou:
>
> How's my sweet but mixed up baby? I saw a guy at a bus stop yesterday who was frantically patting himself all over, probably looking for his wallet or whatever, and I immediately thought of you, for some reason. I suppose that isn't very nice of me, especially because we haven't seen each other since Christmas. What have you been up to?
> Alice got drunk last night and threw up in the elevator. Guess who was left with the cleanup job? What was really exciting was that I had to drag her into our suite and flop her down on the bed, and then go after the elevator, which had descended with the puke to pick up two other girls, who were really thrilled with the mess. I got on and tried to explain, but they just gagged and got off at the next floor while I just swabbed away with a beach towel, trying not to barf myself.
> She really should stay off booze. This is the first elevator mess of hers I've cleaned up, but there have been others in stationary locales. Funny, but when she gets drunk she often talks about you. I know you think she's dull, so I can tell you something without worrying too much about consequences. She thinks you're weird, but I secretly suspect she's got weird hots for you. She and I have other things in common, too. But don't let that go to your head.

Why don't you come to Milwaukee for spring break? The weather is bound to be yucky, but I could get you a free room with one of my many suitors. We could go to the world's greatest German restaurant and have sauerbraten, and I could give you a haircut and a neck massage. And maybe even a kiss. But only one. Let me know. If only you—

Lou turned to the next sheet and was immediately disappointed at what she said next.

—would get a telephone like the rest of the civilized world we could actually talk more easily about such things. I guess you could call me from someone else's phone and reverse the charges. Hint.
Speaking of which, I got a call from my mom yesterday and one of the things she dropped on me was some half-baked story about your brother in law. Could you fill me in on those details? Maybe I could call Louisa and see if I can do anything to help her out.
Please respond to all of the above soon. If you don't I may permanently write you off, even if you are cute. --Maggie

Lou had a picture of her up in his room, but he really didn't need to look at it to refresh his memory of what she looked like, the gleaming eyes and a smile like joyous illumination. She was fair skinned with dark hair that puffed slightly at her forehead, and dropped to her neck in slow swirls. In the wind the locks at her temples became feathery, and the strands covered parts of her face like thin netting. Her eyebrows were dark, and her brown eyes looked the same when she was being sarcastic as when she suspected him of lying about something. Her uncle Jim told him once that she had the map of Ireland on her face. Other people said things like that, but the uncle put a certain pride, even honor, into the way he said it.

Lou smiled every time he thought of her.

Upstairs, the musicians had opened a window and begun to share another joint. When he stuck his head in the door they passed it to him but he shook his head.

"Ah, yes," Lee said. "He wants a clear mind to fantasize about his lady love."

Jake laughed. "So what did she say? Did she admit she's fucking an ex-priest?"

"Hey, man," Milner said to Lou. "Don't pay attention to that asshole. Anyway, she's 300 miles away. Just put on something cool and you can make hay with a chick at the ATO house."

"Yeah, and get rid of that stupid chin hair."

"You guys ever hear about a killing on campus, involving—"

Jake interrupted him. "Oh, yeah. There was that guy who got knifed over on Eighth Street last summer."

"No, this was some time ago, maybe six, seven years ago. The victim was a guy from my old neighborhood. I was just a little kid when I knew him. Some professor was involved in the death."

"Seven years ago. Man, even I haven't been here that long," Jake said.

"You're talking about the English prof," Milner said. "I read about it in the Times."

"The New York Times?"

"There is no other. It was on an inside page, like a survey story on campuses. The guy was cleared of the charges, and there wasn't even a trial. But there was some controversy because the only eye witness was a female student the prof had been screwing."

Lou didn't think it was a good idea to share with the guys the fact that the female student had once been his babysitter. "Is the prof still here?" he asked. For some reason, he was curious enough to want to talk to the guy, maybe get information for Louisa. Then again, he realized that didn't make clear sense.

"He stayed here through the following year, I think. Then his wife divorced him. I guess the university didn't think it was a bad enough scandal, but the wife did. He took a job somewhere in the south. I got that part of it from the Beta house mother where we had a gig.

Lou crossed the hall to his own room and threw the letters onto his bunk, which nestled under the slant of the roof between two windowed gables. He liked the bunk in that spot, for it gave him the feeling of safe sleep in a secure cave. He went to his desk and started a letter to Louisa, but nothing emotionally coherent took shape in words.

He decided to go to the gig, though he had no intention of pursuing a sorority girl.

8. *The Breeze Across Her Face*
1968-69

It's May, and the soldier, his sweaty uniform over his damaged body, hopes for a ride from a sympathetic driver on this unusually hot night. Various poses have brought him through Ohio, across northern Indiana to US 41 at Merrillville. He knows how to act to get the rides, although the fantasy performer dwelling inside him has stepped out only a few times into an actual spotlight on an actual stage. He chooses new poses if one doesn't seem to be working, or he alters his step. Tonight he limps, a slightly twisted leg reserved for the lights rushing up from behind him. His real wound is in his midsection, but he figures it would scare off drivers if he lifted his shirt to show the big scar. Still, it isn't hard for him to convey his need for help. A desperate face, unsteady movement, the uniform.

The limp does it. He gets a new ride in a well-kept Olds 98 with power everything from a deep-voiced black musician who smiles at him but then says how much he hates the war because soldiers who didn't volunteer were getting killed, even so. The musician drives smooth and slow, conscious always, he says, of white state troopers. He talks of his own foot wound from World War II, and how it prevented him from working the pedals on a piano, so he switched to alto sax in the late forties. He talks fast, and he makes a wrong turn near East Chicago, and when he loops around he accidentally brings the soldier a mile closer to his destination.

The soldier doesn't mention his real wound, fairly healed, but bad enough to earn him the medical discharge he keeps safe under the strap in his duffel bag. He sustains the limping lie and says his is a minor knee injury, a bad twist from jumping out of a helicopter. He asks the driver to stop and he opens the door.

"You all right?" the driver asks. "You're not gonna hurt that knee worse, or anything?"

"I'm fine. The docs told me walking is good for it." says the soldier, pulling his bag from the back seat, then bouncing a bit on one foot. "I appreciate the ride. This helps out a lot."

"Hey listen, kid. I'd take you farther in, but I've had a couple of bad experiences with cops in Whiting. Once I got thrown in the slammer there, so I wouldn't want to get stopped again. They might start diggin in their files for some shit they can use."

"No, this is good. The midnight shifts are letting out, and I'll probably get another lift."

"Okay. In Whiting they don't take too kindly to the brothers."

"Well, that's their problem. Thanks again, man."

The driver laughs nervously. "Hey listen, kid, I can probably take you down to—"

"No, I'm good right here." In truth, he wants to get farther north, but he knows the dark skinned man isn't exaggerating about the selective diligence of Whiting patrols. "Hey, maybe I'll run into you when you're playing in a club somewhere around here. I'll buy you a drink."

The driver grins, as if the soldier has said something foolish, but he doesn't want to make anything of it. Then his smile goes away, and he nods. "You take care, young man."

The soldier lifts the duffel bag to his shoulder so he can take bigger strides. It isn't far now, anyway, maybe three miles. Gnats and beetles dart crazily around streetlights down the boulevard as it slopes upward and over the tanker channel at the edge of the Sinclair refinery.

The channel bridge still unsettles him with its steel waffling through which he can see the gleam of murky water reflecting light, 50 feet below. And the way it bounces when cars pass over the crease in the center, prompting him to briefly imagine it rising, separating or even collapsing as he tries frantically to clutch the steel grating, his legs dangling just above the masts of ships that blow their deep whistles at him. But then the wild vision vanishes. It used to be his buried phobia: crossing a bridge, trying not to fall in. He knows it has always been a stupid fear, and he tells himself he doesn't feel it now, even though he does. Just a bridge, nothing more, over dark water streaked with oil spillage, rippling rainbows in the reflected moonlight.

Then he's back on concrete. Northward he can smell the refinery stills giving off something chemically stronger. Even though the night is warm, there are fewer bugs than you would expect in the thick air. Apparently not even the insects can take much of the air that hurts, the soft breezes with tiny stings of acid, like carbonated bubbles that bite. The soldier takes a deep breath and coughs, and feels pain in the uneven center of his abdomen, right under the big scar. He shifts the duffel to his other shoulder, as if to confuse the pain, which isn't sharp, but seems keyed to his leg movements.

He doesn't want to stop and thumb another ride, for the driver might be someone he knows, someone from Whiting who might ask why he was only in for eight months and did he have a wife, a girlfriend, a baby, and which church did he go to, and did he know Teddy Kreevich, still back there on the other side of the world, in the jungle for another tour. So fella, he hears the voice like a stage prompt, why is it that you were only over there for eight months? So he'd have to fake something threatening, like heavy nausea, and improvise: let me out right now before I puke on your leopard skin dashboard, right below the Blessed Virgin with her hands outspread, bestowing impromptu miracles. Then the irregular pain subsides as he moves straight in a dark stretch of sidewalk where a streetlight has burned out. But he remembers other pains so recent he can still feel the sharpness pounding into him like a fist strapped with chisel tips. The pains so intense they blacked him out in the big room in Saigon.

He keeps moving ahead now, but on his mind's stage he sees himself against the refinery fence, sweating and immobile, Maggie not knowing where he is, her dark eyebrows slanting down in worry.

Lou kissed both her eyebrows as they sat in adjacent webbed chairs on her lawn, but she looked at him angrily, a stare of exasperation he had lately seen often.

"I'm sorry, Maggie."

"For being a jackass?"

"I'm sorry for not paying attention to your stories about helping little kids to read in summer school."

"Ohh—" she pushed him lightly in the chest.

"I am, I mean it. My trouble is I hear something you say that makes me think of something else, and my mind drifts fully into the thing I'm reminded of, and I miss the rest of what you say."

"Because you're acting out some alternative version in your mind."

"What are you, a witch? How do you know?"

"You've *told* me that's what you do sometimes."

"I guess I have."

"The worst part of it," she said with fatigue in her voice, "is that in your version you'd be one of the kids in my room. What role do you want to play? In the artful universe."

"In the artful universe, I would want to be one of Shakespeare's fools."

"That's typecasting."

"Hold it," Lou said, as if he had come upon a new idea. "Maybe I could be the misunderstood thief, who really isn't a thief. He steals happy moments from the greedy rich, and delivers them in the form of happy songs to people who live under overpasses."

"That sounds rehearsed."

"Well, it *is*. I have to figure out the best way to get on your good side."

"Never mind that. What about the artful universe, where you could create atmosphere and crises, and all that?"

"How about if I would slouch at my desk in the front row and behave like Stanley Kowalski?" He took a deep breath. "And then I might drop to the floor and look up your dress."

"Lou, your trouble is you're not following your dreams, you're just groping. And thank God you're nothing at all like Stanley Kowalski. You've always misread Tennessee Williams, because you think Stanley's cool, when in fact he's a brutal slob who—"

"Come on," Lou said. "He's a slob who's jealous of his sister-in-law."

"So he *rapes* her!?"

Lou stuttered, "But maybe—"

"He rapes her while his wife is in labor, and you—"

"Maggie, it's a *role*, for Christ's sake! Not a model for behavior."

"You say that, but then you yearn to play the part, even though you're nothing like Stanley except for your ethnic connection, which is really pushing it, if you ask me."

"So what's more my speed, Irish cave mother?"

"Anything else, asshole," Maggie said, though she couldn't help cracking a smile. "Irish cave mother? Where did that come from?"

"Intensive research. What should I be? Que sera, sera?"

"Anything you actually try out for, with a real theatre group in a real auditorium, like the Goodman. They've got summer programs open to anybody."

"I've been drafted."

"And you didn't even answer that ad I gave you, the one about ordinary people needed as bit actors in clothing store commercials. It's a longshot, but if they picked you it would be like getting your foot in the door."

"I'll be carrying a gun in 23 days." He touched her hair.

"At least it would be a credential you could show after you serve your term."

"Why don't we get married?"

"I can't stand you. And anyway, you'll still have to report in 23 days. You just said so."

"Well, we could have a baby, and I'd get a deferment."

"In 23 days?"

She moved her legs, so one of her feet rested on his. Her legs were perfect, aside from a couple of tiny shaving scratches. From thin ankles they rose up in smooth slopes to rounded knees that looked almost boneless when bent. She picked up a book. "I don't want to marry you," she said loudly, even though his face was only a couple of feet away. "Why would I want to marry a 22 year old adolescent?"

He stood up. "Hey—tomorrow my days of freedom will match my age. Maybe I should go to the race track and bet on anything wearing 2."

"With what? You going to sell your baseball card collection?"

"If I did, I'd buy you an engagement ring." He knelt next to her chair.

Her eyes softened. She looked directly at him as he moved closer. "I wouldn't accept it."

"Why not?" he said as he leaned closer, and made his lower lip protrude, and even managed watery eyes.

"How do you do that?" She touched his face. "You can cry whenever you need to."

"It's the one thing I got out of acting classes. I was one of the best weepers on campus. It's not actually fake, because I think of something terrible, like my dog dying, or my sister having such a hard time, and I can generate deep sadness." He sat down, and tugged at her wrist to come down to him on the cool, shaded grass, where they could get closer in the fading light of late summer. They shared secrets with each other—he that he didn't actually have a baseball card collection, and she that she just needed to unload once in a while about the stresses of teaching little kids, and that she didn't actually blame him for not paying attention.

He held her, and she brought his hand up to her neck. "I probably would accept it," she said. "The ring. Whenever you give me something I love it, even if it's dumb."

"Like what?"

She shook her head as if there were no answer, then pulled his face down to hers, and they kissed and clutched and rubbed against each other in the evening wind, as automobile headlights from passing cars streaked through the tall shrubs that ran across the front of her yard. In the year during which their friendship had grown stronger, they had stopped short of anything fully sexual. They enjoyed each other but were afraid perhaps of crossing a line which, though they knew would inevitably be crossed, they backed away from because of something like foundational Catholic fear—premonitions of senseless, endless punishment. To them the wild noises of life in the 60s pounded outside their own cautious walls; everyone else seemed far ahead of them in the pursuit of pleasure.

But on this evening they touched each other in the ways that felt unusually good because they were supposed to be sinful. When their breathing became irregular, even uncomfortable, they pulled away from each other, but then stared at each other's eyes. She turned to the house, which was dark and soundless. Her mother and both sisters were gone.

"I have something for you," she said. "My cousin Sarah gave it to me."

She rose and took his hand and they walked to the dark house, its west side discolored by the gold tones of evening sun. She felt softer as they walked, and he stopped at the foot of the stairs to the back door to kiss her again, and her lips were warm and they moved against his and opened to invite his tongue. He knew the house must be empty because otherwise she wouldn't have kissed him so passionately and pressed tight against him.

He grew nervous. His tension mounted as she led him quickly into her small bedroom next to the kitchen, a room too small for anything but sleep and sex. It was a room she could lock, and when they stood inside in the near dark she reached into her underwear drawer. She handed the small plastic package to him as she sat on the bed and pulled off her shorts and underpants. The deliberateness of her movements rattled him, his own hands seemed to lose some of their feeling as he undid his own clothes. She lay back as if luxuriating. He didn't look directly at her, but out of the corner of his eye he could see her raise one knee.

He fumbled with the wrapper, his hands shaking with uncertainty, since he had never opened one before. Then he put it on wrong, and then he wasn't able to get it on, and he looked down at her weakly and with embarrassment. Dim light crept under the window shade, and her eyes seemed to glisten. He trembled increasingly, and she reached out to his shame.

She leaned forward to him. "It's alright. It's alright."

"It isn't," he said. "I've wanted you so much, and here I just don't know what I can do. I don't know why it's not happening."

She touched him but he continued to shake and breathe with difficulty. "It's alright," she said, kissing him as if they had actually done everything to each other.

He turned, and tears welled up in his eyes. "It's awful."

"It's alright." She held him, and kissed the bridge of his nose.

The pain subsides after he puts down the duffle bag. Then he realizes he doesn't immediately need anything from the bag except the special discharge papers under the strap, and the medical documents and pain pills. And the tags explaining his susceptibility to hemorrhage and his newly discovered allergies, and occasional infectious swelling brought on by emergency medications. He digs into the bag for all of it—all the proofs of his wounded identity. Again he imagines a drive-up critic—a World War II vet with a sneer on his pockmarked face—growling how'd you get out, slacker? Fed up and cowardly, eh? Deserter? No, he would say, here's my proof, and that's a shitty imitation of Lee Marvin. Where's *your* scar?

Then he could tell them what it felt like to touch the membrane of his own intestines, or what it looked like to watch Francisco's head crack and bleed, and see his shin bone poke through thin flesh. Or what blood smells like when enough of it is smeared everywhere inside a packed tent with a low ceiling.

A big tanker truck roars past on the otherwise clear boulevard, probably heading for the Sprout & Davis dock a few hundred yards north of Stieglitz Park. He stuffs the appropriate papers and pills in a side pocket, and pulls the tags around his neck and goes on, dragging his duffel bag across an alley, then to the corner at 129th Street, right in front of the Clipper, the heart of Stieglitz. It's still the heart but there's nothing else around, just barren cinders and cracked pavement. He hasn't been this close to the old tavern in several years. He almost went inside on his 21st birthday, but he was with a girl and another couple who insisted on something classier for his special day.

The tavern gives off a familiar stench, dried alcohol and nicotine, and there's the neon night light on inside, indicating the place is closed. In the old days, so he has been told, the bar probably would still be open, and Ace would have shouted in his gravel voice "last call, this is no drill!" But no one lives here anymore, and Ace's only customers are probably millworkers at changing shifts, and maybe a few the old timers who come back out of curiosity, or to talk about the explosion and fire that eventually drove everyone away. He looks at the empty sky where once the big still rose high, then one day, the worst day, the black smoke took its place.

The duffle bag seems harder to drag, so he pulls it up on his shoulder again as he walks farther up the sidewalk along the boulevard. To his right, in the east, is the rebuilt section of the refinery, the glossy painted structures with their irregular lights: red, blue, or yellow, decorating shiny replacements that hum and hiss and give off steam. Away from the sidewalk to his left is an empty flatness for hundreds of yards, cinders and dark, oily soil. In the same space years ago there were frame houses and coal shacks and chicken coops, all sticking up from the dirt and cinders. Now there's just the leftover asphalt streets, running pointlessly across each other, creating big empty squares—a gameboard where nothing meets nothing.

He can see a couple of blocks ahead that SOCO has already extended their fence a few hundred yards south, so that a storage tank surrounded by a protective ridge of dirt and gravel now occupies the Grace Street space where Gary Gajewski's house and garage used to be, as well as the house and back yard where Crazy Erma lived. Her chicken coop had been home run territory when they played baseball on hot July days, all day. What great, memorable exhaustion from playing eight hours in July heat. Anything hit to right field was an automatic out—the reason being that a ball hit there would go into the passing traffic, causing big trouble, potentially. It was easier to dicker with Crazy Erma when they scared her speckled hens than it was to explain to the cops how they shouldn't be to blame for traffic accidents. Left-handed hitters were inclined to go that way naturally, but Pat McCardle, the only lefty in the neighborhood, had from an early age taught himself not to pull anything. He took all pitches to left field. Lou remembers himself with pride, having been the youngest player then, just out of the fourth grade at St. John's. He was five years younger than some, but he could hit almost as well, just not as far.

The duffel bag begins to get heavier again when he gets to Louisiana St., just up the road from the middle of the empty space where his house once had sat. A bit closer this way used to be the brick place owned by old Mrs. Springer, who talked about the dignity of Thomas E. Dewey even as she accidentally dropped a turd on the linoleum floor of the Fronczek kitchen, next door. Terribly embarrassed, she wept as Mrs. Fronczek wrapped it in toilet paper and flushed it. The soldier remembers how his mother invoked a kind, sensitive tone when telling the story. But she told it fairly often, even so.

His abdominal muscles twitch and hurt, and he considers taking a pain pill. They give a nice feeling, even a buzz, but he doesn't want that now because he's got to keep going without getting woozy. So he drops the duffel bag on the corner of the street where he used to live. No one will want to steal it, he thinks. No one is here to steal it.

Without the bag he walks much more quickly, and even breaks into a jog, the first gallop of any kind since he went down, fresh out of the helicopter five months ago, after one step into wet foreign grass. The running feels good, a slow trot past the barbed wire-topped fence around the tanks, past the Sprout & Davis truck entry gate and the rusty viaduct over the boulevard. But after what couldn't have been more than a quarter of a mile, he slows to a walk because his stomach muscles seem under pressure, as if the twitching will become violent.

As he cools down he recalls a long walk home, along this same stretch of sidewalk, when he was seven. It was right after his lone stage performance, as a kid in blackface, humming while a white baritone, also in blackface, sang "Old Man River." After the show he didn't know how to remove the greasepaint, and he missed a ride with another kid, so he just walked home in the dark. He knew it was dangerous to walk alone, but he hadn't yet been carefully taught how dangerous it could be to navigate the streets of Whiting with black skin.

He crosses the tracks just past the refinery and remembers there used to be a phone booth outside Ingy Andersen's drugstore up ahead, at Schrage and the Boulevard. It's still there, and he can call, but it's so late, nearly one thirty. He doesn't want to wake Maggie, or her mother, just to ask for a ride from this spot, not all that far away.

Maggie's mother is Ellen Marjorie Conroy, but she denies her name, for some reason, demanding to be called Sis. He has always called her Sis, and has always tried to make her laugh, occasionally succeeding. In conversations over the years she would look him square in the eye when he had, say, given a vocal imitation of W. C. Fields, and her eyes expressed no reaction. In time he learned this meant that at that moment she was doubting his sanity. At other times, though, she would tell him a joke in return or an old Irish tale about the foolish ferryman of Galway, implying he should get the message. After he and Maggie became romantic she called him Dear once in a while, and once in a while she would look at him hopefully. She was a gloriously contradictory Irish matron, and a bit more love spilled out of her than she was willing to acknowledge.

When he gets closer to Ingy's he sees the booth doesn't have a phone in it anymore, so he doesn't need to feel tempted to call. But he stops anyway, for the wind has strengthened, growing slightly cooler in bursts that scatter gnats and mosquitoes away from street lights.

On the day before Lou was to leave for Fort Leonard Wood, Missouri, Maggie gave a going away party for him at her house, across the tracks from Lake Michigan. Lou appreciated festivity even when he was emotionally down. He knew she was worried about him because she hadn't gotten angry at him for a couple of weeks.

When Maggie asked him if he really thought he could kill someone, he thought for a while and admitted it wouldn't be difficult if the other guy were one of those robotic pianists who played what he termed paralytic rock. Then he tickled her at her rib cage, causing her to jerk quickly and fend him off.

"You know I hate tickling more than anything."

"Ah, you exaggerate. More than Patty Perkins' wardrobe?" Maggie loved new clothes and Patty, an only child, always had more things to wear in high school.

"Well, maybe not that much."

For a few minutes they were alone in the kitchen, so they embraced quietly. She asked again if he thought he could kill someone. He didn't answer directly because had a premonition he himself would be killed before he had to decide. He said nothing.

"Are you afraid you'll get killed?" she whispered. He still said nothing, despite his amazement she could apparently read his mind. "You *are* afraid you'll get killed. Then why did you say you wanted to get married?"

"I didn't have the same thoughts then," he said, lowering his head a bit. Their intimacy may have been strained, but she had transformed herself into something greater than a friend, bringing gentle fun to him in his anxiety, giving him her radiance out of those dark, warm eyes.

In the crowded living room Maggie's mother tried to make sure everyone had enough of everything, while managing at the same time to suggest they all go home soon. It was her way, to be slightly surly even as she made people think they were pleasantly welcome, thus assuring herself that each young visitor would remember the night later with a smile.

Whoever was nearest the stereo increased the volume to "Eleanor Rigby." A husky guy named Jerry, who had also once proposed to Maggie but now had a separate, quieter, pregnant wife, openly talked about how lucky he was now, having served his reserve time just out of high school, before the Gulf of Tonkin, so that now his number was low enough that they could have a kid (at this he squeezed the girl's shoulders) and be fairly sure he wouldn't have to go back, certainly not into combat.

The guy's words sounded hollow, as if he were trying to convince himself most of all. What he said brought back uneasiness into the pit of Lou's stomach. Maggie, noticing this, went to him with a scotch on ice and an arm to lead him outside. A passenger train thundered past, not fifty feet from the side door to the house, which vibrated perceptibly with the heavy noise. Maggie once told him she was almost envious of people whom others described as 'living on the other side of the tracks,' because she had always felt she lived right <u>on</u> the tracks.

They walked down the back stairs to the lawn, and Maggie pinched his buttocks as if to revive him. "Pay attention to me, okay?" she said.

"What?"

She kissed him quickly, like a shake of the shoulders to someone in a stupor.

"You're going away tomorrow and you feel bad about it, but make me laugh anyway, because you'll be alone in your own cocoon soon enough."

"And I'll come out a moth, with fuzz around my mandibles."

"What do you know about mandibles?"

"Nothing yet, because they're still developing." He pressed his arms against his sides and tucked his chin down to his chest. "I'm still a larva, or larvum."

Then Brad someone, whose last name he never could remember, came up to them, trailing his girlfriend Lucy Bedford, who idolized Maggie to the point Lou thought she might be a lesbian, or at least bisexual. They were grinning as Brad was lighting a twisted cigarette.

"For God's sake, Brad," said Maggie. "My mother will chase you away with a broom if she smells that."

"Ah ha. Notice the breeze, my dear," said Brad. "It carries the fragrance from this spot to the cooking oil factory, and Sis will not get a whiff."

"Well, move away farther, anyway," Maggie said. "Go down there by the shrubbery."

Lucy said, with melodramatic emphasis, "Maggie, you *have to* try this, you and the guest of honor. A friend of mine brought it at great risk from Juarez. That's Mexico."

"I know it's Mexico," Maggie said.

"Well, you were always confused by geography, so I couldn't be sure."

"I helped her find Sumatra once," Lou said, "and she improved after that."

They shared the joint with Brad and Lucy, coughing at first, then enjoying the gradual buzz. Behind them in the house, Maggie could see her mother, in her nightgown and robe, trading stories with a couple of the young guests. Brad and Lucy split a piece of chewing gum before going back toward the house.

Lou shoved his hands into his pockets as he walked under a streetlight and spun around on a heel. Maggie just looked at him, her eyes sleepy.

"I'm not coming back," he said, but when her face showed shock, he quickly added, "I mean not here, not to Whiting. Except to get you."

"What if I'm not here?"

He looked perplexed.

"Would that surprise you?" she asked.

"I don't know. You've always been in the thick of things, with your uncle in politics and you settling into the teaching job. You're sort of part of the establishment. I've always been of Stieglitz, *de Stieglitz*, the eternal periphery."

"That's stupid. It no longer exists." Then she looked nervous, as if everything they both said was the wrong thing. "What do your parents think of you going off to war?"

"Well, they're not happy about it. I don't really give a shit what they think."

"Don't talk like that. That's not you. They did their best."

Lou shrugged. "I don't know about that. They've always been afraid of life. Now they're fulfilling the East Europe model, which is to avoid sin and pray a lot while growing old. I wish they treated Louisa better, since she cares about them more than I do. "

"They love you."

"I love them, too. I just don't *like* them."

She made a disapproving face, but he quickly held her hand as they crossed many sets of railroad tracks on their way to the strip of beach next to the power plant. As the puffs of marijuana gradually affected them, they both babbled as they walked over the boards and rails. Halfway across, Lou's foot slipped into a space between iron and wood, and he raised his arms in mock terror.

"I'm stuck at the mercy of the onrushing iron monster!" he shouted.

"What do you want me to do?" she said, in an intentionally flat, emotionless tone.

"Just remember me as one who gave his life for better rail service."

"There aren't as many trains as there used to be. Less noise."

"Less danger," he said with a gasp.

She kicked him lightly in the foot that was stuck.

"I actually *was* stuck once," he said. In the distance they could hear a whistle, and he could feel vibrations on his stuck foot. "Just like this, with a train down on the middle tracks, running through the refinery, speeding this way toward Chicago. And my foot was skinnier, so it slipped deeper in the crack. My mother was screaming all the while, anyway, because the Pere Marquette flyer was bearing down on me, blasting away with its Baaa! Baaa!"

"Baaa," she echoed softly. "I've always thought of it as obnoxious noise."

"Oh, no. Not at all. God, I love trains," he said, pulling his foot out without any trouble, as the train got closer with more warning blasts.

"How did you get free?" she said, not concerned about the train's noise and headlight, because they were walking free and clear on other tracks. "I mean back then ."

"I didn't. I got mangled." He took her in his arms, but she pulled away.

"What a jerk," she said quietly.

"My right eyeball bounced all the way to your porch."

"And I saved it," she said in a melodramatic voice, "as an omen of love in the next life."

"Seriously, it was a dangerous situation," he said, "my mother was shrieking like some kind of jungle bird, or like the *Psycho* shower music. I finally relaxed and pulled out my foot. It was a dangerous situation. I'm not kidding."

"Lots of things are dangerous, baby," she said with droopy eyes, and rubbed her nose against his.

He kissed her, then took her hand and they trotted over the rest of the tracks toward the stretch of sand next to the power plant. They called it NIPSCO beach, after the public service company, who owned the land but didn't patrol it outside the security fence. The waves on Lake Michigan were high and loud as they got to the sand, and the train behind them rushed noisily. He took off his shirt and jeans and put them on the sand. When he sat, she came down and held him and for the first time nothing mattered to either of them except the other. They didn't talk about feelings or futures or reasons, and perhaps because they hadn't planned to make love, they did.

Then they rushed naked into the surging lake, with Maggie shouting over the waves that if she splashed the right way, it would be like taking a douche. She also told him he could help her out in that regard. When they came back wet and naked they lay atop their clothes and did it again with new energy and familiarity, as if they had been doing it for years. And although Lou withrew from her before ejaculating, they held each other for a long time, whispering lewd nonsense, kissing and clutching, then dozing for a few minutes while still wrapped around each other, holding each other sweet and numb, trying to delay the sadness that would come soon.

The next morning she drove him to his departure point in Elgin, and he hated himself for not breaking the law, not running off with her, the only person who had ever made him think about life as something that could go on forever. He hated himself for leaving her cream colored face which for him defined love with thick, sad eyebrows that also managed to be hopeful.

Basic training at Ft. Leonard Wood was as physically challenging as he expected it would be. Because of the distant war they prepared for, the angry conditioning of the troops was harsher than what he had been led to believe by guys he knew who had served during peacetime. It was a shattering thought that the great distance to the real hostilities on the other side of the world could be closed in just a few days, if necessary. In preparation they all went through a variety of infiltration courses. At any moment each of them could get blown apart by automatic weapons strafing the air above them as they crawled toward the muddy completion of the drill, after which they were promised only more gruelling tests, hazards as threatening as actual warfare. They waded into swamps, occasionally upsetting resident cottonmouths that slithered and hissed in the water. Stories circulated about mistakes like dropped grenades that maimed or killed recruits before they had the opportunity to go to that part of the world many of them couldn't even pronounce, and get maimed or killed there.

Five weeks into the program the minds of the various troops had been altered to weak acceptance of just about anything. For confused, educated city guys the idea of sacrifice for the greater good became an absurdity, for they realized acceptance of a deathly fate was really irrelevant, since their fate would never be any less deathly, whether they believed in something or not. Belief, said Lou's friend Francisco Torres, stopped with the heart. Those who wanted to be with their Lord thought otherwise.

Some didn't want to share space near their Lord with black believers, but they never openly exposed that side of themselves.

Just when Lou had begun to think that the civil rights movement was influential even in the Army, he learned otherwise first hand. During war games on a hot day he accidentally dropped his rifle into a muddy gully. His commanding officer, a smooth-talking, serious black man named Warren, scolded him mercilessly. He was, the Captain said, a pathetically weak representative of a strong nation, and he should be ashamed of what he might do to endanger the other members of his squad in the future.

Lou stood at attention before the angry captain, and muttered "no, sir, "or "yes, sir," then started to slide down into the gully when a guy from Southern Indiana named Wilfrey came up to him after the captain walked out of earshot.

"Soldier," Wilfrey said softly but with fake authority, as Lou made his way back up. "You gonna let that nigger talk to you like that? Huh, soldier?"

Lou couldn't think of anything good enough to spit back at the blond, skinny fellow who seemed so pleased with his own words of challenge and contempt. Lou just shook his head and mumbled disbelief, then wiped off his rifle.

Behind him he heard Francisco lace into Wilfrey. "What business is it of yours, shitface? What's he supposed to do, get courtmartialed to preserve *your* redneck honor?" Wilfrey laughed noiselessly and moved away.

For days Lou relived the scene, thinking how naturally the retort came to Francisco—the Cisco kid, as he called him. He envied that strength and angrily regretted his own inability to verbally retaliate against the smirking Wilfrey. Why didn't he come up with his own wise crack, at least? When he shared his feelings of inadequacy, Francisco laughed. "Don't worry about it. Guys like that are all over the place, and put-downs come easy for me. I'm used to that kind of crap. Maybe you're not, coming from the enlightened north."

"I don't know about 'enlightened.'"

The toughest period of training ended late in the still-hot summer, and each battalion was given ten days leave. Lou took the train to Union Station in Chicago, where he was picked up by Maggie, looking tired but exquisite in a bright red silky blouse, short skirt, and sandals. Her black hair flaired out in the wind and smelled soapy and clean when he hugged her. Trying to save money she had parked at a meter on Columbus Drive, in the heart of Grant Park, a good distance even on a cool day. Lou flipped his soft baggage onto his shoulder and began to walk, then jog, laughing at her efforts to keep up. After six blocks he could see Maggie didn't appreciate his quick pace. When they crossed Michigan Avenue and walked up the slope near Buckingham Fountain, she staggered a little and slowed down. From the overpass Lou looked down at a South Shore commuter train, fresh out of northwest Indiana, slowing as it changed tracks below, electric sparks flashing atop the cars as they curled into a new track. Maggie didn't look at the train, but moved slowly on the overpass. Lou offered to carry her the rest of the way, like baggage on his other shoulder. He showed dramatically how he was filled with fresh enthusiasm, and did a clumsy tap step to demonstrate his fitness. She forced a laugh, then rushed to a hedge at the end of the overpass railing, bent over suddenly, and threw up.

He went to her, touched her on the hips, and started to ask something, but she shook her head and then vomited again. He put his hands gently on her hips.

"God, Maggie, I'm sorry. It's my fault," he said.

"It certainly is," she said, out of breath and looking pale. "Just because you're in great shape you don't have to pretend this is a track meet."

He gave her a gentle hug, but she wasn't particularly receptive. They cut through a hedge to a bench in the green area, where they sat quietly, looking at pigeons and listening to traffic noises from every direction.

He loosened the tie to his starched uniform shirt and wiped the sweat off his face. He took her wrist. "Are you alright?"

"I'm wonderful. I'm sitting here near the lakeshore of this beautiful city with the man of my dreams. And he's in perfect condition to go off to war."

"Nah, war for me is still in the future. Way in the future."

She didn't look at him, but she moved her lower lip slightly to one side, suggesting she didn't believe him. He rattled on like a nervous salesman.

"I'm a lousy shot, so they'll probably stick me in a supply depot or kitchen. But I *am* in perfect condition for other things." He reached into a pocket and took out a condom.

Her eyes dropped to it but she continued on something else. "Don't supply depots and kitchens get bombed, too?"

"What?"

"Nothing." She popped a tiny mint in her mouth and rolled it around. "Now I'll be safe to kiss."

They did, but she kept her lips together.

"You okay?" he asked.

"Definitely." She got up and struck a pose. "We can go to the Thunderbird Motel. I even made a reservation."

"Ah, the Thunderbird," he said, squinting. "That sleazy place on the South Shore."

"We can get sleazy," she said, reaching into the hand that held the condom. She took it away from him. "And you won't need this."

"Why? Are you using something?"

"No, nothing. Don't have to. At this point birth control is irrelevant."

He didn't say anything.

"The running didn't make me throw up. I've been puking for a couple of weeks now, especially in the morning."

He still said nothing.

They walked between picnickers; she held his hand and they walked without saying anything else until they got into her car. The meter next to it had just expired.

"Well, at least you didn't get a ticket," he said. She gave him the keys to drive. They got inside, and after a quiet minute, Lou took a deep breath and spoke. "I figured this could happen."

"You *figured?* When, Lou? While *figuring* stories about the supply depot?"

"No, let me finish what I was going to say. It's okay. No, it's really okay, since we were going to get married anyway."

"Lou!" her eyes welled up in anger. "I never agreed to marry you, and the baby doesn't change my mind. Why would it change my mind?" She tried to suppress the sobs but they came anyway. "The baby doesn't change anything." She paused and dried her eyes. "If I have it."

"You didn't say you'd marry me in so many words, but you tell me you love me, and you know what we mean to each other. You're the dream I keep inside me, reminding me I'm only important when I'm with you. Why—"

"No, I don't know that. I don't know any of that," she said. "I don't know the blissful shit you ramble on about, like some kind of Don Juan, which you aren't because no other girl would be dumb enough to listen to it."

"It's always true, what I say." He touched her face, then pulled his hand back and put it on his head. "What did you mean, 'if I have it?'"

"What do you *think* I mean?"

"That's illegal and dangerous."

"My cousin knows a doctor that's safe."

"You'd rather get rid of it than marry me?"

"Yes!" she snapped fiercely.

"God, Maggie, please tell me you don't mean that."

"Why, so you can feel better about yourself?"

"Maggie, I know goddamned well you don't want an abortion. Tell the truth."

"Oh, shut up! Marrying you would mean two children—an infant and a grownup child who does performances for me. Like show and tell."

"Honey," he said, moving toward her, but she held him off and stared at him.

"We don't need to get married," she said. "You left for boot camp August 10th. The baby won't come until late spring, probably the middle of May. I can continue to teach until it's born, and I'll just need a sub for a couple of weeks. Then I'll take care of the baby in the summer, and when it's time to go back into the classroom in the fall my sister Ruth will help out, and my mother."

Lou said nothing.

"Don't you get it?" she said. She spoke in a flat, clear tone. "Whether we get married or not, it will be the same. You're over there on the other side of the world, and I'm here having the baby. What difference will marriage make? And don't tell me the baby will 'have a name.' He'll have a name. She'll have a name. My name."

"What'll I have?"

"You'll have—" She tried to regain the flat voice but the flat words weren't there. "You—You'll go off and get killed, and that's that. Or you'll come back safe and what? Work at Socko? Do we get a house on a street with trees and a back yard where we can talk to neighbors. Talking across the fence about recipes and preventing the blacks from moving in. *I want to get out!* You got out of Stieglitz Park!"

"It isn't there anymore," he said.

She took a deep breath and looked ahead at the windshield. "I guess a bigger explosion is too much to hope for," she said with a sneer.

He leaned his head on the edge of her seatback, close to her face. She shook her head.

"What am I going to do with you?" she whispered. "No, don't answer that. What are *you* going to do when it's all over?"

"Take us out of Whiting and make a life."

"How?"

"I don't know. Sell widgets. Or maybe I could follow up on your suggestion and get some kind of an acting job. I'll play a widget."

She touched his face; her hand was still slightly cold.

"All I do know," he said, "is that if I'm with you—even thousands of miles apart—the confusion will make sense, and we'll always be a part of each other's conscience. Hey—" He squinted. "You ever notice that—a part and apart? We could be a paradox."

She punched him gently in the head with the fleshy part of her fist. He just stared at her. She punched him again. "Damn you," she said, then she kissed him, just for an instant.

"I don't want to get close to anyone else, ever, " he said.

They kissed for a longer time, then held each other, and she told him she loved him more than anything else in the world, even if he *was* immature. Then they drove off to the Thunderbird.

The soldier stops again, this time to loosen the brass clasp and adjust his canvas belt, purely for comfort. Probably a mile more, he thinks. In training they would do that distance in ten minutes, with full pack. Tonight it will take him longer. He looks across the boulevard, where White Oak slants across into another neighborhood. The bare benches and posts chip and peel in the area where Vasilko's market once stood, where John Zmudka shot it out with Ditcher Hathaway. Instant legend, local fame. Vasilko's itself benefitted from the shootout, for people came to look at the famous scene, then stayed to buy corn or cabbage as an offering to the notoriety, almost like lighting a token vigil in a quiet church.

After the refinery explosion, however, things slowed down at this end of town, and Vasilko's gradually died as a shopper's stop. Only White Oak neighborhood regulars and occasional commuters on their way back to South Chicago pulled in for fruit and vegetables. Eventually their ranks thinned also, and the owner piled up the tables and benches and chainlocked them against potential thieves.

The soldier notices how they are still stacked up as they were six or seven years ago, while under the corrugated roof the wooden posts and supports, untouched and flaking, have gradually begun to rot. He remembers a rumor before he went away, that the owner of the funeral home next door wanted to buy the market, probably to turn it into a parking lot, but the deal never happened.

The funeral home is literally a home, a big house which years ago was transformed by the Wojciechowski family into an establishment for embalming and layout. People walk into it as if visiting for coffee and donuts, but actually to witness death in a satin casket.

Two cars roar past, side by side, much faster than the speed limit, headed south. The houses facing the boulevard from either side are all dark, including the one still owned by the parents of Ricky Magyar. Ricky married early, to a quiet girl with angelic eyes who always wore a soft look, as if Ricky were love's incarnation. The soldier recalls a blind date Ricky had set up for him, had in fact begged him to accept, to help out a friend with a visiting cousin. The cousin was intended to be Ricky's practical joke, a homely, heavy girl that would make him feel uncomfortable all evening while Ricky and his future wife enjoyed each other in the front seat. The soldier remembers less what the cousin looked like than what fun she was to talk to. She loved baseball and the Marx Brothers, and she explained to him different ways to avoid getting poison ivy, to which she was as susceptible as he. Eventually he kissed her goodnight, a warm kiss, making sure Ricky saw the kiss, just to spite him, just to let him know his practical joke backfired because there can be no such joke when people like each other.

Ahead, highlighted by the flashing glow of a late-night yellow traffic light, is the plain brick façade of St. Adalbert's Church, which rests for the most part along 121st Street. Other steeples poke the air almost everywhere in town, though not in Stieglitz Park. There never was a church in Stieglitz Park.

He crosses over to the front of St. Adalbert's just to read the bulletins inside the glass case next to the entrance. A card announces a feast day in bold Polish print, then the same thing in English: "He ascends that we may follow." The accepted image of Christ is the background for the words, plus scattered baby-like angels, carrying gold branches and leaves. All of this is bordered in plain white behind the glass. A fluorescent tube is at each side of the case, but someone has turned them off. He squints and sees his own reflection. He wishes he looked better for her, for their first meeting in so long.

They told Maggie's mother and Lou's parents of their hectic marriage plans. Sis seemed relieved, or perhaps pleased, and she gave Lou an eagle-eye smile, plus a squeeze of his shoulder that passed for a hug until he deserved better. Lou's father laughed and almost shouted, "for cryin out loud!" while his mother, without being told Maggie was pregnant, sensed the truth and immediately put on a tortured face, as if condemned for having raised two children into sinfulness. She asked no questions, however, and congratulated them anyway. Then they left quickly to set up the wedding at Sacred Heart, the Irish parish, an old red brick building with steps in front and someone's laundry lines at the side. Properties fit tight in this part of town.

"And why do you want to marry?" Father Broadhurst asked, from behind a desk in the rectory. He was a middle aged man with pointy features which he seemed to cultivate by sucking in his saliva every few minutes, both his cheeks pulling in so that they probably met, just above his tongue.

"Well, we don't have much time," Lou said, quickly trying to explain when he saw Maggie rolling her eyes. "That is, we don't have much time before I ship out. I don't know when, but it won't be more than a few months, that's for sure."

"That doesn't answer my question, at least not the heart of my question."

"We love each other," Maggie said. Lou looked at her eyes, which often looked fatigued when she meant what she was saying, or when she was in an especially loving mood. Up to now neither of them had ever mentioned love in the presence of anyone else, so this might have been one of those special pauses in life had not Fr. Broadhurst, clearing his throat and pulling in his cheeks, moved on disinterestedly.

"Yes," he said, "that's of course the expected response. I'm sure you're sincere, but people who love don't always marry, and Holy Mother Church, of whom you are a part, expects more than physical love and mutual living."

"Well," Lou said, "we do plan to have children."

"Yes, well, that's admirable and also to be expected." The priest's mouth curved to signify a smile, but his eyes coldly pierced the space between him and the two young petitioners. "Why do you want to marry in the church?"

Neither of them could formulate anything beyond an open-mouthed uncertainty as they struggled for the correct answer, even though they both could see that the priest knew they didn't know what it was, and he seemed almost pleased they didn't.

"Such a fine couple, a handsome couple you are. In love, feeling passion for each other. But you need more, you need to understand why this great sacrament continues through time." The priest paused, and Lou felt they were being quizzed without having had time to study. He opened his mouth but could not yet bring anything out. The priest continued. "You need to understand that you marry because God wants you to marry."

Again the priest paused, and he looked downward—at their feet, or at a scuff mark on the linoleum tile. Then he sucked in his cheeks again, and put his hands behind his head and gazed up at the ceiling. Such gestures and mannerisms seemed designed to keep Lou and Maggie outside the border of what he recognized as the true import of the meeting.

"We—" Maggie started to speak, but when she looked at Lou and saw his eyes widen, she stopped.

"Well, no disrespect, Father," Lou said, "but I haven't really put God in the forefront of our plans. Religious thinking is kind of a luxury when you're faced with separation and combat."

"Not a luxury, my son. Not a luxury. Perhaps you both need to reconsider. Too many mistakes have been made through the years when people rush just as you're rushing."

"I don't think we're rushing, and I don't think we'll reconsider. But we won't bother you any further. To be honest, we don't have *time* to bother you any further." Since it was her parish, Lou expected Maggie would make some half-apologetic gesture to the priest before leaving. But she rose first and turned to go without another word, and he followed. He caught up with her at the outer door of the rectory, and when she looked sideways at him he sucked in his cheeks. She squeezed his hand and laughed.

"You want to go to a justice of the peace? We've got everything else we need."

"No," she said. "Jamie Curran will do it. He owes me lots of favors. If he doesn't want to, I'll get his mother and sister to threaten him." Father Curran was a traveler, the brother of Maggie's oldest friend Brigid, who now lived in the southern part of the state.

"I thought he had been kicked out of the order."

"No, just cautioned. He's been warned about things. Probably about fooling around with women. But he's still a priest."

"So if he says the words they count."

She nodded, then just looked at him with the slightest upturn in the corners of her mouth. The dense heat made him sweat, but her face was smooth, soft-looking. The only sweat he had ever seen on her were drops of his own, while they made love feverishly at the Thunderbird.

They stood at the corner opposite the church as the afternoon sun shot through the oaks in front of the Shanahan house. Dappled shadows moved briefly on the bridge of her nose and her forehead, then she turned to him with a smile and put her arms around his neck. He wrapped his long arms around her middle, and clasped his hands just above her buttocks. They stood there embracing quietly for several minutes. A few cars passed by in that time, and an elderly woman walked diagonally up the front steps of the church without looking at them.

Two days later Father Jamie married them at the chapel in the Community Center, with Mrs. Curran and her wastrel youngest son Billy acting as witnesses. Billy was scheduled to enter the Navy the following month. Sis was there, and Lou's mother and father.

Sis let them have her car for the time they could be together in Missouri, and they left after a glass of wine and quick goodbyes. But after a few minutes on the streets of the town, Lou drove back toward the Curran place because Maggie felt they hadn't thanked Jamie and the Currans enough. Lou reluctantly agreed, for it would have been a dumb thing to argue about on their wedding day. Then he saw Sis walking by herself, and he stopped the car and got out.

"Has he changed his mind?" she laughingly shouted to Maggie, then gave Lou a peculiar smile as he came close.

Twice Lou started to express gratitude or simply affection, but nothing came out. Finally Sis reached out and took his chin in between her thumb and forefinger. "It's like I say," she said, as if she had told him something before. "I know little about your parents, but I see how royally your father treats your mother. If you treat Maggie the way he treats her, I won't ever worry. At least not about Maggie."

She gave him a hug. "Come back to us, Dear." she said. It was a quiet intimacy that Lou thought would stay with him forever, if there really was a forever.

At the car, Maggie's eyes were wet. "Forget the Currans," she said. "Let's go."

The boulevard slopes upward for several blocks until the big intersection at 119th street. In the quiet thick of night no random light can be seen, only a couple of globe streetlamps and the traffic signals at the intersection. Darkened houses seem to sag, black with sleep, deathly still, some open for the rush of wind cutting around them or into opened windows. A gust pushes against the crest of his cap, and he takes it off and stuffs it into his back pocket. He's out of uniform now, so he loosens the tie and unbuttons the collar and the next one down. The breeze cools his damp neck.

Belchik's gas station at the corner is closed, but a neon clock inside glows red, showing ten minutes after two. He remembers it was always fast back when he would pull in with his father's car for a fill-up, but two ten seemed about right. There is a clock across the street, outside on a post at the parking lot for the Burns Funeral Home, but it always says 4:30. It hasn't worked for years. People have always made morbid jokes about it, but maybe Tommy Burns thinks of it as good public relations. Any thought about his establishment is better than no thought at all. Somebody dies, they think of the clock that stopped, and they call Tommy.

The soldier remembers his only visit to the big room at the Burns Home. The lights were dim around the walls, and there were muffled sounds of recognition and grief. In the center front, just behind the brass kneeler, was the coffin with Martin Conroy in it, an austere face that matched the one he had in life, or at least the piece of his life the soldier could recall: sitting with him briefly on a Friday night, watching a televised boxing match. He said little then, but every few minutes he would groan angrily, as if both fighters disappointed him.

They were only a couple of years out of high school and Maggie was just his friend then, but a good friend, and when her father had a stroke and died, he went to the wake respectfully and briefly embraced Maggie, who kissed him and thanked him for coming. He remembers how warm her lips were. Years later, after they had become intimate, he realized her lips are warmest while she weeps, or when she's sexually aroused.

Although Lou had managed to get placed in a clerk-typist preparation slot for signal and supply support, he still had to undergo further rigorous training with weapons and field pack. The training was physically demanding, but his worries about Maggie still fogged his thought every day. They couldn't live together in the cottage they rented off base—the one in which they discovered a scorpion on the first night, just after unpacking. Lou had to be in his bunk each night by ten, so Maggie would visit the Guest House as often as she could, which was every other night, trading reservations with a Chicana girl whose husband was in a different platoon but under the same restrictions. Francisco had told Lou about the other couple shortly after secondary training began.

There was something wonderfully dramatic about going to that plain door at the Guest House with a crooked 8 on it, the dim hall making it look for all its worth like a whorehouse, even after Maggie opened it an inch or so and he could see her eyes and the whiteness of her teeth. Her smile betrayed her eagerness to play the slut for his waking dream, wearing a silky blue and pink kimono that rode her skin and moved easy with his hands.

The Autumn interludes always went too fast, but he made it back to the barracks without fail, and he never washed until the end of the following day, because he wanted to keep her scent close, above the oil and metal smells of combat preparation.

He did risk trouble not long before shipping out, when the luck of odd-even random service-number nonsense dictated he had to stay within the company grounds for assorted details during an entire weekend. Soon he would be packed in a transport and flown to a makeshift station on the Mekong, or some other dangerous venue, so he couldn't bear the thought of not seeing her. A couple of friends were willing to trade passes with him, but he was sure he would get stopped and questioned at the base entrance, and thereafter punished disastrously. He took one of the trades anyway, and then paid a corporal with a full car to stow him away in his trunk until they were far enough away from the gate.

Maggie was angry with him for taking such a risk, but thrilled even so that he would do something so impetuous just to be with her. They stayed in bed for two days and indulged in each other while listening to Oscar Peterson, George Shearing, and Aaron Copland. On Sunday night they caressed and kissed gently right up until the moment the corporal drove up to the wooden deck next to their cottage. The final movement of Cesar Franck's Symphony in D played behind their farewell.

"Think'st thou we shall ever meet again?" he said to her when their faces were inches apart next to a wall near the doorway.

"That's Juliet's line," Maggie said.

"I know, but you weren't saying it."

"I was thinking it."

Close by in the rumbling car the corporal and the others were laughing through hangovers. Lou and Maggie weren't laughing as he went out the door, then kissed her one last time through the dirty screen. They separated, but neither heard the other soldiers' laughter, for they were inside the notes of the climactic passage in the Franck Symphony. The sounds rolled out of their cheap stereo atop a folding chair, ten feet from Maggie's sad face.

Two days later, his unit was flown to Southeast Asia.

The soldier takes off his right shoe to remove a stone, a small piece of gravel or asphalt from the newly resurfaced intersection. The light changes but there's no traffic, so he crosses a side street and walks in front of the bright shine, the smooth alabaster of White Castle, open all night, usually for the few who can't sleep, like the old guys sitting at separate raised tables reading the early Tribune, probably mumbling to each other about taxes. Framed by big picture windows and underlined by the sidewalk that slants up to the restaurant wall, their scene might look to a passerby like an allusion to Edward Hopper. If so, it was not on purpose.

A heavy-set man with a thick speckled moustache starts to wave at the soldier passing but, squinting in the middle of the near-wave, realizes it's no one he knows, and turns back to the market quotations.

The soldier is reminded of Billy Shanahan, a longtime regular with political clout who has always called the place *the* White Castle, so that all the old Irishmen and even some of the younger ones tacked on the definite article as if it were part of an accent. "The best coffee is at *the* White Castle," they would say, "especially late at night." Typically, someone else would make a joke out of it, or a goodnatured insult. "That's cause you only drink it there when you're drunk as a skunk and your fuckin taste buds are numb."

Even the thought of coffee stresses his stomach, reminding him he hasn't drank any for months, not since whatever pieces of shrapnel that didn't rip into Francisco cut across the left side of his own trunk near the navel, like sharp hooks unable to grab onto bone, peeling away slices of nonessential flesh. He doesn't really remember any of that because he had just fallen from the rope ladder, and the chopper noise pounded in his head.

Atchison Avenue is the municipal boundary at which point Whiting becomes Hammond, except no one calls it Hammond. Neighborhood names dominate, so that one section is Robertsdale, another Water Gardens, and still another Roby, with its neglected swamp of a village and shacks unoccupied except for rabbits and raccoons.

The neighborhood divisions make the soldier think of Benjy Popovich, who lived back in the Goose Island part of Hammond. Nobody knew he lived on that side of the line until he got really good at basketball. A back court man with great instincts even as a sophomore, he scored 26 points in a losing cause against East Chicago Washington, which made the state finals that year. Before the start of the following season the father of another, lesser player, a man with a close friend on the board of education, found out about Benjy's address and notified the board, which promptly informed the boy he was an ineligible non-resident. Presumably he could have played for one of the Hammond high schools, but he never looked into it. Instead, he approached the teammate whose father had blown the whistle, lured him into an alley behind the fire station, and beat him bloody. Only later did the kid understand why Benjy attacked him.

The soldier remembers Benjy's wild look, his big round eyes that never narrowed or softened, regardless of what the rest of his face showed. A couple of years later, after high school, Benjy had tried to kill himself with aspirin, but his old man found him doubled up and took him to the hospital. Angry and ashamed, the story went, the father had him locked up in some place for lunatics. But then Benjy was the sort of person about whom people told long stories, with subplots, maybe because Benjy himself sometimes boasted how crazy he was.

Thinking back on that wild look, the big eyes and the sudden laugh sometimes accompanied by spit, the soldier wonders if a prophecy can actually be considered self-fulfilling if other people intervene to make it so.

He stops in the midst of trying to recall more about Benjy, then loses interest suddenly, because he finds himself standing in front of Elmer's barbershop near Myrtle Avenue, where his father took him for many years. He didn't especially care for the barber, but perhaps out of habit he periodically went there whenever he was in town and excessively shaggy, the last time being late November, 1963.

Elmer had heavy jowls that seemed to bounce when he talked. His mirror reflection barely showed movement above his upper lip, but the bottom half of his face opened and flapped as if an unseen ventriloquist were manipulating his jaw.

"What're you, a senior now?" he asked, giving off the faint odor of mustard from lunch.

"No, I'm a freshman. Just got started."

"No kidding. You play football?"

"God no, only guys with talent and scholarships play. It's the Big Ten, man."

"Wait a minute, you in *college* now? Wow, you look young—even with all this hair."

Then the radio station which had been playing music suddenly went over to a loud, serious voice describing a shooting in Dallas. The voice said the president had apparently been hit and was being rushed to Memorial hospital.

Elmer stopped cutting for a few beats, then said something like "well, what do you know," as if he were taking the news as a pleasant surprise. "Him and that brother of his." He still hears the barber's deep voice and sees the jiggling cheeks and neck. "Nigger lovers."

Lou recalls standing up and pulling off the striped cover, tossing it into the chair. "That's enough. I don't want any more."

"Here, just let me even it out a little."

"I'll just keep it uneven." He paid and left, shaking. Minutes later worse news came through the open door of Darla's Bar. The president was dead. Faces reflected the death.

As he walks, now years later, his hand still shakes, and the president is dead again, and his trembles are no less strong. His hand shakes and he touches his own wound through an opening between two shirt buttons. He shares lost blood with his friend and his president as they die, senselessly.

Six of them were to follow the boxes below out of the chopper. The boxes contained some kind of electrical stuff, though the smaller ones had medications inside. They were supposed to pull the cargo toward a dirt trail a couple of hundred yards to the north of the drop-off clearing. It was their first mission, and it seemed strictly simple. Down the rope ladders they moved, then swung just above the ground. But suddenly a couple of grenades rolled in out of nowhere and went off, at first sounding like dirt splattering from explosions, but then cutting into his own belly. Before he could shout or even think straight, he saw Francisco's leg bone bare and sinking down and his head seeming to come apart. Then there was loud firing from above, in the chopper, but the sound grew muffled as he touched his own body. For an instant, death was the feel of his own open stomach. He touched bleeding skin, then the slippery corrugations inside of himself, for his inside was no longer inside.

Francisco was motionless. Other explosions cracked the air, and then a long blank.

In his confused unconsciousness, pain surged and disappeared, and then came back in swells. Then there was a dream that developed on the downside of a pain surge, a dream he had dreamt at least once long before the grenades, and had it again long after them. It unfolded in an urban place, inside a classroom crowded with beds and desks. The desks were piled double, and students sat in the upper rows. An officious man in horned rim glasses told students to go forward and backward and they would all be safely home soon. Some of the young men cheered, but the young women acted as if they heard nothing. He stepped away from the others and went outside into a crowded square, or circle, with iron bar fences marking the outer edge. Vendors shouted and vendors sold. He moved to the fence and felt the points on some of the bars, and something growled. He moved back again, and eventually he was in the thick of a crowd. Just when he saw a storefront he knew, it was next door to a bakery where people spoke French. He turned and jogged with stomach pain, and a dark uniformed man smiled broadly and said step up to the next level, but it wasn't a bus, rather a line to register for prizes. The pain made him turn.

He came out of it that first time, or maybe it was later, in a wide space where windows were dirty. His mind was frantic, but he barely moved.

"No, just relax, Louis." Speaking was a medic, who smiled as he would at a party, not in a low-ceilinged room where bandaged men were lying or propped up everywhere. "You're supposed to be in a coma," the medic said in a strange, soft voice, "and lo and behold you come out of it just when you're supposed to be lying still so the medication will spread evenly. What kind of cooperation is that?"

When he tried to speak he only gasped, his tongue and palate so dry the tight mouth tissue seemed ready to crack. A tube ran out of one nostril; he could breathe easier through it.

"Just lie still." The medic put a warm hand on his forehead. "Right. That's it. I knew you weren't going to die on me. You've developed some bad infections, but you're a strong young man. You might get hit by a car when you get home, but you won't die here in this bunk." The medic moved his hand down a bit and patted him gently on the cheek.

He still had scattered pain, and dull pressure, as if something clutched his abdomen and kept it from tearing loose. The stomach muscles tightened into terrible spasms when he tried to voice words, so he whispered. Then again, with more air. "What—?" was all he could bring up.

"It's a long story, and you don't need it all at once. Bad news is you missed Christmas and New Year's. We had a nice party here, too, while you were zonked out. Good news is you're going back to the states where they can deal better with these infections. It's trouble enough to get ripped up by shrapnel, but then your own body turns against you. Such a nice body, too. One wouldn't think it would be so cruel." The medic smiled and clutched his hand.

A corpsman came over and withdrew the syringe from the cylinder which ran into a tube which ran into his arm. The uniformed guy replaced the whole system with another, and then went on to other patients on other bunks. The soldier could feel the new medication creeping into his system. When he moved his buttocks he could feel another tube inside, emerging from the tip of his penis. It was constant discomfort, but he was at least relieved his penis was still intact.

He wanted to tell the medic about his dream, but pain came with even a loud whisper.

"When—?" he was able to breathe loud enough.

"When—let's see," said the medic. "When are you going back to the states? Any day now, especially since you're awake." The medic put a warm hand again on his face. "I'll miss you terribly, of course, but that's the way it is in love and war. Let's see, what other 'when' could you mean? When are you going back into the foray? Never, my friend. Stomach wounds will set you free quicker than toes or fingers getting shot off. When will you be able to eat popcorn? I don't know. You'd better count on applesauce and jello for the near future. Your mother, or your—" The medication rushed heavier into his body and dulled his senses. His mind drifted and seemed to sway. He could see the medic nodding and grinning as he moved to another bed. He wanted to thank that medic, but then everything sank into blurred images.

Weeks later he was still mostly prone, but at a hospital in Maryland. He wasn't fully healed, and his periodic fever and fluctuations in blood pressure concerned the doctors enough to delay his release. The uncertainty aggravated him, which then led to the fever and rise in pressure, which in turn caused further uncertainty. He telephoned Maggie every four or five days, but he didn't lead her to believe he was coming home soon. He wanted good news to be absolutely definite before he would pass it along. And he urged her not to travel east for a weekend, since that would mean flying and heavy expense when they had no funds to speak of. They would be together soon enough, he said, immediately regretting the word choice.

On the phone they talked about their separate worlds. Her voice was altered by the mediocre connection, but it was still her voice, and it quietly thrilled him. Her teaching job was good, except for the two Grenchik boys, who were cousins but seemed to hate each other like feuding families hate. She said her goal was to get them to enjoy a game of something with each other, and not fight. He in turn avoided talking about his injury except that he was doing well enough to walk around and go to the toilet voluntarily. He didn't tell her about the pain, which kept coming back, almost whenever he thought it had stopped for good. The dream was like that, also. He told her about the dream, and she said it sounded like he just wanted to come home, or maybe that he still regretted losing his home.

"Stieglitz Park?" he said.

"If that's what you think of when you think of home."

Daydreaming about anything has always made time go faster for him, and as he slants across the parking lot on the way to Davis Avenue, her street, the wind and lights glow to make shadows, moving shapes in front of the closed buildings that in some instances look like caricatures of people—long noses, big feet, frantic behavior in gusts. He remembers there used to be a market at the foot of Davis, Gatto's market. There were big plywood flaps that pulled up and attached to support poles in front when the little place was open, and one of the young Gatto boys, who looked a little like Kirk Douglas, was in charge. That Gatto proudly told him how wise he was to buy large eggs because they were double-A grade. His only regret as a vendor that day was that he didn't have any *extra* large eggs, since they were *triple*-A grade. There probably was no such thing, but Gatto's grin, with the deep dimple in the middle of his chin, suggested no further validation was necessary.

The street darkens as he walks farther into it, surrounded by thick Norway maples and sycamores, darker still as he moves away from the boulevard lights. The scrape of his Army oxfords across the sidewalk makes an unpleasant sound.

He thinks of the last time they talked on the phone. He didn't tell her much, and she knew he was withholding words about pain or bleeding; he tried to steer the conversation into something else, but he could hear her crying. The best he could do was settle her down with indefinite promises and possible dates of arrival.

He remembers the day of exit, and how his starched shirt rubbed against the big scar, ready to go, ready to get out, not feeling perfect but wanting to look bright and smiling so they would give him his last orders and not take his temperature again. If he saw they were going to stick another thermometer in his mouth he had saved small cubes of ice which he could shove under his tongue to give a lower reading. They didn't bother, however, and at the very moment the papers were in his hand and the warrant officer on duty wished him luck with a vacant expression, he relaxed and all pain went away. In the last phone call to Maggie he didn't tell her he was leaving at that moment but he said it would be soon.

Now on the dark street he feels the papers, moistened by the heat in his side pocket, all the verifications and official seals and embossments texturing the sheets that give the feel of never, that announce how long the never is, the never qualified by his damaged flesh, the never that he'll go back in to give sudden death another chance, never.

He takes a pain pill from the little plastic vial, chews it and swallows.

Amid the dim array of houses, a horizontal light breaks through the dark at the end of the street, an engine lamp from a slow train going back up the night rail to Calumet Park. Just the engine and a supply car, with no other cars trailing. The engineer honks because by law he must, even though there's no sign of traffic anywhere.

The house at the end, in the middle of a lot shaped like a rubber doorstop or a slice of pie, bordered with tall oaks and thick hedges, is Maggie's. As he gets close everything that has always been Maggie rushes to the stage of his mind: his sneaking up on her through the hedge as she sunned on a blanket or in a webbed chaise, reading John O'Hara, or his closing the living room blinds to prevent the neighbors from snooping, or his kissing the bridge of her nose and marvelling that a face could be so radiant at a distance of one inch.

As he stands in front of the house he can see vague patterns of light within, glows against the edges of a window or doorway, perhaps from a small night light. He moves through a break in the hedge to the sidewalk that leads to the little porch that juts out from the kitchen. Another train, a much faster one on the farthest track, rushes past the beach where he and Maggie clutched and went into each other months ago, and rolls toward Chicago with a high-pitched squeal of a whistle, just as the screen door swings open slowly at the top of the steps.

The soldier stands at the bottom step and looks at her as her left hand guides the door softly shut while her right hand touches her chest above her swollen breasts. She wears some kind of white silky thing he's never seen before, and it slopes over her enlarged midsection, which he also hasn't seen before. As he goes up to her she seems even taller, as if carrying their child has forced her shoulders back in added support. Her lips don't shape into a smile, but her eyes tell him how she feels, and she reaches to his face with both hands. Then she touches his shirtfront as if she knows precisely where the scar is. He moves closer and their stomachs touch.

"Are you—" she stutters. "Don't you have a duffle bag, or anything?"

"I left it in Stieglitz Park."

"I thought that didn't exist anymore."

"It doesn't, but I do." He holds her close and tastes her face as he kisses it, and the baby inside her moves with a suddenness that he can feel against his scar. "How could you be waiting up for me if I didn't tell you when I would be here?"

She kisses his lips, and runs her hand over his shoulder against the damp spots on his shirt. "I could smell your sweat. And the starch."

"Pregnant women have that kind of power?"

"You'd be surprised."

They hold each other as all the muffled ambience of the industrial heart seems to stop. She undoes a button on his shirt and slips her fingers through to touch his scar more intimately.

"Why didn't you want me to come to the hospital?" Tears well up in her eyes, so close to his he almost shares the wetness.

"I'm sorry." He whispers. "I'm sorry. Please, it's over." He touches her midsection

"What if you had died on that hospital bed?"

"I didn't. Please don't be angry. I'm here. Here's my body and here's yours."

Her wet face changes and she laughs. "Yeah, for better or worse."

The wind gusts, and when she turns to feel its coolness, the breeze lifts her long black hair and trails it across his cheek. Their faces then join under the dark silk strands, wind-blown and feathery light.

He half-sits on the railing of the porch and looks up at her, tall in the moving shadows of the big trees. He touches her stomach again, and she holds his hand there. The wind swirls lightly, an uncertain breeze, waving the silky strands across her face as she looks back at him with eyes of liquid shine in the suddenly wonderful depths of night.

9. Stieglitz Park in Chicago
1969-1970

Lou rested that first day back in Whiting, and found occasion to stare at Maggie, who returned some of his stares with an easy smile touched with lustful promise. Directly below the smile was the big swell and the pale, smooth legs, stressed but still perfect to his eyes. She was a wonder to him, a glory he had almost forgotten during his days of blood, pain, and healing.

But he barely looked at her on day two, for he got up very early in order to get into Chicago and follow some job leads. Maggie's sister Ruth, who was three years younger and worked for a law firm in the Loop, gave him a couple of tips and also a ride to the South Shore station in the north part of Hammond. She herself was doing research that day and, she told him in semi-secrecy, spending some time with her new boyfriend, whom no friend or family member had as yet met. One of the tips Ruth gave Lou was about a guy who had dated a friend of hers for a while, a facilitator named Rod at the Strong Case Employment Agency on Michigan Avenue.

When Lou walked into his office, Rod pointed out a spot on the left collar of his brown suit jacket. Brown was not a good choice to begin with, Rod said, but what looked like grease was simply unacceptable. Lou figured he had to deal with stuff like that in order to pay bills, so he accepted spot remover from Rod and applied it while the latter described the late morning job interview he was setting up at the First National Bank. Lou initially was skeptical about such an opportunity, since he had no business or economic training whatsoever. Rod explained how the bank was looking to expand its base of potential officers to include people with liberal arts degrees, for they (presumably) had a broader understanding of life, rather than prepared skill in prime rates and financial risk. And of course, Rod said, the bank would pay his agency fee, a not inconsiderable amount.

During their conversation Rod asked Lou about his early discharge from the Army. When Lou said it was a medical discharge stemming from a wound and subsequent infection, Rod became excited.

"You were wounded? Did you get the Purple Heart?"

"Yes."

"My God, why don't you <u>wear</u> it?"

"On my suit?"

"Yeah, right over the spot."

"Hey, what the hell. I could bring along the commendation letter."

"I'm kidding. But maybe you could wear your uniform, with the medal. I'll change the appointment to tomorrow morning."

"Look," said Lou. "I understand what you're saying, but the medal is purely for formal gatherings and military moments. And I'm not putting on the uniform again for anything. Ever. Anyway, guys in uniform aren't exactly admired and praised these days. "

"Maybe not at rock concerts or street demonstrations. You're lucky this isn't last summer, when all hell was breaking loose down on the streets." Rod shook his head and took a deep breath, as if he had actually survived the violence outside the Democratic convention. "No, the bank will be different. Make sure you mention the medal to Jon Clark . He's the personnel officer over there. Jesus, the Purple Heart! Clark'll probably presume you're pro-Nixon. Or at least not a radical."

Rod proved to be right about the medal. At the First National Bank, Clark was so enthusiastic he called over a couple of other officers, who shook Lou's hand with vigor and mild reverence. At their insistence he had to explain the circumstances of the wound, but he left out the death of Francisco, for he needed to protect that memory. The officers welcomed him aboard, even before Clark handed him the application, describing it as a necessary formality. Despite all the respect and praise, his salary was set at just $600 per month.

During his physical the next morning, the examining doctor expressed some concern about his badly scarred abdomen. But then he changed his tone, and said bank work wouldn't tax his physical strength. "If you have to carry a million bucks from one safe to another," he said, "make sure the batch isn't made up of one dollar bills."

Within hours he hated the job, which essentially was structured tedium, with every activity aimed at expanding wealth, then measuring it. Riding the South Shore commuter that first evening, however, he promised himself he would not complain to Ruth or Sis, who picked him up at the Hammond station, and certainly not to Maggie, who didn't need to hear anyone else's gripes. Their dinner that night was in fact a happy event because of the job.

Within a week Lou got to know many of the other new hires, along with some of the veterans of the group called General Clerks, who liked to think of themselves as troubleshooters. When, at the end of the day, a specific department could not balance their receipts and expenditures, the General people and the new trainees would go in and start counting slips from adding machines and other receipts. Lou couldn't see how this could be considered "troubleshooting," but he kept his opinion to himself, for the time being. Besides, the extra half-hour or so at the end of the day brought each worker a cash payout of four dollars which, to ward off any objections by advocates of unionizing, the bank officially called "supper money," rather than overtime compensation. Even a few days of sampling downtown Chicago eateries was enough to convince Lou how ludicrous the term was, since four bucks could only get supper at street vendor stands.

On the second weekend after his return, they moved from Sis' back bedroom to a house on Green Avenue, about five blocks down from where Lou's parents lived. They rented the main floor and basement from a grizzled man with the unlikely name of Marcus Antoniak, who lived above them and shared the back stairway. Occasionally they could hear him stumble above, despite the thick carpeting he bragged about. Marcus snickered when Lou mentioned he grew up in Stieglitz Park. Later the older man admitted he himself had lived there several years before the big explosion. Still later, Maggie was informed by a neighbor that Marcus was an ex-convict, paroled from a sentence for accessory to grand larceny while working as a night watchman at Inland Steel.

Neither one of them warmed to the idea of living in the same house with a convicted felon, but at least he wasn't a pervert, they reasoned, and anyway the rent was dirt cheap--$160 per month, including utilities. If they moved to Chicago or the Illinois suburbs, they'd have to put up twice that, or more. In addition, their portion of the house was fully furnished, so the move was relatively easy.

Three days after moving in, while Lou worked in the currency department separating raggedy five- and ten-dollar bills from still usable ones, Sis drove Maggie to St. Margaret's Hospital in Hammond, where she gave birth to a six pound, 7 ounce baby boy, whom they named Martin Francisco Fronczek, after Maggie's father and Lou's friend, whose own death had probably saved Lou's life.

Lou thought the child looked like Maggie, and Maggie thought he looked like Lou. Sis said they were both wrong. "Give him a couple of weeks," she said with a laugh. "Right now he looks like Winston Churchill."

In the seventeen months Lou worked at the bank he, like other general trainees, moved from one department to another, the corporate idea being that they would be able to plug themselves in anywhere to cover for vacationing or sick employees in those departments. This mobility didn't in itself alleviate the tedium, but the trainees got a chance to listen to and absorb bank gossip and old stories which, told by many voices, had probably grown away from truth long ago.

His least favorite job was in the collections department, where his duty involved telephoning people who were lagging at least a couple of months behind in their repayment of a personal loan. Each account was represented on a buff colored card with necessary information about the individual borrower, the payments and dates, plus space for "remarks," which in most instances amounted to a few words such as "partial payment in mail Mar 3" or "out of town until Apr 12," written in the scrawl of the guy whose desk Lou was temporarily occupying. Twice weekly a meeting would be called, in mid-morning, by the department head Jack Fisher, an irascible 40-ish man with short curly hair who had recently undergone colon surgery which necessitated that he wear a colostomy bag.. When one of the eight collections clerks asked him how he knew when to go to the bathroom and empty the bag, Jack replied, "I can smell it."

Thinking about such a disgusting signal made Lou realize how relatively untroubling was his war wound. In fact, as it gave him less and less discomfort, he gradually forgot about it.

Lou worked in collections for a little more than two months that summer, and in each case he lowered the number of delinquent accounts. This suggested to him he was doing something right in his phone calls, but Fisher set him straight. "I don't know if you're doing alright or what, Fronczek, because the guys you substituted for were doing such a terrible job even a pollyanna would have shown improvement."

In the late summer he was switched for a short time to the transfers department. All day long he was handed a stack of adding machine tapes to prove, which meant to add up the figures to see if the totals were the same as what the previous person came up with. He never understood how the term 'transfers' applied to anything he did. But the boss was a nice guy, an aging Irishman named Mike Burke whose skin was just a shade darker than chalk. He was afflicted with a rare condition which prevented him from exposing the uncovered parts of himself to the sun longer than ten minutes or so; otherwise he would break out in solar rash and a high temperature. One day he asked Lou about his wound.

"Does it ever bother you anymore?"

"Not really," Lou said. "I think of it only when I get undressed and look in the mirror."

When Lou showed him a picture of Maggie, sitting with Martin on her lap, he grinned broadly. "What a beautiful Irish girl, and your boy looks like her, thanks be to God. How'd a hunky like you wind up with such a beauty?"

"I guess she felt sorry for me."

"Ah, go on. I'm just teasing," Mike said, then lowered his voice. "And I see the way Loretta over there eyes you every chance she gets. Course, even if you were available she's way too tall for you. Stay with your little colleen."

Actually, the woman Mike referred to was shorter than Maggie, who never wore high heels when they went out in public. Lou changed the subject to the White Sox, a change that brought a frown to Mike's face, since the team had been doing poorly since opening day.

"Do you take the el?"

"No," Lou said. "I come in on the South Shore, but I know what you're going to say."

"Every goddamned day, twice a day, I have to listen to those Cub fans."

"So do I, and it looks like they're going all the way this year."

"Yeah, well if that happens I might retire, just so I don't have to ride the el so often."

Mike and others were friendly, but most of the workers Lou met who weren't officers were openly racist. Perhaps the officers shared the bias, but they may have reserved it for closed door meetings. In departments, casual conversations regularly focused on what they called "changing" neighborhoods—where "they" were at this point, in geographic terms: north of 83d street? Jesus, are you kidding?—or they would talk in mufflespeak about newly hired men and women of dark skin at the bank. The white veterans, and many of the younger workers, talked loudly about welfare cheats and other blacks getting favors from the city and the federal government. They only toned down their voices when telling vulgar racial jokes, but that may have been because they didn't want to offend some nearby woman with crude language, rather than in deference to a nearby black person. One spring day, when asked about an extended lunch hour he had taken, Lou mentioned he had gone to the mayor's tribute to the late Dr. Martin Luther King, on the second anniversary of his assassination. No one in the group said anything afterwards, as if he had violated some racist code which dictated only bad things could be said about the murdered civil rights leader.

During such unpleasant circumstances he sometimes thought of how the bigots must have been somehow indoctrinated gradually, so that they considered racial bias the natural order of things. For once he was thankful for his own parents, especially his mother. She was raised in Indiana Harbor, and went to school with black kids, and later worked alongside them in a dime store. If she ever spoke of them it was only to say how cheerful were the ones she knew. Her sanctimonious brand of Catholicism angered him increasingly, but at least she wasn't a bigot.

Later that spring he did manage to land a couple of situations at the bank with some degree of responsibility. One came about, Lou was convinced, because he used a particular word which impressed one of the vice presidents, a self-congratulatory hotshot who had gathered Lou and a dozen other trainees into a conference room adjacent to his personal office. It looked like every other conference room featured on television and in the movies, but most of the young men gathered rhapsodized about its special character, and the long table, and the dark walnut shelves, and how there probably was a wet bar somewhere if only someone knew the right button to push.

Then the grinning vice president, tanned and muscular with streaks of gray rushing back through his brown hair, came in and sat at the head of the long table, looking around at each of their faces and continuing to grin.

"I always feel great after a workout," he said. "I hope each of you someday get the chance—sorry, gets the chance—to have your own key to the Executive Club on the 24th floor. I try to use the facility as often as I can, simply because I feel so great when I get back to my desk." He paused then, but continued to smile, as if waiting for someone to tell him he also looked great.

"At the risk of being redundant," he then said, "I'm Mark Wainwright."

Lou didn't hear everything else the man said, for he was trying to figure out how "redundant" fit into the man's self-introduction.

"I'm vice president in charge of what I want you gentlemen to create, which is a central file. A file of all accounts and all people who come to our bank. What do you think of that?"

Wainwright seemed proud of the bait he had just thrown out to them. There was some mumbling, then a couple of statements of support, and some comments about the capacity of the data processing mainframe, and a question about what sort of training they needed in working with IBM cards. Wainwright told them the proper name for the cards was hollerith, since different companies made them. He then continued his good-natured pedantry by responding to each comment and question while retaining his grin, apparently happy at such eagerness in the group. Then he pointed to Lou, who had raised his hand.

"Sir, I'm wondering—"

"You don't have to call me 'sir,' Louis. You're not in the army anymore."

"Yes, well," Lou was momentarily taken aback by the simple fact that Wainwright knew his name. "I'm wondering. Since the bank is a hundred years old, with all the history, isn't it kind of an anachronism to want a central file at this point?"

"Anachronism," Wainwright said, and then laughed, and nodded a sort of approval. "I don't think so, not with the capabilities of modern data processing. But let me take the matter up with you after we break up here."

Wainwright apparently both loved and hated Lou's use of the word 'anachronism,' for he took Lou out of the research group and put him on an assignment which required verbal skills and writing ability. He was to summarize the various accounts at the 1st National maintained by key officers of companies whose headquarters were in the Loop. At first Lou thought he could bring opinion or evaluation into the task, but Wainwright told him to stick to the facts and records of the people. As such, what looked promising at first turned into merely a different form of tedium. And, like so many other jobs inside the big vault, as he privately nicknamed the bank, it was easy, made to order for the laziest of workers.

The other department at which he had some responsibility was no challenge, either, but it offered him the opportunity for genuine overtime—a half day's pay, plus meal money and carfare—on Saturday mornings. Maggie hated to see him go off to work the extra half-day, but they needed to save money, especially if he wanted to follow through with his plan to go to graduate school, with help from Lyndon Johnson's Vietnam GI Bill.

It was called Out Mail, the last department in which Lou would work at the bank, and it sprawled with long tables across the middle of a long room on the fifth floor. There were machines for wrapping packages, strapping bundles, and stamping postage on all outgoing mail. The employees were all male and almost all temporary, working flexible hours while taking classes at Loyola, DePaul, Chicago Teachers College, or other local colleges and universities.

The full time exceptions in the department were a burly assistant head named Ed Veltman and the red-nosed boss, George Carter, who resembled Walter Brennan.

Veltman had been at the bank for 30 years, and frequently brought up the subject of Carter's retirement.

"For Christ's sake, Dog," Veltman would say, typically. "Dog" had been Carter's nickname from the time he was a southside kid, back in the days following World War I. "For Christ's sake, you've got enough socked away to retire tomorrow."

Dog would then lean back in the wooden swivel chair at his desk, and put on a bloodshot grin, which usually signified he was about to talk about hot pussy in his past, but sometimes about money and power. In either case, he would look toward Lou while responding to Veltman. "How do you like this vulture? Circling the wagons, looking for a weak sister. Jesus, if I retired tomorrow, what would I do? Sit home watching TV while Edna drapes her fat ass on the front seat of the Cutlass and goes out to spend more of my money."

Sometimes Veltman would bring Lou into his appeal. "Give the Hoosier kid a break, Dog. If you retire, not only do I take over, but Hoosier-little-whosis gets some permanent authority. And you can drink all the Ezra Brooks that Foremost Liquor sells."

Everyone knew about Dog's drinking, in as much as he would take extended lunch hour every other Friday or so, only to return with a redder than ever face, walking past the ten or fifteen young men at the working table, and singing some standard like "I've got you under my skin." But he never got into any real trouble, perhaps because his supervisors knew Veltman would cover for him on those alcoholic Fridays, and anyway the new kid seemed to know what he was doing, knew how to deal with the part-timers, who weren't much younger than he.

When drunk, Dog often waxed nostalgic about his old south side neighborhood, and all the fucking he used to do with what he called his well-honed bone. When he talked like that Lou was reminded of characters in books by James T. Farrell. But when he mentioned the novels, Dog just shrugged and said he knew who Farrell was, but he didn't read much. Then he would started talking about himself again. More than once, after returning from an early afternoon of shots and beers, he seemed to drift off into a private narrative, a quiet, paradoxical reverie of joy and lamentation.

"And we're lyin' on that upstairs bed," he would say. "She's got one knee up and her hand over her bush. I'm on my back, startin' to think about going in for a second round, and I could feel the captain slowly rising to full attention. But she's got this wet face, and she says oh God what have we done? What have we done? Your wife is my friend. What have we done? Shit."

Whenever Dog mumbled through this apparently adulterous scene out of the past, Lou said nothing, figuring the old guy needed no comment from someone 40 years his junior. The others in the big room weren't close enough to hear. Sometimes Dog would resume his mumbling minutes later, but the private narrative would then address a totally opposite topic: his current impotence.

"Isn't that somethin'?" he would ask himself, as his bloodshot smile turned ironic and his hand scratched his crotch, or massaged his flaccidity. "All that equipment, and it's useless."

During dinner each day Lou told Maggie stories about the bank, but he made them brief and even less interesting than they actually were, for he didn't want her to think he was having a good time while she struggled to meet the tough challenge of raising Martin, who was changing their lives so drastically.

Martin was a good but mischievous baby who brought out childishness in both his parents, especially Lou. But Maggie had to follow the broad variations in the little boy's temperament. At times he exhausted her, and whenever he was around, Lou was able to recognize those moments just from looking at her through a doorway. He would then take over, though sometimes Martin balked and began to cry or otherwise become bratty when he saw Maggie go to the big bedroom and lie down. On the baby's brattiest evenings, Lou felt the heaviest kind of guilt, for he realized Maggie had to give so much of her energy every day, while he only had to smile and be polite with customers at the bank, or pretend to be interested in high finance with his supervisors.

After his return on Saturday afternoons they always tried to do something as a threesome, piling into the used Oldsmobile F-85 Lou had bought at a lot near 63d and Halsted, on the recommendation of a funny black mechanic named Cyrus, a bank customer he had met while working a cashier's window. Cyrus said the car was swift and true, and nothing was wrong with it. Sure enough, Lou had no problems with the car, and as often as he could he left it at home for Maggie to use, after she drove him to the South Shore. Some evenings he caught a ride from the station with his uncle Fred, who worked at SOCO's Loop office, or simply rode a bus.

Even though they didn't spend much time talking about their future, Lou recognized signs of dismay in Maggie, a visible fatigue not solely tied to her daily routine, but a fear that they might be stuck in Whiting. He began building a resume he could take back to Rod at the employment agency. When he showed the finished document to Maggie she cheered up somewhat, happy to see he wasn't sinking into a soft bank slot. He also resolved to take Martin to Whiting Park or Wolf Lake on Sundays so Maggie could sleep in. He even began cooking weekend meals. She still feared he wasn't following his desire to become an actor.

But in a small way he *was* exercising his penchant to act. In front of his peers during coffee breaks or lunch hour, he sometimes broke into impressions of officers and supervisors at the departments where they happened to be working that day. For his spontaneous skits, he would give speaking parts to other trainees, such as Leroy Watkins, originally from Keokuk, Iowa. Leroy was such a precious rube that Lou let him play himself, in a momentous confrontation with Mark Wainwright concerning the arrangement of banners on the streetlamps outside the bank. Leroy bought into the routine, perhaps because he seriously thought Lou was already an important, successful person just waiting around, as if the bank job was a mere vestibule in the cathedral of prominence. Whenever they worked together on a job, Leroy would ask him lots of questions about buying a house and acting and talking to girls. Once he asked Lou to show him a picture of his wife and baby and, upon seeing the wallet sized snapshot, said in a swirling Iowa drawl, "shoot, she looks just like a movie star."

"She was going to be one," Lou responded, "but I ruined everything." He could see that Leroy probably believed him.

Lou had particular fun mimicking individuals who wore their officer's sense of power on their sleeves, but he also developed a short routine about an elevator operator who seemed to be on the brink of lunacy. Riding up and down in the tight square of anticipation, the guy created an adventurous persona for himself, complete with floating hormones and a strategically placed cucumber in his crotch, which served as an invitation to any equally lonely lass who didn't mind taking a chance on a pervert.

When Lou told Maggie about the imitations she not only wasn't entertained, but she sternly told him if he wanted to do comedy, why didn't he see if Rod the agent could line him up with something real, to show his talent.

At his next lunch hour he went to the agency and posed the question about any kind of acting slot. Rod shook his head in exasperation, saying that's not how it works in the world of actors' unions and theatre companies. It wasn't Broadway, but even in Chicago there were thousands of would-be actors waiting tables in restaurants, hopeful that their clever delivery of menu highlights and eccentric observations would earn them better tips.

Nonetheless, Rod promised he'd keep an eye out for him.

In October, Maggie did three days' worth of political telephoning for her uncle, who paid her nicely, even though everyone else who did the same thing got only a thank you for their services. She thought of buying clothes for Martin, or fixing the car radio, or other practical expenses. Lou's suggestion was to blow it all on a second anniversary date, complete with dinner, dancing, and a lake view motel room.

"Maybe we could get one with a vibrating mattress," Maggie said, buying into his idea immediately and grinning.

"Hell yes," Lou said, covering his mouth. Martin was on the couch next to him, grinning like Maggie, then putting a hand over his mouth like Lou. "You can't come, though, young man," Lou said. "Because mommy and daddy want to do wicked things to each other. Uninterrupted." Martin, whose sounds were gradually developing beyond "dah!" and "mah!" stared at his father and shaped his lips as if to make a "woo" sound, but it didn't come out.

Happy at the prospect of their first genuine night-out date in over a year, Lou made the necessary reservations for the Thursday night which was exactly two years since the wedding they had slapped together. The General group leader at the bank gave him the following Friday off, continuing a new policy to give trainees occasional paid leave for special days, though no more than a couple per year.

All was well, then, in advance, until they found out Sis was scheduled for tests at the hospital early that Friday morning. When she learned of the babysitting problem from Maggie, Sis offered to reschedule, but Maggie said they would get by, although she was troubled that her mother was evasive about what the tests were for.

Since Ruth was in New York, they were forced to ask Lou's parents to care for Martin while they had fun. Lou wanted to make the request, but Maggie argued she had more time for it, and she took the boy along, after putting him down for a nap and making him promise to be at his cutest. Louie's expression betrayed his disapproval, and he pointed out he had to work the 8 to 4 shift that Friday. But Lois loved the idea and said she could hardly wait, as she walked around their living room, bouncing Martin lightly in her arms. She told Maggie to have fun and not worry, but Martin grew cranky just before they left, and Maggie couldn't help but worry.

On the night of their date, Lou realized he hadn't allowed sufficient intervals of time. He didn't get home from the bank until just before six, and even though Maggie had already dropped off Martin with Lou's parents so they could toss their overnight bag into the car and scoot up Lake Shore Drive in 20 minutes to the 50th On the Lake Motel, they had to check in fast, negating the possibility of quick sex before dinner, since Lou had set the dinner reservations for 7:00 at Scampi, a 25 minute drive to the southwest. Standing in the middle of their second-floor room, staring at each other, deciding if they should bag the restaurant date and eat via room service or go to the great place, eat paella and dance, then fuck thereafter, they went to the car.

As they sat and drank white wine before and after a wonderful meal, and danced to sharp tango beats and other sensual rhythms on the crowded floor, they were happy they had gone through with their original plan. They also hungered for each other, and when the band at the Scampi took a break at 9:00 p.m., they rushed back to the motel.

They had brought along a pint of Johnny Walker Red, but once in the room their only appetite was for each other. They stripped, and she was first into the bed, looking out at him, seeing in his eyes the same desire she felt. He in turn looked down at the slopes and peaks of her creamy skin, interrupted only by pink nipples and the thick black patch of hair. He intentionally gasped before bending to her, kissing her like a dying fool. He stuck the tip of his tongue into her belly button. "You're not ticklish when you're turned on," he said. She laughed, then reached to the bedstand and unwrapped a condom and slipped it on him as she fused her passion with his.

The night was quiet as they slept, even quiet when they stirred from mutually peculiar dreams. They decided to indulge in the Johnny Walker without ice, in turn sucking the bottle until it was empty. As if ordered by the proprietor, the bright moon made thin ribbons of light on the rippling waves of Lake Michigan beyond their picture window. The walls of the room reflected other random glimmers of the night from passing cars. Dizzy from booze and easy sleep, they looked into each other's shadowed faces with the kind of peaceful lust available only to people who lie together in memory as well as anticipation. Through exchanged hypnotism they soon were fully joined again, pushing a crazy power of feeling into each other.

"Oh, what a night we had," Lois said as soon as they walked through the entrance late Friday morning. "The poor baby kept waking up and asking for mommy, and then he'd quiet down and I would put him back down on the bunk and he'd start whimpering again. So I would sit down on the bunk and stretch my back muscles, they're so sore this morning, but—"

"Is he okay now?" Maggie asked, moving into the living room. "Where is he?"

"After he ate, I put him back down on the bunk because he was still tired. Maybe he just doesn't like that mattress, or it's cold so close to the floor."

"It was warm last night," Lou said.

"Maybe it was cooler here," Lois said, "since we're so close to the lake."

"We were almost *in* the lake."

"And you never told me where—oh, look at sweetheart! With the tsuntsies in his nose."

Martin stood in the doorway just as Maggie reached it. She picked him up and he smiled.

"You're so happy to see mama, aren't you? Such a pretty smile!"

"Grandma, when he cries the best thing is just to give him the pacifier," Maggie said, kissing Martin's forehead.

"Well, I didn't know. Louisa never wanted her babies to depend on the sassy."

They hugged and kissed Lois, then packed up Martin's things and left. In the car, Lou spoke right after starting the engine. "She won't have to worry about how to calm him down, because he's not staying there anymore."

"Lou, don't be such a—"

"Such a what?"

"Prick."

"Nice talk in front of our son."

"Lou, they mean well. Don't be so judgmental. They didn't ruin your life."

"I wonder."

"I wonder if you wonder," she said, poking his shoulder.

"Double Indemnity! But *I* should have said it, because it's Fred MacMurray's line. And he was an insurance agent, a standard nothing job just like mine, a goddamned bank clerk."

"As you said, nice talk in front of our son."

Their bickering died down when Lou decided that, instead of going home, they would pick up some food at the Parkview Market and have a picnic in Forsythe Park. It was a blustery, warm autumn day, with the south wind carrying the smells from the Lever Bros. plant northward across the lake's edge. Wolf Lake, inland by a half mile or so, looked murky as ever from the spot in the park where they had put down their picnic supplies. Martin moved forward in uneven steps toward the bullrushes in the shallow water.

"He wants to play Moses," said Lou, rushing forward to grab the boy before he walked into the swampy soil. He swept Martin up in the air, then brought him down to rest with his butt against Lou's armpit, so that Lou had to look wide-eyed up at him. Martin began to laugh down at his father's face, and Lou laughed up at his. Maggie sat at a picnic table on a slightly downhill slope, looked out at her two loves, their hair blowing in the wind gusts and silhouetted against the bright sky and the bending willows. They laughed with wide open mouths just inches from each other, and Maggie registered it all, a most wonderful moment in their life together.

Just after the new year began, Rod called him with excitement in his voice about a possibility with Lakeside Advertising Enterprises. One of their clients, Consolidated Baby Foods, had decided to trash their earlier infant-centered commercials and, for the coming year, to see if they could direct consumer attention to young parents, maybe even young fathers. Lou would need no equity credentials, Rod told him, just his good looks, his degree, and his first-hand experience. Rod was also excited because his Lakeside contact was a woman he had dated a couple of times, a beautiful blonde who once lived in Whiting.

"Small world, eh?"

Lou responded, "I guess that's true, since it's just over the skyway. What's her name?"

"Geraldine Stillman."

"Jesus."

"Is there a problem?"

"No. It's just that I haven't heard that name in a long time. She's a boss, you say? Wow. She couldn't be much more than thirty."

"More like thirty-three, but she's a looker. And a go-getter. That's what you need to be. The interview is tomorrow, just after lunch. Can you skip out of the bank? If they like what they see, it could last an hour or two, maybe longer."

In as much as Dog owed him several favors for Friday binges, Lou said it wouldn't be a problem. He floated through the rest of the day absent-mindedly, trying to think of ways to impress advertising people. Perception is all, he remembered someone saying. Should he exude confidence, or simply restructure the ass-kissing strategies he often used at the bank?

He rushed enthusiastically into the house on Green Avenue, lifted Martin in his arms, and told the child about his day—loud enough that Maggie could hear before he walked into the kitchen, where she had just burned pork chops.

"Hey, no worry," Lou said, "you know I like a high charcoal factor on my meat. Did you hear the news I was conveying to this lad?"

"So it's tomorrow, the interview?"

"Right. Are you happy?"

"I'll be happy if you get the job, I suppose."

He could see her face didn't reflect happy feelings. "Honey, what's the matter?"

"Nothing. Let's just sit down and eat. Pull the high chair over here."

They ate quietly, but Lou kept trying to invade her mood. Finally she told him she and Martin had run into Patricia Gregorovich, who used to be Patricia Janacek, who thereupon launched into a presumably envy-inducing saga of her and her successful engineer husband, who had bought and remodeled the Callahan house on LaPorte St. and turned it into something Patricia had always dreamed about for her two perfectly coiffed daughters to grow up in.

"Did Martin poop, on cue?" Lou said, at which point Martin started climbing out of the high chair.

"No, but he chose that moment to spit up part of his lunch on the shoes of one of the perfectly coiffed daughters. Patricia got pissed off, and even though I apologized and wiped off the kid's shoe, she walked away muttering something which I didn't hear and didn't want to."

Martin reached out to Lou, apparently fully trusting his father to catch him before he fell. Lou held him and growled into his neck.

"Why don't you put him in the playpen with one of those teething biscuits," Maggie said.

After putting Martin on the mat, he returned to find Maggie clearing the table with an insistently unhappy look.

"Tell me what's really wrong, Maggie. Please."

She ran hot water over the scraps on the plates, then turned and stared at him for a few seconds before speaking. "When we were at the motel on our anniversary and we woke up in the middle of the night, did you put on a condom?"

"Christ." In an instant he lost every good thought he had been indulging in since Rod's phone call. "I thought I did. Maybe I didn't, or maybe it slipped off, or tore. We were pretty wild that night." He gave a little smile, but she only looked more exasperated. "You haven't said anything about missing periods. In fact, that one night a couple of weeks ago you said you didn't want to screw because you were starting to get cramps."

"Wrong cramps, I guess. And I thought since I didn't throw up even once that there must be some other reason for the missed periods."

"But now you're sure?"

"I wasn't until I went to see Dr. Halfer today."

He took her in his arms and kissed her hair and tried to reassure her with a simple embrace that everything would be fine. The stiffness in her body and her hanging arms suggested she felt otherwise. Without anger, she pushed him away.

"I thought I could begin subbing in the schools next year," she said. "The school system has started a child care center right next to the high school, and I could have taken Martin there in the fall. Now nothing is possible. Another baby, more expenses, crowded house, stupid town. If it weren't for my mother I'd go nuts."

"Maybe this interview will turn into something good, and we can move. Don't despair."

"It's not despair, it's disgust—with myself." She turned away and looked out the window above the sink. It was dark in the house next door, and dark above and below.

"It's my fault," he said. "I should have been more careful."

"No, *I* should have been more careful. It's my body."

"Maybe you should try the pill again."

"It won't do much good now." She put both hands on her head and made a noise of exasperation. "You know those things make me sick! Whatever the opposite of an aphrodisiac—that's what those things are to me."

He started to touch her waist, but knew from experience she didn't want to pull out of a mood too quickly. So he walked into the living room and read the Hammond Times. They didn't talk anymore that evening, and she went to bed early. He played with Martin for a while, then put him into his crib; the child fell asleep quickly. Then Lou went back into the living room, turned off the lights, and relaxed on the sofa while staring out the front windows at a street lamp at the point Green Avenue bent about thirty degrees to the northwest. In his mind the warring factions were worry and anticipation. When the two got mixed up, he tired and fell asleep.

As expected, Dog had no objection to his going off for an extended lunch hour, although the old guy didn't buy Lou's story about an interview, preferring to think his trainee was, as he put it, "off to play hide the sausage with some chippy from the mortgage department."

Geraldine Stillman came out into the lobby at Lakeside Advertising Enterprises as soon as Lou walked into the entry lobby. Stunning in a knit black blouse and silver skirt, she introduced herself by asking him to be as well-behaved as he was fifteen years or whatever ago, when she babysat him at their house on Louisiana Street in Stieglitz Park. She talked fast, telling him not to elaborate on their mutual background if the subject arose in the interview, but otherwise to be as honest and casual as possible, and think of himself as what he was, a young father. She seemed pleased to have him re-enter her life, and when she touched his hand, her face was bright and pleasant.

They went up to a spacious room on the 10th floor, where one wall was almost completely window, showcasing the frozen lakeshore and the blue beyond in the dimming afternoon sunlight. Six men sat in chairs, showing no inclination to greet him with more than a glance. Lou realized the gathering was probably more important than what he anticipated. Geraldine introduced him to the company president, who gave him an extra squeeze on the handshake. He insisted on being called Bert, and he stared at Lou's face throughout the ensuing conversation. The guy who was personnel director also watched him closely as he answered questions; his face and body language suggested to Lou he didn't have a chance.

"Are you agile?" Geraldine asked; the personnel director turned toward her with a squint.

"I, uh, never thought of myself that way," Lou said, grinning back at her grin. "I suppose I'm closer to being a klutz than a ballet dancer."

"That probably is preferrable in a young father who doesn't know what he's doing," she said to the others, as if confident in knowing exactly what she was looking for in a performer.

Bert, the president, continued to stare at Lou's face, as if committing it to memory. Then he spoke for the first time, in a deep tone, and in a different direction from what the others had been pursuing. "Mr. Fronczek, Lou? Lou, how was it for you when you got back from your hospital stay with your wound? Did you fit back into the peaceful part of the world? Let me put it differently. Were you *allowed* to fit back into it?"

"Well, I got a job, if that's fitting." He stared back at the graying man with the deep voice. "It isn't what I want to do in life, but I have a wife and a son, and the job pays bills."

"We've been talking to several other young men lately," Bert said. "They all look pretty good. They too want to pay bills and do something with their lives. That's fine, but those aren't good reasons for us to hire somebody. You know what I mean?"

"Yes, sir."

"What I'm much more interested in is what *you* can bring to *us*."

"I understand that, sir. I have a talent which I haven't had the opportunity to exercise yet. I'm flexible and I think I have a good sense for comedy. I'm not cracking all of you up right now because I'm nervous, but give me a funny script and I'll run with it."

He regretted saying it, but Geraldine gave a muffled laugh and some of the others smiled.

"Let me put it this way," Lou said. "The necessary factors needed to make a product attractive come clearly to me, I think. I can cozy up to *dog food*, if that's what you need. I mean, I can be someone who will help you earn the confidence of a client."

Bert got up from his chair and began to walk slowly around the table to where Lou was sitting and shaking his right knee nervously. The older man had the look of a chemist who, having seen the right results of an experiment, wanted other proof, confirmation of a more dramatic nature. "Lou, you're a veteran. What should we think of you in that sense? How does your having served in war make you more ready to serve in peace?"

"Well, I didn't get much chance in war. I hope peace will be better for me."

"What's your <u>stake</u> in the peace?"

Lou remembered what Geraldine had advised him about honesty, so despite his presumption that the company president wanted him to voice some form of rah rah patriotism, he instead brought into his consciousness the image of Francisco being ripped apart by the grenade, and tears began to well up in his eyes.

"Sir?" he said, seizing the moment to put the test to, as Maggie put it, cry on cue, because the company president was supplying the cue.

"Lou, vets like you have lately been getting fucked over from all sides. Your bosses don't care if you have put your life on the line against the enemy, and the goddamned flower children don't care, because they think you sold out by going over there and taking metal in your stomach, instead of staying here and smoking dope and screwing pseudo-liberal ex-debutantes with beads around their neck."

"Uh, Bert," the personnel guy said, "we should—"

But Bert raised his hand, signalling him to shut up. Then he leaned against on the table and gently slapped Lou on the shoulder. "Go take a chair in the other room, where you were sitting before. Go on. I want to talk with my people for a while."

Lou went in the other room and sat. On the one hand he could see that the president was interested in him in one way or another, and that Geraldine Stillman was on his side, probably because she attached some value to their common background. On the other hand, he could see objections from some of the others, who probably weren't impressed with his sketchy degree from Indiana, while glittering prospects from Northwestern or DePaul or wherever were applying by the dozen each day. He sat and thought and stared, and almost jumped out of his chair when the nearby receptionist asked him if he wanted a cup of coffee. He didn't.

A half hour later, Geraldine came out with a faint smile and sat down next to him.

"How do you feel?" she asked.

"Fine. I'm fine."

"Do you want anything? A cigarette?"

"No, I don't smoke. I guess I must look like I need something."

"No, you look great." She touched his hand again. "And you were great in there. Bert sees something in you, so give him more of—what you are, I guess."

As she spoke, a tall, sandy haired man came through a different door and casually sized up Lou, as if he were going to put him in a container.

"Edgar, this is Lou Fronczek," Geraldine said, and the tall man shook his hand. "Lou, we're going to run you through a situation with a real baby, whose mother works for us. She's downstairs, and she's being nicely compensated for the borrowed baby, so you don't have to feel you're exploiting anyone. We want you to do an impromptu routine with the child. We'll give you the Consolidated product, but you work out something with the child on your own."

"You mean, improvise?"

"Yes. You've got five minutes or so, to fool around and shift gears, if necessary. Just think of what you can do to make that babyfood in your hand—when you have it in your hand—make it attractive to anyone watching on television."

Recapture moments with your own child. Think of happy things you've experienced and bring them into the scene."

Her pleasant voice and manner were kind and reassuring, though a bit like that of a nurse just before wheeling a patient in for major surgery. Lou took deep breaths and blinked his eyes quickly, for he realized they wanted him to actually audition with a live infant, something he didn't think he was ready for.

"You okay with this?" Geraldine asked.

"I guess I'll find out in short order."

"What's your son's name?"

"Martin."

"This baby is a girl, but pretend it's Martin."

She took his hand and they followed Edgar through a side door and into a small studio, where several others, including Bert, were seated in the dark, away from the production circle. "You'll do fine," she said. "Just keep being yourself. The baby's well-rested and shouldn't be too fussy, so do what comes naturally."

He first got acquainted with the baby, a girl about six months old and very cute. Edgar said they had another infant in the child care section of the building, but this one was happier and would probably work out. The baby made quiet noises while looking him in the eye. A technician handed him a small bowl of babyfood with the Consolidated logos quite prominently painted on the sides of the container. Just before filming, Edgar told him to rely on clichés.

"Consolidated wants *expected* things," he said. "But freshly touched."

Lou didn't understand what that meant, so he launched into his own style as soon as the light on one of the three cameras indicated they were filming.

Lou looked down at the baby in his arms. The food bowl was on a small table just to the left of the infant's face, and Lou held a tiny spoon. "Look," he said to the baby, "I know you think I'm trying to give you something nutritious. You know, something that doesn't taste good. But you're wrong." He lowered his face close to the baby's. "You're wrong, my little sweetheart." The baby gave a little smile.

"Cut!" said a voice in the darkness. It wasn't Edgar, but rather a more authoritative voice. "Go back to the word 'nutritious' and re-work from there."

"I don't think so," said Geraldine, also in the darkness. "He's on the right track, just let him develop it another fifteen seconds."

The deeper voice responded. "I agree he's on the right track, but the people from Consolidated—who, I should point out, are upstairs waiting for a sample of what we have in mind—won't like him saying it doesn't taste good, no matter what else he says, and no matter what clarifications he supplies."

Lou was happy to hear the interchange, since he half expected to get thrown out of the room when the guy shouted "cut!"

Then Edgar spoke. "All right, Lou, take it from the start. Don't worry about the baby's expressions. We edit in whatever we need."

They began shooting again, and Lou stared at the infant, then gave himself a spoonful of the food, which was applesauce. The baby looked as if she knew the man holding her was goofing off, and she laughed. Lou took another spoonful of the applesauce and made an "mmm" sound before bringing his face down close to the child's again. He said softly, "it's okay, sweetheart. I'll get another jar and we can share it. How's that?" The baby stared at him, then jerked a bit when the audience group cheered spontaneously. Even the doubting personnel guy said the whole 30 seconds were almost perfect, a brief and funny skit that would entertain while making young female viewers remember what they had to go out and buy. Bert was impressed by Lou's quick wit, and the ad-lib tasting, and the way he made it look as if he were having fun. It wasn't a getting-up-in-the-night baby scene, but one in which the interaction was eager. He was so enthusiastic about the scene, as shot, that he ordered Edgar to polish it and rush it up to the Consolidated people, rather than set up all over and do it again.

After giving a series of orders to all the other people in the studio, Bert walked over to Lou, who was sitting quietly in a chair in the dark, and told him to go back to the bank; they'd call him before 5:00. Geraldine escorted him back to the entry lobby, complimenting him on his spontaneity.

"I had a hunch about you, and I was right," she said. "I think you'll really be good in this set we're putting together." Her smile was bright and startling.

"Doesn't it depend on what the client says? I mean, they might not like me."

"Oh, they'll like you. If they've got eyes and ears, they'll like you." She touched his cheek as a proud mother might, but her eyes caught him with something more reckless.

He forgot about that look because he felt so airy and slow as he walked back to the bank. He couldn't believe how short and easy the process had been. There was almost no substance to it, but the collective wisdom of the agency said it was great. He had participated in a crazy conspiracy of fakeness, but they defined it as impromptu genius.

He had a brief conversation with Dog, but a half an hour later he couldn't remember the content of it after Bert called him and said the Consolidated people enjoyed what he had done, and they found him perfect for the part. In fact, they wanted to see a whole series of similar spots as soon as possible. Bert also told him to quit the bank job immediately, and if Chuck Hagle (Vice President of Operations) had a problem with the suddenness, Lakeside would compensate them for their trouble. And, speaking of compensation, he was having a contract drawn up for Lou which started him off at $500 per week.

Lou's breathing momentarily stopped when he heard the figure.

He took the train home, barely aware of movement or noise, entranced by the fact he was going to be paid well for something he was apparently good at. The south side slums didn't look as foul as usual, and the smell of garbage near the state line seemed less offensive. As the train slowed at the Hammond platform, he stared at his own reflection in the glass. He looked eager.

Since it was still early, he took a bus home from a stop near the station, and got off in front of a florist's on Calumet Avenue to buy a bouquet. When he walked in their front door, Martin was asleep on the living room sofa and Maggie was next to him, leaning back with her eyes half-mast, as if at the entrance of slumber. He bent to her, then gave her the flowers and a kiss on the lips and the nose, and told her he had a new job that paid $500 a week. She was drowsy, and she thought he was drunk. But when he told her the story of his day, she became increasingly alert, and increasingly stunned. Waking up in dreary Whiting every day would not be so depressing, surely, if she knew they could not only pay all their bills, but even buy some new clothes. Her growing stomach would of course make such purchases irrelevant, yet having another baby wouldn't be so disastrous, after all.

She asked only a few questions about the job because she could see enthusiasm was boundless. He had found something he was anxious to do, and she was happy with him. She embraced him, then said with her lips almost against his, "My hero." There wasn't a touch of sarcasm in the way she said it.

10. Babyfood
Winter/Spring, 1971

In February Maggie began to be concerned about her mother, who looked increasingly tired almost every day. When telephone calls went unanswered, she thought of driving over to check on her. But something would spill, or her own phone would ring, and anyway she was trying not to dwell on worry. Martin, perhaps rebelling against the cold weather, which all but did away with his outdoor play, behaved inconsistently. Now twenty months old, walking and babbling, he seemed to assess any stage in the day—meals, playtime in the pen, naptime, talk with mommytime—according to its potential for mess and mischief. He would shake his spillproof cup so that milk squirted over the kitchen like holy water; he would demonstrate ambidextrous potential by throwing toys out of the pen with both hands; and he would fake sleep so he could scrawl on the window with various colored crayons after Maggie left the room.

"No, Martin. You must not do that," she would say after witnessing his latest mess. "See how hard Mommy has to rub to get that off? Write on the paper, honey. Okay?"

Usually he just laughed and muttered something like "bad," and Maggie would laugh too, and pick him up and kiss him on his cheek, which often was messy from chewing on the crayons.

A lesser concern for her were her breasts, which swelled again only a few months after shrinking, barely after she had finally convinced Martin she was no longer his milk tank. But now, seeing closeup how they were enlarging once again, the boy sometimes moved toward them. When this happened, she took his chin in her hand and spoke softly to him, but in adult tones.

"Mommy can't nurse you anymore, honey. You have to get milk from a bottle, just like a big boy. To be a big boy you drink milk from a glass, and speak clearly in words."

Martin stared at her wide-eyed.

"And pee-pee in the toilet," she added with a squeeze of his ribs.

"Pee pee," he said, then he laughed.

Suddenly she looked at the clock and realized there were only a few more minutes before Lou's new commercial would run, in the middle of an afternoon soap opera. Having missed the morning version of it out of simple forgetfulness, she felt compelled to watch it carefully with Martin. Turning on the TV in the living room, she told him daddy was going to be on with a baby and was going to pretend to be the baby's dada. Martin stared at her, more out of curiosity than understanding.

The show was called "Another Sky," and it seemed as dumb as any of the others she had glimpsed during bored moments of recent life. As a scene ended with melancholy strings and tense melodrama, the screen went pale, then abruptly showed a closeup of Lou, in a plaid shirt, staring at the camera, but actually staring at an infant. "Trust me," he said, and then the baby's face was shown, staring back at him. He looked haggard but handsome, with a few strands of black hair intentionally strewn across his forehead. She presumed this was the way he was supposed to look in order to sell babyfood to impressionable young mothers.

Martin stared wide-eyed at the screen.

"You are going to like this, my dear little Bonnie," Lou said to the baby, who squirmed as if she wasn't ready to trust him. The jar of Beefy Good was then superimposed over the space between daddy and baby. "This is Beefy Good for Bonnie, only for Bonnie." The infant squirmed again. He started to feed her, but then stopped in mid-feed. "Except for one teeny bit for Dada." Lou then tasted a spoonful, and the infant looked wide-eyed again. Then, having tasted the stuff, Lou himself was shown to look wide-eyed, but also with absolute delight. Then the infant giggled and Lou fed her the Beefy Good, and Lou giggled, and both said "Mmm." Then there was a closeup of the Beefy Good jar, and finally a shot of Lou hugging the infant.

After the hug, Lou had a couple of straight lines, but Martin began to cry, and turned to Maggie as if to say his daddy was a traitor. Maggie tried to explain to him that Daddy was just pretending, and that his job was to pretend. She even brought out a jar of Beefy Good for both of them to taste, but Martin didn't like it. Maggie thought it tasted like a pudding version of bouillon, but she made no face. Even so, Martin wept quietly for a couple of minutes.

Later Sis showed up and, after Maggie explained his upset, took the boy in her arms, telling him that daddy was doing the TV stuff as training to be a better daddy.

"Do you want daddy to be a better daddy?"

Martin's crying stopped, and he nodded his head.

"Then you should be a better Martin," Sis said. "Isn't that fair? Daddy's working hard because he loves you so much."

People had always told Maggie she looked so much like her mother, but now, in her mid-fifties, Sis looked simply like a tired woman who was holding on, and Maggie could only see her physical heritage in hand gestures or eye movements. Sis was thin, but the inner parts of her upper arms were loose enough that they jiggled or swayed when she raised them, even when she tensed and held Martin up. Her ankles were a bit swollen, suggesting high blood pressure or water retention. But her eyes were still bright, almost sparkly when she smiled.

"You look so tired, mom. Have you been sleeping well?"

"Fine. I sleep fine."

"Are you taking anything?"

"You mean for sleeping? No. Well, lately I've been having a tiny glass of Southern Comfort before I go to bed. Everything is soothing after that," she said with a short laugh. "Listen, if you need something to worry about, think of Martin's response to the new baby. If Lou's commercial with another baby upset him so much, what will a permanent baby in the same house do to him?"

Maggie didn't answer, because what her mother said had unintentionally triggered new thoughts of being trapped even worse. While Lou worked and played in the glistening big city, with its Art Institute, great restaurants, and svelte women in short skirts, she would have to juggle her powers of attention between two little ones who might not even like each other.

The next day she went with Martin to a baby shower at Mildred Sullivan's house. Kathy Cleary was about eight months pregnant, and Mildred had taken care of the various store registries in Whiting and Hammond. It was convenient that a controlling person like Mildred would handle things, for Kathy was such a quiet mouse Maggie couldn't even recall what her voice sounded like. And, looking at her bloated abdomen, she couldn't envision her in the midst of anything so strenuous as the sex required to bring about the bloated abdomen. Kathy was, however, the first to say how impressed she was with Lou on the tube.

"Yeah," said Mildred. "What a star! You must be proud."

"Well, I don't know about proud, but I'm happy he's enjoying what he's doing."

Just then Patricia Gregorovich walked in with her two daughters, and Maggie instinctively reached for Martin, who was sitting on the floor playing with plastic spoons.

"Does Lou really eat the baby food?"

"No, they put applesauce in the jar, no matter what they're supposed to be sharing"

"Does he really use the same spoon for the baby? Germs!"

"No, they—"

"So are you guys in big bucks now, with him being a star?" asked a fat blond woman whose name Maggie couldn't remember.

"Well, it's only commercials, so he doesn't think of himself as a star. But he's—"

"How much does he make?" a voice behind her asked.

"Is it like thousands?" another voice trailed in.

"I can't remember," Maggie said. "Lou handles that stuff. It isn't so much we—"

"Well that's not good if he handles all the money," Mildred chimed in.

Maggie was about to clarify a misunderstanding, since she herself took care of bill-paying, but she decided to shut up, in the hope that they would, too.

Another voice said "I heard those advertising people do things in groups, like brainstorming, partying, sex orgies."

The fat blonde said with a laugh, "Lou's gonna be tempted when you get real big and you have to stop doing it."

They kept on spilling out such things, so after a few more minutes, she told Kathy she had to get Martin home because she had forgotten his medicine.

"What does he take?" asked Mildred, who had overheard.

"I can't remember the name of it. It's for an allergy."

Driving home, she recalled, as she often did, that all her best friends from high school and college were far away—in San Francisco, Albuquerque, New York, Washington D.C. No interesting human being had stayed behind in Whiting. Few of the women she had just walked away from had even enrolled in college, let alone completed work for a degree. If they were just weird, or senselessly unusual, she could think of offbeat dialogues to have with them. But they were dull and witless, unwilling to cut the ropes that kept them from examining each other. She couldn't imagine having a conversation with any of them that would last more than ten minutes. To be fair, she couldn't imagine that any of them would want to talk to her, either, for more than ten minutes. They probably found her uninteresting, even with her husband's "notoriety."

Lou was much luckier, she thought. Not only was he surrounded every day by urban excitement, but he had creative people to work with, including a former neighborhood honey. As stupid as the remarks about group sex were, she couldn't get them out of her head, especially when she recalled what the Stillman woman looked like, having briefly met her one afternoon when she drove with Martin downtown to pick up Lou for shopping and the Lincoln Park Zoo. She had a great body and a certain sophistication; she probably could have any man she chose.

Lou got home late that night because the snow had begun to fall again, mixing with sleet and rain to slow every form of travel.

"Christ, what a mess," he said as he stomped his feet on the entry tiles. He gave her a silly look as he pulled off his shoes and began hanging up other parts of his winter outfit.

She told him about Martin's reaction to the commercial, and he said the easiest way to address the problem was simply not to let him watch. "No one besides the Consolidated people have to like the crap I do, anyway," he said.

"And your boss. She's got to like it, right."

"Stillman's not my only boss. Yeah, they've all got to like it. What about you?"

"It was alright. But I'm not a boss. I just keep the homefires burning."

"Okay." He shook his head, not knowing what to say at that point. "What's wrong?"

She picked up Martin and carried him into his bedroom, where she put him in the playpen with a biscuit. Then she walked back into the living room, where Lou had flopped into a chair.

"Before you get too far into this new job," she said, "we should re-address the subject of graduate school, getting an MFA."

"Okay."

"Have you sent off the applications?"

"No, but I figured with the kind of money I'm making we could hold off for a while so we could build a kitty."

"Whether it's 'I' or 'we,' you've still got to apply well enough in advance of the fall semester. And you've got to get an acceptance from somewhere in order to get the GI Bill."

"All right, I'll send them off, but I've still got to get a couple of recommendation letters." When he looked at her, at that moment, she saw none of the desperation so evident before his recent success. "You know, of course," he went on, "that the LBJ Bill is nowhere near what the World War II guys got. I mean, it's one month's money for one month's active duty. That means for me it would run out in seven months."

"Come on, Lou, you know that's not right. You were wounded in action, so for you, the money will go on indefinitely."

"You're exaggerating."

"It will keep on coming until you finish the degree."

"Okay, but $400 a month from Uncle Sam doesn't compare well to $600 a week, now, does it?"

"I thought you were getting $500."

"They kicked it up another hundred today. I was going to tell you as soon as I came in the door, but then I saw your unpleasant look, and I figured I'd save the good news for later."

"They gave you a twenty percent raise after <u>six weeks</u>!?"

"The Consolidated people subsidized it. I guess I must be their darling this month. But stay tuned. Things happen fast in the advertising racket."

He reached out a hand toward her, but she didn't feel like being hugged. "I hope you're not getting money-conscious," she said, "like your sister."

Later, when they were in bed, he was more sensitive and tender, but it was obvious to her he just wanted to have sex. She found his lust irritating enough to start an argument, or extend the one which had only reached the introductory phase, but just then the phone rang. It was Ruth, speaking in a chaotic, stuttering voice.

An ambulance had just arrived, but they couldn't help. Sis was dead.

The air was clear and crisp on the sunny, cloudless day in May when they gave Martin a party for his second birthday. An easy south wind pushed the pinch of industrial air northward into the big lake, replaced smoothly by the fragrance of spring fruit blossoms. To Lou's surprised admiration, Martin seemed to understand the terrible thing called death, and his behavior, especially when he was physically close to his grieving mother, was much calmer than anyone would expect from a child of two.

Martin enjoyed his party as much as they hoped he would. It was the closest thing to collective joy that anyone in the family had felt in the three months since Sis had passed on. Maggie's brother George and sister Julia were there, faces with whom Martin was briefly acquainted, albeit sad faces during the time of his grandmother's funeral.

Ruth brought her boyfriend Benjamin, who had finally revealed himself to the rest of the family at the funeral. He was a big, strapping, handsome man fresh out of the University of Chicago, and he was black. The color of his skin became irrelevant after random conversation, but it was conversation taking place in Whiting, where skin color would always be a cause for alarm, rather than socializing.

Louisa showed up with her son and daughter, dressed nicely and well behaved. They were still living with Talbot, but he did not come to the party. At a quiet moment, Louisa embraced her brother and told him how proud she was of his apparent success. Lou in turn told her how great she looked. Louisa said Talbot's indiscretion may have been the best thing that ever happened to her, since now she knew she had to make her own life. She had begun working for a lawyer in East Chicago, and she tried to disregard Talbot as much as possible. Although she didn't actually say so, Lou understood she was going to seek a divorce.

Louie and Lois brought jigsaw puzzles and a savings bond as presents; when Martin opened a puzzle box he stuck a couple of pieces immediately into his mouth. Lois was unusually soft-spoken and helpful toward Maggie, perhaps because now there was no reason to resent Lou's affection—in fact preference for—his mother-in-law. Lois also appreciated how Lou's televised face had begun to enlarge her otherwise dismal social scope. People now would stop and chat with her about Lou, whereas in the past all she could see in their faces were dirty looks which in her mind transformed into condemnations of the family for Louisa's troubles.

After putting Martin to bed that night, Lou crawled in beside Maggie, who wasn't quite asleep. Lou cradled her head against his armpit and kissed her hair, but said nothing, and she fell asleep in the dark as he lay awake remembering other times when he held her gradually sleeping body.

As often as possible, Lou cooked more of their meals. At first it was just a Saturday and Sunday thing, but soon he was cooking sauces and casseroles in batches which could be frozen and heated later. Since Maggie didn't especially enjoy cooking, except for special occasions, she encouraged him and praised whatever he whipped up.

He in turn tried to be as open as possible, and he listened carefully to the distress and regret she periodically voiced, without introduction or context. "When I wanted to stay and help her," she said in one typical instance, "help her through that weekend when she had the stomach flu, she ordered me out of the house because she said my place was with my husband and child." He recognized her need to say it, and nothing he could say in return would have made a difference to such impromptu memories.

Lou's shooting schedule was irregular, which sometimes worked to his advantage, for he was able now and then to stay home late in the morning or come home early in the evening. But an extended day was almost as likely, particularly since Lakeside had started using him in connection with products other than babyfood.

He was shooting a series of spots for Sears Roebuck when Geraldine approached him.

"You look like a dorm representative in that outfit," she said, referring to the medium blue sweater he was temporarily wearing.

"I don't know if that's a compliment," he said. "But whatever, I've got to get out of it as soon as possible. It's 100% wool, and it makes me itch."

"Well, maybe that'll put a touch of intensity to your pose," she said, and moved closer.

"If Sears wants a guy who desperately needs to scratch, but isn't allowed to scratch, then I suppose I'm their guy."

She laughed. She was wearing a black knit sheath which stressed her shape while making her look tall. She was, in fact, more dressed-up than usual.

"Listen," she said in a low tone, "I hope you remembered about lunch today. A couple of the writers and Bert himself will be there, so it'll be important for you. We'll meet at one o'clock at the Pump Room."

"I'm supposed to be out at Navy Pier around 2:30. Where's the Pump Room?"

"The Ambassador East, near north. Just tell the cab driver and he'll find it. And don't worry about the Navy Pier session."

He watched her walk away. The dress was snug enough around the hips that it caused the fabric above her buttocks to ripple with each step. When she got to the exit sign she turned and smiled, as if she knew he had been looking at her. He turned almost as quickly toward the cameraman, who was also smiling, suggesting they had both been eyeing the same movements.

"It looks like you're following me," she said in front of the hotel. Their taxis had pulled in one behind the other. A moment later, after he had paid his driver, she added "from Whiting to Bloomington to Chicago to this place."

"Well, I only do what I'm told. Anyway, you forgot Stieglitz Park."

She ignored his reminder, and took his arm with a smile. "Bert couldn't get away, and the writers didn't want to do this if Bert wasn't along, so it's just you and me. I hope you aren't too disappointed."

Lou could only guess whether she was making a legitimate excuse or simply toying with him. "Since I had no idea what the agenda for lunch was," he said, "I'm neither here nor there."

They went up the short stairway lined with pictures of famous guests like Eddie Fisher and Debbie Reynolds, smiling next to Chicago standbys like Irv Kupcinet and Mayor Daley. The hostess took them to a quiet corner table in the rear of the long room, but they did get a look at a radio program being broadcast from the opposite corner.

"Hey, I know that guy," Lou said, indicating a moonfaced man sitting in front of a radio microphone."

"Really?"

"Not intimately, but I know who he is. That's Bob Elson. He announced White Sox games for a hundred years or so."

"And the other guy, don't tell me," she spoke excitedly. "God, it's Walter Matthau!"

"You want me to go over and get his autograph for you?"

"No," she said emphatically. "Don't be stupid." The words seemed to come out prematurely, and she immediately clutched his nearest hand. "I don't mean that. I guess I've gotten used to you being naturally goofy in those silly babyfood spots." She made an obviously fake face of sorrowful regret. "I meant no harm. Go ahead and be whatever you want to be, but don't go over there."

"Well, as my former babysitter, you certainly should have dibs on ordering me around."

"Dibs?"

The waitress interrupted to take their order, and Geraldine told him to shoot the works, for it was on the company.

"I should already know things like that, I suppose," he said. He wasn't going to order a drink, but when she asked for wine, he followed suit.

"Dibs?" she said again.

"You know, ahead of the line, a sort of privilege because of something else. It was one of those Stieglitz Park expressions that filtered in from elsewhere. Most others were pretty vulgar."

"I'm afraid your recollection of Stieglitz Park must be quite different from mine."

"Did I say something to offend you?"

"No, no." She reached across the table. "It's just that the first thing I think of in connection with that place is my father's death."

"I barely remember that. I'm sorry for bringing it up."

"It's alright. Really." She touched his hand. "Do you 'barely remember' my babysitting?"

"No, I remember that vividly. I think you were the only person who ever babysat me who wasn't a relative. And I remember thinking you looked like jewelry— your lips were bright red, and your hair was like gold, and—"

"Oh, God."

"—No, I'm serious, that's what I thought. And your eyes were green. I guess they still are. To me you were human jewelry." He paused as she smiled, looking as if she was enjoying what he said. "I think I was afraid of you."

"I don't know why," she said, making her eyes look sad. "Your mother was probably more afraid than you were. Maybe she thought I would molest you, or something. By the way she looked at me, I knew she'd never ask me again. And here we are. What is it, fifteen, sixteen years? Is she still alive, and your father?"

"They're both hanging in there."

They finished their wine and she ordered another. Lou declined, saying he didn't want to breathe alcohol on the afternoon babies. She ate her chef's salad and he his ham sandwich, and they continued to make small talk between swallows.

"You know, when Rod called me—"

"Rod?" She had the look of genuine, rather than polite, curiosity.

"The guy at the employment agency who sent me over to you."

"Right." She grinned, apparently remembering. "How is dear Roddy?"

"I don't know, I suppose he's okay. He mentioned you two had—"

Retaining the half-smile, she rolled her eyes. "Go on."

"Well, nothing. I guess I was leading up to a question about how you came to Chicago and got your job. You've obviously done well."

She reached over and touched his hand again. "Strangely enough, I was hired in the same way you were." She paused, but he said nothing. "When I graduated from Northwestern I shopped around from one ad to another, trying to find something where I could fit. Bert was a personnel guy at the time, and he wanted to, as he put it, bring more women into the idea center at Lakeside. I guess he liked what he saw, but he wanted to challenge me. So he gave me a case study problem on monkeys in the Lincoln Park Zoo. I was to write two pages on how to make the primate exhibit more attractive to young families. He loved what I wrote, and he hired me."

"And you obviously worked your way up the ladder."

"Well, envious people would differ with your choice of verbs. But I did *work* hard."

Eventually they talked about Bloomington.

"He was the first man I ever loved," she said of Stephen Coble. "I knew it was wrong, and I even knew he was going to dump me eventually, since he had this goddess of a wife who made three times as much money as he did. But I was young and impressionable. I wanted it to go on longer."

"How did Richie Bowman come into the picture?"

"Do you remember him?"

"Yeah, I knew Richie back in Stieglitz. He'd tease me once in a while when I wanted to play baseball or football with the big kids. But sometimes he would *let* me play, so I guess I liked him."

"Did he ever hurt you?"

"*Hurt* me?" Lou laughed.

"Well, he was a bit violent."

"I suppose so, but there were a lot of violent guys in Stieglitz. He tackled me in football sometimes, but mostly he'd just make fun of me, like calling me a boy-girl because of my eyelashes. "

"Oh, God," she said with a big grin. "Your long eyelashes. They're still longer than most guys'."

"Yeah," he said, shaking his head while grinning. "Was Richie your boyfriend?"

"He wanted to be. In his own mind he thought he was, and that's what did him in."

"Wasn't it an accident? I mean, when he got killed."

"Yes, but Stephen was the wrong person for Richie to attack. He was a World War II veteran who had killed Germans in hand-to-hand combat. Don't get me wrong, he didn't kill Richie, but I'm sure he could have."

Lou didn't understand, but he asked nothing.

She ordered another glass of wine, and tried to convince him to have one more, but he declined. She went to the women's room, and Lou thought of ways to ask her for a graduate school recommendation even as he realized she wouldn't really be open to such a request, since she ostensibly took him to lunch for Lakeside-connected reasons. When she returned she was more fragrant and her green eyes were glassy but captivating.

"Well, now that we've addressed one scandal," she said, "let's do the other one."

"I don't know what you mean."

"Your sister's husband."

"You know my sister?"

She put her hand to her cheek and looked down, in embarrassment or mild shock. "No, I don't. Thank God I don't. Don't you know what I'm talking about?"

Lou felt foolish for trying to seem like he was totally in the dark.

"Vaguely." He wanted to hear her own view of what had happened. In the empty space between them at the table, with its impeccably clean white cloth under their finished lunch plates, he recalled the letters from Louisa and various rumors. "But I guess I don't really understand," he said.

"Talbot and I were friends, but we were never more than that. I didn't know he was stealing, or embezzling, or whatever kind of fraud he was perpetrating. It had nothing to do with me. He didn't buy me furs and diamonds, or any of the crap the prosecutor would have used if the thing had gone to trial. Thank God it didn't." She stopped, then drank the wine which had been set down in front of her just minutes before. Then she moved to a chair to her left and pulled it next to his.

"Anyway, let's talk about more important things. I haven't got around to talking to you about the main reason for the lunch," she said quietly. "Bert wants us to work together on new scripts. Not just for the Consolidated account, but for other clients. Carson Pirie Scott, say, or the CTA."

"That sounds good, " he said.

She stared at him with a puzzled smile. "What do you want to get out of this job?" she asked, moving her look from one spot to another on his face.

"Well, things have happened quite fast since I signed on with the company, so I've not had time to set up goals, or anything."

She stared again, focusing on his mouth. "Have you considered the possibility you might become more than just a performer in commercials?"

He shook his head. He thought of explaining his plan for graduate school, but as she moved her face closer to his he knew she wouldn't want to hear of any such thing.

She reached her hand over to cup his chin, and then kissed him softly and warm on the lips. When she pulled her face back he could see the tough yet yielding beauty and he felt nervous and aroused at the same time. He hated himself for feeling lust, even as he knew she must have wanted to make him lustful, for when she gave him an embarrassed smile and said she was sorry for kissing him, her free hand was on his thigh.

She took care of the bill, and they walked down to the lobby level.

"This is a very famous hotel," she said, as they stood next to the elevator. "Not only because Bob whomever does his broadcasts from over there, but also because right where we're standing, Alfred Hitchcock showed Eva Marie Saint going up to her room on the fourth floor, while—"

"North by Northwest," he said.

"That's it. Cary Grant watched her from right over there, at the check-in desk."

"I feel like I'm part of movie history now."

"The other thing you should know about this hotel," she said, looking at him clearly with desire, "is that Lakeside has a suite on the 25th floor which we use for meetings and brainstorming sessions. Would you like to go up and take a look at it?"

Lou looked at her beautiful diamond-shaped face and fought the urges he hadn't felt in a long time. He also thought of Maggie and the contradictory pains of death and new life she felt each day, and he forced shame upon himself as convincingly as he could.

"I told Edgar I'd be back at the shoot in time to re-work the biscuit commercial." He looked at her, knowing she didn't believe him. "I wouldn't want to incur his wrath."

She gave him another stare that wandered about his face, but before she could say anything to further persuade him to go upstairs with her, he descended the few marble steps and went outside. Then he got into the first of several taxis lined up at the curb. As he gave directions to the driver, he could see Geraldine standing at the elevator doors as they opened. She got in just as the taxi moved away.

"Wait," he said.

"Sir?" the driver said.

Lou took a couple of deep breaths, then put his hands on his knees. "Nothing. Navy Pier."

As the weather grew inconsistently mild and blustery, Maggie's daily agonizing over the death of her mother began to subside, for no other reason than she was big and uncomfortable with her pregnancy, preoccupied with the life growing inside her, rather than the emotional, psychological loss of her dearest connection. At first she would think positively about going out and seeing a movie or even dining with Lou and friends he had made at Lakeside. But then she would reconsider, and just lie down for a nap, sometimes leaving Lou to explain why they couldn't be wherever they said they were going to be.

So it didn't surprise him when she said she didn't want to go to Bert's 50th birthday party at the Agency, even though Bert had specifically pointed out to Lou that his one exposure to Maggie, some three months before, had made an indelible impression on him. She was, as he put it, like a beautiful spirit he previously could only have imagined. She smiled at the compliment when Lou told her, even though she guessed that advertising people were simply full of shit.

Lou finally convinced her it would be good to get out of the house and into a different social climate. Besides, his argument went, her condition could serve as an easy, believable excuse for them to leave early if they so chose. He also worked into his persuasion the fact he had sent off to Michigan State a couple of one-inch videotapes of his commercials, on secret loan from Edgar.

"Maybe that'll save me the trouble of going to East Lansing for an interview. I don't want you to have to travel, and I don't want to go myself and leave you here without a car."

"Have you had the DePaul interview yet?"

"I cancelled it, since you want to get out of the area so bad."

She smirked. "Yeah. Chicago is beginning to feel like Whiting. I've never been to East Lansing, but I dream about it. Did the Stillman woman give you a recommendation?"

"I didn't ask her for one, since she probably wants me to stay here." When she didn't comment, he added, "she wants me to do some dramatic things for a toy company, so I figured it was pointless for me to ask her to help me. It's okay, though. A couple of my I.U. profs are writing letters for me."

He looked at her, and when their eyes met she turned away.

"Maggie, you know there's no reason for us to rush out of here for the fall semester just when the money is so good."

"Ah yes, in the 'advertising racket.' Do you really enjoy the shit that you do?"

"Of course not, but I just want to fatten the bank account a little more." He knew as soon as he said it she would jump on him.

"Oh, that's impressive thinking. Great integrity. Get the money while it's available. Maybe after the baby comes I can work out and get back in shape, and then start walking the streets of Calumet City. Probably could make a four or five hundred a night."

He tried to make a joke out of it. "Oh, honey, you're worth a lot more than that."

"Shut up. I'll probably be as sexy as a hippo the rest of my life."

They turned to see Ruth drive up to watch Martin while they were gone. Maggie spoke more quietly, "You want to be an actor. We don't have to change our plans because of the 'advertising racket' or anything else. As soon as my part of my mother's Socko stock is sold, we could leave the next day. That should be in the next two months, according to my uncle."

Lou took a deep breath and held it, then let it out slow, a tactic he had been employing to fool himself into thinking he was calm. "Okay, but let's air it out for a while." He said aloud.

Just as Ruth came through the door, Maggie said, in just above a whisper, "like newly washed sheets?"

They circled around to Calumet Avenue, then turned left at Indianapolis Boulevard and went up the Skyway, exiting at Stony Island to snake through Jackson Park and around the big Museum of Science and Industry before swinging onto Lake Shore Drive, past the motel where their half-drunk passion had yielded the new pregnancy. It was a clear evening, and lights were just starting to come on. The distant Loop skyline sparkled most brilliantly at that first curve just beyond the university. The different spires looked dark against the deep evening sky to the north, while late streams of muted sunlight shot through them from the west, some streaking onto the smooth water of the lake. It was a sight Lou rarely looked at from a taxi or the train, but spread out across the wide lanes of the highway and the green slopes of the green park this side of the water and the big rocks, it was pleasantly hypnotic.

"God, isn't that gorgeous? A waterfront to end all waterfronts." he said.

"I would have thought you'd almost be bored with it by now."

He glanced over at her and made a face. "You don't mean that."

They approached the Soldier Field area; just east was the Shedd Aquarium where they had taken Martin a few days after his birthday.

"Lou, how available are you going to be if the baby comes during the day? I mean, Ruth will probably be here in the city, so my only option will be myself, with Martin in the car."

"You know the emergency number at the agency. If I get a cab I can be at the house or the hospital in half an hour—forty minutes, tops. Or if your pains are close, call an ambulance, or even my father."

There was a pause, and she looked at him, and he briefly glanced at her while maneuvering into the left lanes of the drive.

"You're not serious," she said.

"No, but as a worst case—"

"Look, I know I tell you to ease up on bitching about your parents, but how reassuring is it to be in a car with a man who won't exceed 30 mph on an entrance ramp because he thinks he'll burn up the motor if he goes faster."

"If you hammer away about the safety of grandchildren he might ratchet it up to 35," said Lou. She said nothing. He glanced over at her. "I saw the slightest crack of a smile."

"My lip itched."

They parked in the underground at Monroe Street, then pushed through warm air as they went up the escalator. At street level they passed a couple of young women who stared at Lou, and then one loudly whispered to the other, "hey, that's that babyfood guy." When Maggie turned, the women laughed and walked on at a faster clip.

Maggie laughed, and said, "Gee, I wonder why she didn't ask for your autograph."

"Yeah. She should have handed me a TV Guide, and I could have asked her name, and then written 'for Hortense: all my love, the babyfood guy.'"

The party had commenced before they arrived. Everyone was on the ornately designed mezzanine floor of the company building. Waitresses moved through the crowd of about 75 to a hundred with platters of shellfish, meat fingerfood, and different kinds of paté. Champagne was also being poured around, and temporary bars supplied cold beer and hard liquor.

To Maggie everyone in the room looked glamorous or trim as they moved effortlessly from one section to another, as if delivered by slow conveyor belts. She on the other hand felt big and stationary, balancing an enormous bowling ball on her pelvic girdle. "With a martini," she said, "I may be able to make it through the night."

Lou brought her back the drink, giving a hug to a matronly but attractive brunette along the way. He told Maggie she was more beautiful at her worst than any of the other women looking their best. She took his remark not as a compliment but as confirmation that she did indeed look her worst. She finished her drink quickly and asked for another. When he cautioned her she gave him a dirty look and walked to the bar. He followed, introducing her to a couple of men he barely knew. One of them had a wife at home who was almost as far along in pregnancy as Maggie, but had decided to stay home because she was inclined to get nauseous from the smell of rich food and booze. Maggie tried to ignore what she construed as an insult.

Bert came over and bowed a bit galantly. "A change has come over you since our previous meeting, " he said.

"Yes, I've grown," Maggie said. "Happy birthday."

He took her free hand in both of his. "Thank you. You know, up until now I never believed it when someone would say that a woman is especially gorgeous when she's pregnant."

Maggie rolled her eyes and smiled. Then Bert leaned over to her face, kissed her softly on the cheek, and said in her ear, "your guy is wonderful. He deserves someone like you, and babies that look like you."

He moved away as quickly as he had appeared in front of her a few minutes before. His quickness cheapened the flattery. Lou signalled to the nearby cameraman who, with a smile, introduced himself to Maggie before Lou could speak.

"I'm Edgar," he said. "I'm the reason Lou looks so good on television."

"You're a plastic surgeon?"

"She's in rare form tonight," said Lou. "Edgar does everything, He's producer, director, editor—"

"He's exaggerating. But he left out collaborator and conspirator," he said in a low tone, and then looked at Lou. "And also out on my ass if anyone else finds out about those duplicate tapes." Lou nodded and walked away, toward a pretty woman in a yellow cocktail dress. Her stomach was flat and she had big breasts which were emphasized by the knit fabric; she looked like Rhonda Fleming. Maggie then remembered the face. It was Geraldine Stillman.

Maggie turned back to Edgar, who had resumed talking to her."No one else knows about the tapes, so be sure you don't accidentally refer to them. Let me tell you, the people at Michigan State will see him at his best. He's got good instincts, he's a great improviser. I'm sure he'll do as well on the stage."

Even as she listened appreciatively to Edgar, she looked past him to see the shapely, flat-stomached Stillman turning away from the people she had been talking to and embracing Lou, kissing him briefly, then holding onto an arm while never taking her eyes off him, as if she were ready to engulf all his protrusions.

"Does the boss take hold of all the actors that way?" she asked Edgar.

"That's Stillman. Bert's the boss, but she's our boss in production. It's the occasion—hugging and kissing are expected."

As she finished the second martini Lou was bringing over Geraldine, and the closer look gave Maggie a sinking feeling just above the upper edge of her frontal hump. Geraldine sustained a smile all the way to her, but for all Maggie's effort to be civil, she didn't feel civil.

"Another fellow Whiting native, " Geraldine said, extending a hand. "So nice to see you again. And," she looked down at Maggie's midsection, "your fellow traveler."

"She just moved, so I guess that's acknowledgement."

"Do you know it's a girl?"

"No. I just say 'she' because most people say 'he.'"

"And you like to be contrary." Geraldine looked toward Lou before Maggie could respond, and then actually pulled him away to say something to him privately. Even if Maggie hadn't been quietly fuming, and even if Geraldine's stomach hadn't looked so smooth and flat, she would have thought it a rude gesture for the ostentatious glamor girl to suddenly pull her husband away.

Maggie traded the empty cocktail glass for some water, and watched Geraldine say something into Lou's ear, then break away to another part of the room.

"What was that about?" she said as he got close and looked at her with uncertainty.

"Nothing, really. She wanted to talk more about getting me into other things."

"What, like women's underwear?"

Shortly thereafter Maggie lied and said she had stomach cramps, so they left quietly.

"Maybe you shouldn't have had the martinis," Lou said.

"Maybe you should fuck off."

The ride home was almost soundless. Stars flickering amid smoky wisps of clouds and the glow of an imprecise moon did nothing for them as they looked out the windshield and adjusted their sitting positions separately. In so far as people who have for years been intimate can suddenly feel uncomfortable in each other's presence, they were uncomfortable. When they got home, Maggie went into the back bedroom and told Ruth to stay in bed, while she would sleep on the cot in Martin's room. She told Lou to sleep on the couch.

"Wait a minute," he said. "I will gladly sleep on the couch, but I won't do it because I'm ordered there senselessly by you."

"I don't feel like arguing. It's late, and I don't want to disturb my sister and our son."

"Let's go outside."

"God, what for?'

"I just want you to tell me what's wrong."

She looked around the living room, then walked out the front door, and kept walking until she got to the big oak at the foot of their driveway. He followed.

"I don't understand your—" he started to say.

"Why the hell did you want me to go with you tonight?" She made the question sound a harsh accusation. "All that warm persuasion you put on me, for what reason? You usually save that kind of sweet-talking bullshit for the bedroom."

"Maggie, I wanted you to get out and just socialize with interesting people."

"Oh, spare me the phony self-sacrificing tone! Interesting people. You wanted to display yourself as the prince of the airwaves, as confirmed by your voluptuous boss."

"Maggie—"

"Jesus, she looks at you the way strippers look at guys in the front row!"

"Maggie, they're advertising people. They're demonstrative. I didn't think anything of the way Bert was nuzzling up to you because that's the way they are."

"Don't give me that crap. He was just being polite, humoring me while I've got this eight month tumor sticking out in front of me. Stillman was much keener on what might have been sticking out in front of *you*."

"Maggie—"

"Stop saying my name. I know who I am. I'm not sure I know who you are."

"She had a few drinks and she was feeling giddy. She probably went around and—"

"Just went around and what? Just feeling your giddy crotch?"

"She didn't feel anything! Goddamn it! There's no reason for you to talk to me like this."

She leaned back in the shadow of the tree, while he stood in the light of the street lamp, shaking his head and looking around as if for clues to this trouble.

"Look me in the eye, Lou. I know when you're not telling the truth. Look me in the eye and tell me, say to me directly in my eyes that you haven't fucked her. Don't turn away."

"I'm not turning away! I've not done anything with her, and I don't plan to do anything with her. I'm looking at you, and I'm not lying. You know I'm not lying, so be decent enough to say you believe me."

"Decent. What is decent? Be decent enough to look at me and say you've never *thought* about fucking her."

"You know, Maggie, this is one of the stupidest arguments we've ever had, and we've had some doozies."

"No, I want you to look at me and tell me you've never thought about her in that way."

"You know why it's stupid? Sexual thoughts pop into guys' heads—"

"You have! God, you have!"

"Maggie, for Christ's sake, *Edgar* probably had sexual thoughts about *you* in the few minutes you talked to each other."

"Oh, your point is something like 'despite the unsightly mound of flesh between us,' eh?"

"No, no! I'm just saying it's part of the environment. People think about desire a lot more than they actually feel it."

"Oh, how philosophical, how broadminded and understanding. Shit, you've probably thought about her sexually since day one, and I've stood in the way. If it weren't for me, you could be having great sex every night."

Lou put his hands on his head as he shook it with exasperation. He walked in a small circle as Maggie leaned back against the tree.

"Tell me something, Maggie. Why do you encourage me to be an actor? What if one day I land a role in a passionate drama where I'm required to *feel* lust for a woman, or desire under the elms, or within dried-up sumac? What then?"

"I don't have a problem with your role-playing, though I should probably wonder if *you* will have a problem with it." She put her hands on her stomach. "Just don't play roles with me."

He grabbed her hands and squeezed them gently as he shook his head slowly. Tears welled up in his eyes and he turned away. "Maggie, you know who I am!"

"Oh, shit! Don't do this. Your manufactured tears don't hit the right chord now."

"Maggie, I'm not manufacturing anything. You're still hurting from your mother's death, and I haven't been the guy you needed me to be. And it probably *was* selfish or thoughtless of me to insist that we go to the party tonight. But don't shut me out."

"Go to hell." she said it coldly, without hatred or passion but sorrow, instead.

Neither of them said anything for about a minute. Then she looked at him with the sort of flatness of expression reserved for exchanges at the subway ticket counter. "You know you've got all the options," she said. "No matter what I say or do, *you* have all the options. You can do anything you want. You can do any goddamned thing you want, without a thought for this place. I don't have *any* options! None! I have Martin and this painful body with another body inside it and no hope to sustain things on my own. And what do you have? Television spots and glib professional partners and a blond bitch who dangles your paychecks in front of her, and who's dying to get you in bed. I'm sure you *know* that, but if you don't, you're a lot dumber than I thought."

She took deep breaths, trying to control her tone. "You could leave me tomorrow," she said, "and you'd have anything you choose. I'd be back here with no chance to survive."

"Maggie, none of that is true. *None!* I don't have any options, because I'm incurably in love with you. Why would you ever say what you just said? God, you're my everything—I know it sounds stupid, so don't make fun of it."

"Ohh. It *is* stupid!" Maggie angrily fought back her own tears, then walked around him and up the sidewalk to the steps of the house. "Let's just go to sleep."

He watched her go in, and pulled his hair in frustration. He ached even worse as he thought of all the things she said, and how they all were understandable, really.

In the middle of the night Maggie awoke to revolving lights outside the windows, and several voices. Lou was in the kitchen, looking through the screen at the back door. When he saw her, he waved her back toward the bedroom.

"What's wrong?"

"Just stay back out of the way. At first I thought someone was sick, because the first thing that arrived was an ambulance. But right after it got here, two police cruisers pulled up. Just stay in here, in case there's trouble."

"You mean, like gunshots?"

"I don't know. I'll get Martin, and both of you go in with Ruth."

As he spoke there was a knock at the kitchen screen door. The policeman asked him a few questions about noises in the night, and Marcus' apartment upstairs. Lou could see Helen, Marcus' girlfriend, talking to another officer in front of the garage door, which was now open, and a dissipating cloud of car exhaust floated over the dim light inside the stall where Marcus' car was parked. Her look of pain suggested she was the reason the ambulance was there, but just as the nearer policeman went up the stairs to the second floor, Lou saw the emergency crew wheeling Marcus out on a cart to the ambulance. They were in no hurry, and there was no mask or IV connected to the man on the cart.

Minutes later, Lou went into the bedroom where Ruth lay in a foetal position, with Martin on his back between her and Maggie, who sat on the bed's edge, the swirls of emergency lights reflecting in her wide open eyes. He bent to her and whispered, "I've got to go out there and answer some more questions."

"Why? What happened?"

"Marcus committed suicide. They just want to know about the living arrangements here."

Maggie pulled her knees up and covered her head with her pillow. Lou started to reach for her hand, but changed his mind when he feared she might push it away.

She said something quietly. It was either "get out of here," or "get us out of here." Whichever, he knew he no longer had any place in the room. He went into the kitchen, and saw for the first time how small the room was, and how linoleum and tile and white paint could collaborate and become oppressive.

After the police left he felt like getting drunk, but it was already 4:30, so he decided to stay awake. He made coffee, and brainstormed on a legal pad: questions and observations as they leaped to his mind:

--quit the agency? Right away or after hearing from MSU?

--Not right away, need medical insurance to cover birth

--What if Maggie leaves me? Pump Room, God was with me and wasn't

--God must have told her, but not everything

--Am I really only thinking of myself?

--Has she really been a bitch lately, or just someone clinging to a ledge? And what do I do, but step on one of her hands

--Dear God, give me a clue

--let me recognize some good in me and put it to use

Religious fall-back, he thought, the last refuge of a moral weakling. He wondered if Marcus had sat in the car, in despair, thinking God-thoughts because he had committed some irrevocable sin, hoping God could put the money back or whip up order out of chaos, but God said no to his prayer. No, Marcus, you have grievously transgressed, and verily you must start your engine and pump death into your lungs.

Lou took the yellow sheets he had just been writing on, and tore them into strips. The stress in their lives wasn't about him, it was about Maggie. And the resolution of conflict wasn't his to make; it was Maggie's.

Two hours later, as he rested his head on his forearms on the kitchen table, she came into the kitchen, walking unsteadily. Ruth followed, wiping the floor with a towel as she entered. Lou rushed toward Maggie, and she stared at him weakly.

"Let's go, chief," Ruth said. "Her water just broke."

"But it's not due until—"

"Well, I guess 'it' changed its mind."

So they left as a foursome and drove to the east, where the dark factories spit fire into the air, blending industrial power momentarily with the orange sunrise. At St. Catherine's Hospital Ruth cared for Martin while Lou, much to the dismay of the doctor and nurses, insisted on being in the room while Maggie pushed out their child. He was no help to anyone but himself for, having missed the birth of Martin, he only knew he wanted to share Maggie's shrieks of pain, and to complain that they weren't doing enough to alleviate it. They told him to shut up and stay back, but all he could see and hear were the weakening cries and the stronger ones, and the veins in her eyes as she did all she could. He looked at those bulging eyes and wished he could somehow absorb all her pain, especially that which he had caused in recent months.

And then, as she would have with or without the help of her father, the little female body they later named Evelyn Marjorie slipped out into the world all gooey and dark pink, looking angry that her mother now rested easy in her exhaustion. One of the nurses put her atop her former dwelling, just below her mother's heart. Lou rose and looked down at the tired mother, and then at the soft new life, all puffy and rippled.

"I'm going to quit the agency," he said at her bedside.

Maggie gave the tiniest of smiles, then fell asleep.

11. Going North
September, 1971

As he rearranged things in the U-Haul trailer, Lou listened to a night-time disc jockey who pointed out how Chicago area temperatures were rising and falling unpredictably in this September of 1971, just as they usually did, which meant they weren't unpredictable after all.

Almost everything they had accumulated in two years and eleven months of marriage was either in the U-Haul or in the trunk of their used Oldsmobile F-85. Ruth and Benjamin had helped them pack that day, and they had all gone to Phil Smidt's later for a perch dinner. Their waitress was cute and friendly, especially to Benjamin, a flirtation which irritated a couple of nearby customers who weren't used to seeing a black man doing anything in the restaurant but clearing tables and hauling away dirty dishes. After the meal they said their goodbyes, and both Maggie and Lou told Ruth they would miss her terribly.

From the beginning of her life, Evelyn was a blessedly calm and happy baby, radiating a pleasantness which in just a few days had charmed even her brother, who at first had seemed determined to be a rival sibling. Martin loved to make her laugh and then laugh along with her. The grandparents were likewise charmed by the new baby, offering to take care of both kids if Lou wanted to take Maggie out on the town during their remaining days in Whiting. Maggie was open to the idea, but Lou wasn't, and he made up unconvincing excuses to them.

From the brisk, late summer darkness he went inside and poured himself a small glass of Ezra Brooks. He hadn't learned much from Dog Carter, but he had to admit the guy had good taste in liquor. The "E-z," as Dog called it, went down smooth and warm.

He looked in the children's bedroom, remembering he would have to pack the playpen and crib into the remaining U-Haul space the next morning. Then he went across the hall, past the newly uncrowded bathroom and into the big bedroom, where Maggie was asleep in a pink nightie, her legs and one arm extended like a ballerina frozen in mid-leap. Her long dark hair flowed out across the white pillow, and her abdomen was flat.

He took his drink outside and sat in the middle of the first concrete step. He envied the close bond Maggie had enjoyed with her mother, so unbreakable even after death. He would someday have to address his feelings for his mother and father, and try to accept what Maggie often told him, that "they did their best." If their best hadn't been good enough, as he often thought, perhaps he should just accept it anyway. Like millions of other sons and daughters whose parents never took the trouble to know them, he had to stop blaming them for being selfish or stupid, or for being Republicans and devout Catholics. They were getting old, and now he had a family of his own. If he played his cards right he could be a good father, someone whose kids might love him forever the way Maggie still loved her mother.

Then he thought of random things from recent days and weeks, as if he were in the Transfer department at the bank tabulating debits and credits, or testing his memory before launching into an unknown, where memory might not matter.

More than ever before, the best days for anything were weekends. Saturday winds were brisker and clean, and frogs croaked with more satisfaction. On weekends, he got Maggie to admit, even Whiting was better.

One Sunday he urged her to sleep late while he packed the car with kids' necessities and drove off with them. He took them to the lakefront park because there was a full north wind pushing sizable waves against the big rocks near the gun club, and he thought they would enjoy looking at the big splashes. Martin did, but Evelyn just looked up at him with the slightest of smiles, as if she knew more than he did about whatever they were experiencing. They moved to the beach, where Martin repeatedly brought handfuls of wet sand and dumped them in front of Evelyn, who laughed and squirmed forward.

Then they went to the bank, where Lou closed out his accounts. When they exited, the wind had died down and the day had suddenly re-emerged in bright sunshine. He shaded Evelyn with his baseball cap, and decided to get Martin a pair of sunglasses at Walgreen's. Martin liked that idea as soon as he understood what Lou was proposing. The pickings at the drugstore were slim, but Martin liked all of them, especially the ones with thick, brightly colored rims.

"You probably should get a pair for yourself, superstar," said a heavy voice whom Lou eventually recognized as belonging to Chet Puntillo. "I'd say you look more and more like your old man," the cop said, "but I'm not sure you'd take it as a compliment."

He was in street clothes, but Lou remembered his voice and his smile. "Officer Puntillo. My god, it's been years."

"That's true. I see you've been busy."

"Martin, this is Officer Puntillo. He used to live next door to me when I was a little boy." Martin smiled and held out his hand.

"Wow, what a big guy," said Puntillo, shaking the boy's hand. "You've trained him well. Nice to meet you, Martin."

"Well, it's only cops that he's polite to," Lou said with a laugh. "I've convinced him life will be easier if he sucks up to policemen."

"He needs more lessons than that," said Puntillo. "Who's the little dear here?" He bent to look into the baby's eyes.

"This is Evelyn. She's still feeling her way around."

"Hi, Evelyn. Oh, she's a cutie. So what else have you been doing, besides making commercials and babies?"

"Actually, I'm off to graduate school pretty soon."

"Really? What about your television career? I figured you were getting sunglasses for yourself, you know."

"Well, I want to become a legitimate actor. It may not work out, but I think it will. I hope it will."

Puntillo nudged his shoulder. "That's great, kid. I always thought you were weird, but maybe creative."

"Thanks, I think."

"So you're not going to be working any longer for the young woman who was almost my step-daughter?" When Lou didn't react, Puntillo added, "Geraldine Stillman is your boss, right?"

"Yes, she is. Sorry, I forgot about your connection."

"No need to be sorry. The 'connection' isn't there anymore, anyway."

Lou squinted. "I don't get it."

"No, there's nothing to 'get,' kid. You're busy with your own life. Geraldine's mother and I were a twosome for a while, but we decided to break off our relationship some time ago."

"I see. Sorry, I didn't know."

"No reason to be sorry for anything," the cop said again as he smiled and patted Martin's head, then looked up again at Lou. "Life goes on, buddy."

"It does." Lou said.

"Your father still alive? Hell, I *know* he's alive. I just saw him the other day in Sherman's Hardware." Puntillo laughed as he said it. "My old neighbor. I wonder if he's still doing government jobs."

When Lou didn't react, Puntillo said "you don't remember, but that's just as well." He held out his hand and Lou shook it. "Good luck to you, Lou. I really mean that. It's nice to see a Stieglitz Park kid go off and do something worthwhile."

"Thanks, Officer Puntillo. I –"

"Lou, the name is Chet."

"Chet," Martin said. All three of them laughed, and Evelyn yawned. A few minutes later, when he had packed them back into the car, he realized what Puntillo had referred to when he said 'government jobs.' And he also understood why the cop had laughed when he referred to the hardware store.

A couple of days later, right after dinner, he packed the kids into the car again while Maggie went through their collection of paperbacks and folders and journals, picking out only the most essential items to carry off to East Lansing, Michigan.

After an hour she leaned back and ignored everything, dozing off on the back cushions of the living room sofa. By then Lou and the kids had arrived at Louisa's house in Munster, where she had moved just weeks ago.

"I tried to dump all my crap at a friend of mine's garage sale last month," she said, "but some of this stuff, like the coffee table you ruined with a cigarette that time—"

"Jesus, I'm sorry," said Lou.

"No, no big deal. I was just putting it into a context, or whatever. You never knew how to smoke properly. It must have been easy for you to quit. Anyway, the table is out there at my friend's place for a future sale, still with the burn stripe memorabilia, and I've even kicked the price down to $20."

"I think I stopped smoking right after that," said Lou. "God, maybe *because* of that."

"Oh, don't worry about it," Louisa said, rushing to close the screen door, which was flapping in the wind. Then she turned abruptly to her 12 year old daughter. "Andrea! Give Martin some of those grapes you washed before. And keep an eye on him while I talk to uncle Lou."

The girl did as she was told, and Louisa beamed with delight as she cradled Evelyn in her arms.

"My God," she said, barely in breaths. "She's so beautiful. She's got the best parts of your face and Maggie's. Such a sweetie!" She kissed the child, but after a while looked sternly at Lou.

Lou knew what was coming. She was going to tell him how dumb it was for him to give up such a great job and go back to school, so he decided to cut her off.

"So who's this guy you're working for? Is it more than work, or what?"

"I'm not divorced yet, Lou, so talk nice in front of your gorgeous daughter. And explain to me in front of her why you're doing what you're doing."

"Where's Bruce?" Lou said, in reference to her seven year old son.

"He's with his grandparents. His other grandparents. And don't dodge my question."

"I'm not dodging anything. I'm going to East Lansing because I want to become a real actor. I've got a good assistantship there, and Maggie fully supports me."

Louisa continued to grin at the baby in her arms. "Do you think—I mean, if school doesn't work out—that you can go back to the job you've got?"

"I don't know. I don't think I'd want to."

"Would that—" she paused. "Would that woman recommend you to another agency, do you think?"

"Louisa, I'm not thinking in those terms. We're going up to Michigan and make a new life."

"What about Maggie? Is she just going to be a caretaker for the kids?"

"Only for the first year. Then she'll teach. She's got connections. Believe me, Louisa, we'll work it out. We've got money from MSU, from the GI Bill, from savings, and married student housing is cheap. Don't worry about us. Take care of your own problems." It didn't come out right, so he quickly added. "You've always been the smartest one in the family."

She shook her head, then got up and took Evelyn to her kitchen window to look out at an English Sparrow pecking at a bird feeder, while a small squirrel tried to inch its way up the pole beneath the seed trays.

Lou looked at Andrea as she sat and talked in the kitchen to Martin. Then he gathered both of his children, kissed Andrea's head, kissed Louisa's cheek, and went back to the car.

Because Lou regularly took along the kids when he ran various errands, Maggie had time for rest and reverie. After a lot of disapproving expressions by Evelyn, signifying failure, she gave up on her own breasts. The baby's appetite seemed to have increased even as her own milk supply had dwindled. Maggie could almost date the problem to the morning after she and Lou had resumed their lovemaking in mid-July. Perhaps it was coincidental, perhaps not.

But she did remember for certain how proud she was of her newly curvy body—surely now as good or better than Stillman's—and how quickly she was aroused when Lou held her and caressed her. She had initiated the act after both their babies were asleep; she gave him all the tenderness which she had locked inside her during the emotionally difficult pregnancy, all the precious glee she had denied herself during daily attacks of anxiety. They rushed to mutual fulfillment as if they were climbing a steep hill, where exhaustion yielded the highest pleasure.

After that first, unprotected return to enjoyable sex, they were more cautious, but Maggie could sense a familiar development within her, even so. She said nothing to him about her premonition, but she did ask him a key question one hot afternoon on the bright sand at the Dunes near Chesterton.

"How long does your medical insurance last?"

"With Lakeshore, you mean? Until the end of December."

"Then what?"

They sat across from each other on pink webbed beach chairs, the kids between them under a beach umbrella.

"Well," he said, "for a while we'll be doubly covered, maybe almost triply. As in 'the shores of.'"

Maggie poked a toe into his reachable leg because of the lousy pun.

"It's the truth. Uncle Sam will help me out because of my profound bravery."

"You don't know that for sure."

"Well, whatever. At MSU I'm under the same plan as a full-time employee. It's a good plan. Why do you ask?"

She bit her lip. "Don't forget our organization has four members now, and—" She tried to seem bored, or at least only mildly concerned. She actually feared that asking if the plan covered pregnancy would be the signal for him to withdraw his resignation from Lakeshore. "Anyway, I won't be teaching for another year or two."

"I know," Lou said, flicking sand on her foot with his big toe. "It'll be alright."

She replayed his little gesture now in her daydreams, and she further remembered her almost arbitrary desire for him at the moment the sand hit her foot. She put both hands between her legs and smiled.

As the time neared for their departure to Michigan, she was resigned to the likelihood of yet another baby. Once again she had been careless, but she wouldn't throw blame around this time. Another child would be theirs in about seven months, and their lives would be that much more significant, that much more difficult,

In the peaceful air of a late summer afternoon, she tried to convince herself that the medical plan at the university would cover the cost of a vasectomy.

Lou went back into the dark house to pour himself another inch of Ezra Brooks, then repositioned himself on the top concrete step of the house from which he would soon move. As he sometimes did during the last nights in Whiting, he sat alone and recalled his last days in Chicago.

The Monday after Evelyn was born, Lou arrived at the Lakeside office at 9 in the morning, intent on getting a two week paid vacation. He was prepared to compromise; if Bert and Geraldine thought it unreasonable, he would accept it without pay. If they didn't like that, either, he was ready to quit. Surprisingly, they gave him no argument. Go, and take care of your family, they said, essentially.

But when he returned to work after the paid leave, Geraldine seemed less interested in expanding his product horizons, which was just as well, now that he had decided what to do. At the end of July, weeks after he had received word from Michigan State that he would have a departmental graduate assistantship in theatre, he braced himself to tell the Lakeside people of his plans. Bert looked surprised, though what he said indicated otherwise. He told Lou he never showed an understanding of the *necessity* of what they were doing and making, or what he as a specialized performer was giving to the public.

"You're good in front of the camera," Bert said, " but I don't think you've ever recognized the heart of your role, what you represent. So it's just as well that you follow your own private muse."

Geraldine was immediately disturbed by his decision to leave, although more because she found out from Bert, rather than first hand. She didn't speak to him until a couple of days before he quit.

"I shouldn't bother myself with someone so thoughtless," she said, "but it just grates on me. Don't you think you owed it to me, to tell *me* what you were planning to do before you said anything to anyone else?" She looked at him with the pained expression he wouldn't have guessed she were capable of.

"I'm sorry. I was going to talk to you after—"

"Oh, Lou, after nothing. I'm the one who gave you this chance."

"I know. I must seem ungrateful."

Her eyes looked almost as green as they did when she had told him to put on his pajamas and go to bed, sixteen years before. Standing in front of him she moved those eyes to his shoulders and then to the middle of his face, with a very slight smile, as if she were a mother sending off her son, or an inspector disapproving of a product but acknowledging there was nothing wrong with it.

"Well, let me buy you lunch, at least." She paused and fixed her eyes on his, with a look of regret, or resignation. "Not at the Pump Room, and for no other reason than to hear you tell me why you're doing this."

At one o'clock that day neither of them was hungry, so they walked across Michigan Avenue and into the middle of Grant Park and sat on a bench. Not fifty feet away, a couple of pre-school girls were running after pigeons, squealing when the birds quickly decided to fly.

"I don't have any children," she said, looking at the girls. "It's good that my unfortunate marriage didn't produce any. But someday I would like—" she stopped, as if forgetting, or not having an idea fully formed. He said nothing immediately in return, waiting for her to accompany with words her soft stare. She just looked around.

"You become a different person when you have kids," he said.

For whatever reason, she took offense. "You needn't put on an act, since it isn't necessary, and it won't make me any less pissed off. I'm actually very disappointed in you, and not only because of your ingratitude. You're doing something so horribly foolish, a big, big mistake, and I fear it's only the first of many mistakes you're going to make. Putting your family through such uncertainty, and for what? You're giving up the kind of income most 25 year olds would sell their souls for."

"Geraldine, if you can't understand why I'm giving up a good paying job for what I really want to do, then you really don't know me."

"I know you. A young fool throwing away success for some vague dream of glory."

"That's not true. It has nothing to do with glory. You don't know me. If you did, you probably wouldn't like me."

She shook her head and smiled. "I'd always like you."

"Just remember, I'm originally from Stieglitz Park."

"What difference does *that* make?"

"Bad neighborhood." He sneered. "Tough neighborhood. Bad examples. No role models."

"Oh, shit," she said with a laugh that sounded a bit like a cry. "Lou! You were what, a third grader back then? You were barely aware of anything."

"You're wrong. I remember everything. Even little details. My mother was as Catholic as anyone could be, so I would play priest in the dining room, saying mass in an oversized white tee shirt. And the thing I put over the glass that served as a chalice was a doily with small embroidered oranges on it."

"God," she said, with a painful laugh, and then put on an intentionally wicked face. "You were protected from all the evil around you."

"You're making fun of me."

"No I'm not. I'm reflecting on what you're saying. Your mother, the church. If you hadn't been blasted out of your house, you might have grown up as a saint."

"Now I *know* you're making fun of me."

"I'm not, really. Everyone I knew in the couple of years we lived there had such a rough edge. They always seemed ready to fight, or get drunk. You would have been different from them, this screwy little kid."

"You've got the wrong story, Geraldine. Granted, I was protected, but only at home. When I'd go outside into that neighborhood and soak up all the swear words and bad habits of the big kids, it was fairly exciting. My sister overheard me telling Larry Lindquist to go fuck himself, and she ratted on me to my mom."

He laughed, and she laughed with him. "You were trying to be tough. You probably didn't know what you were saying."

"Maybe not, but it shocked the hell out of my mother."

"So that's a fond memory?"

"It's a memory. Just like all the sounds I remember. Even the industrial noises," he continued, ignoring her sneer. "The factory was like a cyclops, or a volcano god. The people worshipped and made sacrifices to it."

"Virgins, I suppose."

"Well, back then I wouldn't have known what a virgin was. Anyway, the volcano god let only a select few escape its wrath."

He waited, but she said nothing.

"Then one day the volcano erupted. In my nine year old consciousness the explosion was like Pearl Harbor. My big yard, baseball in the parking lot, basketball in the alleys, tough guys fighting each other behind the signs that faced the boulevard. Christ, that was my world, and the explosion wiped it out. But I still remember."

"You're romanticizing it. Most grownups said 'good riddance.'"

"You're probably right. I never said it, though."

"Lou, Stieglitz Park was destined to become what it is, a tankfield. Too bad it didn't before—" She stopped and her high cheekbones seemed to sag.

He said nothing.

"Oh, what does anyone know," she said, "why people murder, or why things explode?"

"Fate, factory negligence. Maybe geographical heredity."

"What's that?" She looked at him as if he had spoken a peculiar signal.

"I think," he said, "we are more than products of our environment or heredity or biological makeup, more even than the individual choices we make. There is something else—something like an ongoing *geographical* inner tattoo we carry forth, a constant subconscious reminder of *place*."

"Inner tattoo? Please."

"No, really. It's there forever, but you can't see it or even feel it. And it'll never fade completely."

"You certainly didn't figure that out at the age of nine. I was already a teenager, and I don't carry Stieglitz Park around in my, whatever, soul, or reserve tank."

"Maybe you do, and you just don't realize. It's kind of a paradox. You reject it, but it's still attached. It's beyond simple memory, and we don't choose it or 'unchoose' it, if there's such a word."

"Something mystical," the corners of her mouth turned downward slightly.

"Possibly."

"Have you thought this out the same way you've thought out giving up your job and going up to nowhere?"

He looked at her rejecting face. "You don't think I have much of a chance, do you?"

"I don't know. I don't want you to fail. I care for you. But God, you're even more of a romantic fool than I thought you were that first day, at the interview and the audition," she said. "I could tell you were a dreamer, a guy who could could feel something and convince someone to feel the same thing. Maybe that's what attracted me." She looked in his eyes for acknowledgement, but he turned his head. "I thought your special something would attract other women to the product. And you had— *have*, actually—a sort of silly playfulness in your personality. I don't fully understand it because I've never seen it in another man before or since."

She put her hands over her eyes for an instant, then took a deep breath before continuing. "Almost every guy I've ever known has tried to impress me with strength or charm or self-confidence. You were just silly. You came back from war, lucky to be alive, and you seemed to fit in so naturally with your goofiness. I mean, you fit it into the spots with babies so perfectly, and I was thrilled because you were, you *are*, my discovery, and I also discovered something in myself."

She leaned back on the bench, and looked up at the patches of blue sky above the patchy locust tree. "I discovered something in myself," she said again. "But I put a lid on it, for the most part. I hoped you would--, I don't know. I had to keep telling myself I didn't need another man in my life, not even someone like you, someone as special as--. Oh, shit, everything sounds cheap."

Lou looked at her with a surprising kind of intensity.

"I needed to say that," she said.

"I'm, I don't know, touched."

"No you're not. And you can't possibly be surprised. You picked up the signals a long time ago, so admit it. You're a fool, but you're not dumb. I needed to say it openly for my own benefit." She got up quickly and looked around. "What's clear to me is that you would have a better chance at a good life here, doing the stuff you've been doing. I'll bet even your bitchy wife would agree."

"No she wouldn't. You're wrong there. And why would you think of her as bitchy?"

"Sweetheart, don't argue. She's what I say. I'm an expert on such behavior. If looks could kill, etcetera."

They walked down a gravel path at the edge of a wire fence in the park, toward Michigan Avenue. She told him to wait while she ducked into a public rest room. He leaned against a tree about ten feet from the entrance. She stayed inside for about five minutes, and when she emerged her eyes reminded him of a similar moment when they were at the Pump Room.

"What did you do in there?"

"What do you mean?"

"Your eyes look different."

"Take a closer look." She moved directly in front of him, her face inches away. "We all have our secrets," she said. "One day you'll have your own secret."

When she put her arms around his neck, he put his hands on them. "I saw Chet Puntillo the other day, and he mentioned you."

She brought her arms down, and made a face that suggested she didn't like the way he changed the subject. "Did he say why he broke it off with my mother?"

"Well, he just said things didn't work out, or something like that."

"He's a gentleman. My mother went back to the bottle. He probably figured he was no match for her true love." She put her arms around his neck again. "Like I said, we all have our secrets. Jesus, give me a hug. I'm no threat to your cozy paradise."

The embrace lasted longer than he would have intended had he been the instigator. When they separated she touched his lips with her flattened fingers, then gave him the slightest of kisses. And that was the end.

He tried not to think about how she looked, her green eyes sleepy but oddly intense.

After finally loading the crib and playpen into the U-Haul, Lou and Maggie stood in the living room and bade farewell to the dumpy furniture which stayed with the place. Their relief would be short, they knew, guessing Spartan Village—one of the married student housing complexes at Michigan State—would provide them with something equally dumpy. Martin walked around, saying bye-bye to the porch, the kitchen, and many objects. Evelyn watched from the middle of the dining room floor as her father opened drawers to see if they had forgotten anything.

Maggie stood in pale blue shorts and a striped knit shirt in front of a long mirror in the big bedroom, turning sideways to admire the stomach that was still fairly flat. Lou came up behind her and cupped her breasts in his hands while humming against her neck. As he was about to drop his hands to her stomach, she turned to kiss him. It was lippy and brief, the calmly satisfying gesture of two people about to go where they both wanted to go. Martin walked in and said bye-bye to the mirror.

They drove down the street to say goodbye to Lou's parents. Martin stayed in the car watching his mother feeding Evelyn. Lou went inside and tried to assure his own mother he was doing the best thing, the right thing. She cried quietly, worried he was giving his family such insecurity. Louie, who was planning to retire early from Socko, told of their own plans to move to a place in New Port Richey, Florida. Then he sat down in his favorite chair, looking sad, and said he was scared for them, too.

"Oh, and by the way," the old man said, getting back up. "Never mind that $200 you borrowed when you just got back from the army."

"For God's sake," Lois said, "why bring that up?"

"You know," Lou said over her objection, "I really forgot about that. Honestly I did." He reached for his check book. "I can give it to you right now."

"Oh, don't you dare," Lois said, giving her husband a dirty look.

"No, I didn't mean that," Louie said. "I was just going to tell you to buy something nice for the kids."

"You sure?"

"Yeah, just go ahead. I didn't mean nothing."

Then the young father and the old father embraced, and Lou held him longer than he ever had in his adult life, probably about ten seconds. Then his mother held him and kissed him on both cheeks, and her tears wet his face. All three went down to the white Oldsmobile F-85, at the curb along with the U-Haul filled with their possessions. The old people kissed and hugged the younger ones and their babies, and then the journey began.

When they got to Indianapolis Boulevard and turned south, Maggie reached over and fingered the hair above Lou's neck. "I knew what you were going to do."

"What do you mean?"

"I knew you were going to give a decent goodbye to your parents."

"How do you know I was decent to them. You were out in the car."

"You were. I know you."

"You know me. Do you *trust* me?"

She said nothing.

They drove down the boulevard, past the growing number of tankfields that now occupied the space which sixteen years ago had been houses and yards and an occasional store.

He slowed down, then pulled over across from a sign on 129th Street.

"Maggie, do you trust me?"

"Think about it, Lou. Isn't that a stupid question? Isn't the answer obvious?" She paused and they looked at each other. "I mean, here I am, going off to God knows where or what, with you and our babies, and—" her voice cracked a bit, "and another one on the way."

Lou squinted. "Wait a minute. Are you sort of re-living Evelyn?"

"No, I'm sort of re-living gestation."

"But the breast-feeding? Isn't that—wasn't that—?"

"I guess not. Anyway, my milk supply has been irregular."

Lou got out and walked around the car, then stood next to her window.

"Are you sure?" he asked, in a tired voice.

"Pretty sure."

"Jesus."

"No," Maggie said, "and not Joseph, either. 'Mary' would fit better. I feel a soul-child coming on. A gentle little girl who looks like me. Maybe she can have your eyelashes."

Lou walked around, breathing through his open mouth. He walked over to the sign across the street, at the edge of a big tankfield where houses had once stood, colorless but alive. The sign read "AMOCO Stieglitz Park Field No Trespassing"

When he got back into the car, he didn't want to talk, but Maggie did.

"Did you say goodbye to Stieglitz Park?" Maggie asked.

"I suppose I did," he said, cutting over toward Calumet Avenue so he could take the toll road eastward. Both children were already fast asleep in the back seat.

She touched his cheek.

"Maggie—"

"Shut up. Everything will work out. It always has."

"Maggie—"

She pinched his ear. "Tell me something about the place. What was the highlight of your life there?" she said.

"Stieglitz Park? I don't know."

She pinched his ear again. "Come on, tell me a story."

"Well. Nothing really qualifies as a highlight except for something that happened about a half mile north of it, just off the Boulevard. I was then about the same age as Martin. I don't actually remember it, so it's second hand stuff."

"Tell me anyway."

He told her the story about John Zmudka and his gunfight with Ditcher Hathaway at Vasilko's outdoor market, in broad daylight, back in 1949. Joey Kovacik, who later had told Stieglitz Park kids the story in detail, was working that day at the market, and he told how the shots went here and there, until one of Zmudka's shots hit Digger in the thigh and he bled all over a cantaloupe. When the commotion was over, Joey hosed down the mess except for that one melon, the bloody one he saved for photographs.

Maggie put her seat at a backward slant and leaned her head against a small pillow she had brought along. "Save that story," she said. "Maybe you can write a movie script about it. 'Gunfight at Vasilko's Market.' You could even star as Zoomka, or whatever his name was."

That idea got him thinking about other things as he pulled onto the Indiana Toll Road, and he recalled his final winter break in Stieglitz Park. It had snowed heavy, thick flakes during the week before Christmas. The streets weren't plowed well enough for cars to move through, and the bigger kids decided to play tackle football, using all the property fences as out of bounds. They even let Lou and another small kid play. He remembered vividly running for a touchdown, with Richie Bowman blocking for him, and in fact carrying him into the end zone.

"That's not legal," said Bob Springer. "You can bring it back here."

"You can kiss my ass," said Richie, and the touchdown stood. Cold slop clung to his clothes as he straightened up and played the rest of the game, but he didn't care about cold or wetness because all he knew was his own touchdown, spirited by Richie Bowman.

Then there was a quiet, much colder night a couple of days later. He awoke from a light sleep up in his newly completed room next to the attic in the house his father had rebuilt with hard work and sweat and even some creativity. It must have been about two in the morning when he went downstairs. Mousie, their Rat Terrier, was outside on the enclosed back porch because his father didn't want the dog to mess up furniture, or worse. Lou let the dog inside, and held him in his arms until the dog's excitement subsided. Mousie weighed no more than ten pounds, all speckled gray, his short fur flush against his ribs and tight against his white stomach. Even at that age, Lou could carry him around, feeling his stubby tail wag against his arm. The dog's enthusiasm wasn't noisy enough to wake anyone else up.

Lou and the dog went into the living room and sat in the dark, in front of the big, decorated Christmas tree, immersed in the scent of pine, with the glow of outdoor light and snow reflected on the football-shaped glass ornaments which hung from branches evenly. Mousie licked his hand and lay next to him on the carpet, and there was no sound except for the strains of "Oh, Holy Night" running through Lou's head, as well as some of the remembered noises of street football. He pulled a small blanket off the living room couch and wrapped it around himself, leaving a short end to cover the dog, who took a deep breath and fell asleep.

It was the best time ever in Stieglitz Park, where he grew up. It was the highlight he would save forever.

"What's the matter?" asked Maggie, waking up just east of Michigan City. She reached her hand over to his cheek and touched wetness. "Honey, don't worry."

"Oh, nothing. I'm not. I was thinking about playing Biff, in 'Death of a Salesman.' The scene is sad, but in a way it's a release. He's railing against Willy's self-delusion, and he says they're a dime a dozen, ordinary people like the Lomans, who only dream of being better. 'We're a dime a dozen!'" He says that, and he means it, but he doesn't mean it, in another way. It's a wrenching scene. I mean, how do you face life when you're a dime a dozen?"

Maggie leaned back again to sleep, this time turning toward him and reaching to touch his stomach, just above the scar. "Dime a dozen. Maybe they are," she said. "but you aren't."

"Let's hope you're right," he answered.

Epilogue
1955-56

After the big explosion and fire, the Stieglitz Park community began to be cleared away. On the afternoon of Halloween that year, a few small children and teenagers from down the road in Goose Island trick-or-treated the Clipper and the three houses still standing. At the tavern they got coins, and at one of the houses they got cookies from an elderly woman. The other two houses were empty. One was open, however, so the kids went inside for a spell, out of the wind, and ate some of their loot before walking the half-mile back where they belonged.

By Thanksgiving the rubble had been further cleared, and most of the street signs were gone. Eager to put an end to a near catastrophe, the company settled with all the former residents of Stieglitz Park, paying off generous sums to former homeowners.

Just before a heavy pre-Christmas snowfall, the company graded and surfaced fully two-thirds of the area as part of a plan to expand their tankfield. Commuting steelworkers driving through the dirty slush must have been impressed by the flat whiteness of the big space, unmarked by any feet save those of a lost rabbit.

But New Year's Eve was still celebrated at the Clipper by those coming off the third shift at the refinery or the mills. Inside, Frank Connolly drank heavily and rambled verbally, just as he had for decades. At the stroke of midnight he broke an empty beer bottle against a table, as if acting out an obligatory moment in an old western. Ace the bartender told him to shut up and behave or he would call the cops. Connolly calmed down, and he even cleaned up the glass from the floor, but he laughed at the bartender's threat, for everyone knew there weren't any cops in Stieglitz Park anymore.

Looked at from the outside, the tavern seemed stuck there, a strangely festive tombstone above the cold white, a lonely winter's dream decorated with memories.

# # #